FINDING
JASPER

FINDING
JASPER

Lynne Leonhardt

MATILDA BAY
BOOKS

Lynne Leonhardt was born in the South West of Western Australia and grew up on an orchard in a small rural community. As a young adult, she worked overseas, travelling extensively during an extended six-year period. She later spent four years in the Riverina District of New South Wales. An affinity for creative arts saw her take up tertiary studies in music and English literature while raising four children. For many years she has lived in Perth, Western Australia, but enjoys retreating with her husband to the natural beauty of the South West whenever she can. This is her first novel.

Acknowledgements

An earlier version of this novel was completed as part of a PhD in Writing at Edith Cowan University in 2007. I would like to thank ECU again for awarding me a scholarship to undertake the project, and express my appreciation to all those who were involved in providing advice during my time as a post-graduate student.

I am extremely grateful to Caroline and John Wood of Margaret River Press for accepting my manuscript. I am also greatly indebted to my editor, Richard Rossiter, and other members of the Editorial Board of Margaret River Press, for their insightful comments and recommendations, which have both enhanced the novel and resulted in a far better publication than would otherwise have been the case.

The long-term support and advice of friends has been invaluable throughout the writing of this book and I would like to give particular thanks to Robyn Mundy, Amanda Curtin, and Sally Edmonds. But my largest debt is undoubtedly to my family who have helped in so many different ways: to my wonderful husband, Peter, for his constant encouragement and support; to my grown-up children, Georgia, James, Lucy and William for their various inputs. Lucy's readings and suggestions were particularly helpful, especially in the earlier stages of manuscript development. Others who contributed to readings or discussions were Kate Ozich, James Hyndes, and close members of the Coles family. I thank everyone concerned.

Volunteer guides and ex-servicemen at the RAAF Heritage Museum at Bullcreek were particularly helpful in answering research questions and directing me to the many resources available.

My sincere appreciation also goes to the late David (Paddy) Dwyer, for taking time to chat to me about his personal experiences as an Australian member of Bomber Command, and for volunteering background material and personal copies of war documentation, which I was later able to draw from and incorporate in the novel.

Prior to the 2006 publication of her book, *A Landscape for Learning*, Gillian Lilleyman answered numerous questions regarding the history of the grounds of The University of Western Australia and the foreshore at Crawley Bay, for which I am very grateful.

Part 1

White was never a consideration. It was not appropriate under the circumstances. In the end Valerie opted for oyster, as she called it. The colour suited her creamy skin and emphasised the clarity and blueness of her eyes. There was nothing traditional about the outfit. It was sleek and elegant, a classic shantung suit that could be worn again.

Gin observed her cat-like movements, the slide of her mother's curves into Noel's side. The feathered hat, a furl of cerise, offset the darkness of her bob and its net half-screened her beautiful face. Lips shimmered through the flocked dots. Confetti floated in the air. Then the coloured spots stuck to Noel's shoulder like a broken rainbow.

The black-cloaked photographer dipped and ducked, arranging the couple into all manner of poses. Guests wandered about. Bystanders in the street stopped and stared. Gin stood by herself pulling at her fingers. If only she could slip away unnoticed.

A string quartet started up, penguins scraping and squeezing together in a half-circle. Gin instantly recognised the music as it quavered bittersweet through the air. She must have heard it a thousand times, each note clinked mechanically from inside her trinket box every time she opened its lid. Over and over the music-box played as the china figurine danced in time. Gin never tired of the piece. She could play it on the piano, her fingers finally managing the long, left-handed leaps in the bass with ease. But now the sickly violins were winding their way through the high notes. The cellist was flat.

Everything was higgledy-piggledy. Her new suspender belt felt cumbersome stretched over her cottontails, and the elastic straps pinched her legs as she walked. All of this ridiculous paraphernalia that was meant to make her instantly into a grown woman. Every so often Gin felt the need to turn around and check that the seams of her stockings were straight.

Watch out for snags, was her mother's morning lecture. *They're fifteen denier, don't forget. Of course, a pair of nylons lasts me weeks. I take good care. When I married your father, they were scarce as hens' teeth. War brides had to make do. A touch of Vaseline and a line on the back of each calf with an eyebrow pencil, that's all most of us had.* It had been a quick affair in a London registry office, Valerie had explained, the dress whipped up overnight from a torn parachute silk scavenged from one of Jasper's RAAF sorties the week before.

Gin could see her mother mouthing something and signalling daintily with her kid-gloved hand. As the trembling notes gathered tension and momentum, Noel wrenched his neck from his starched collar and called out to her, 'Quick sticks!' His face was red and shone the same shade as the Boston ivy blanketing the limestone wall behind.

Gin tried to envisage her parents' brief union and what happiness it may have held. Her mother rarely mentioned her father. Over the years any photos of him had gradually been withdrawn from display. Gin could vaguely conjure up a face, young and fresh with dark eyes half-concealed beneath an air force cap, but now, as she stepped out of the gathering shade, it seemed as if he had never existed.

The spent leaves crackled under her shoes as she tried to keep abreast of the flickering light. Here behind the tree, Gin was away from it all, out of sight. The urge to kick one of the dried seed pods which lay half-hidden in the fallen leaves took her by surprise. Without caring, she swished her foot, and watched with satisfaction as the spiky ball spun through the air and ricocheted off the circular drive.

At the bottom of the hill was the river. It glimmered deep and blue against the orange of the tiled roofs, defining their angles into a kind of pattern. Even now, the late afternoon air remained warm and still, unable to produce so much as a ripple on the water's surface. It seemed as if the black-cloaked photographer was trying to hold the world at a standstill, staving off time as he blocked out the entire world to focus on the happy bride and groom.

But despite this air of blissful suspension, Gin could not help feeling that part of her life was coming to an end. She listened as murmuring doves bedded themselves down in the secrecy of their shadowy roosts. Everywhere she looked, trees were beginning to turn. Overhead, broken shafts of sunlight languished through the yellowing branches of a liquidambar.

Gin stood, watching the play of light and shade on the golden star-shaped leaves which lay scattered on the ground. Valerie and Noel were now finally married. That was that, and there was no going back. Dwelling on the changes that would affect her life was pointless. Anyway, thought Gin, you can't really hold things still. Even the smallest things changed whether you liked it or not, for every second, every part of a second was different from the last.

'Virgin-ia!' called Valerie in her high-pitched voice. 'Quick! Over here. The light's fading and the photographer hasn't got long.'

'Come on! Don't dilly-dally.' Noel waved a beckoning arm but she continued dawdling regardless.

'Where on earth have you been?'

'I've been waiting for Attie to come.'

'Dear oh dear, you'll spoil everything if you don't hurry up. This is meant to be my special day,' Valerie hissed.

'It's my suspender,' whispered Gin, as she edged up beside her. 'Look, my stocking's all wrinkled ... I can't ...'

'Well, it'll just have to wait. Good God!' she said, observing the scuff marks on the toes of Gin's new white shoes. 'What have you been up to? Honestly, Virginia!' Her eyes glared. 'Now shush! Stand up properly and don't make a spectacle of yourself and for goodness' sake stop that pouting.'

'Righty-o!' called Noel, with a slight toss of his head. 'You two girls finally ready?'

'Come together a little closer, please,' said the photographer.

Gin flinched as her bare arm touched the buttons on Noel's sharkskin jacket.

*

Within seconds, it was almost dark. The setting sun reminded Gin of a slice of orange as it slid slowly behind the mossy corrugations of the roofs.

'Just a small glass for my daughter, please,' instructed Valerie, as the waitress ushered them into the Masonic Hall. 'Just enough for the toast,' she added, running the tip of her tongue over her two front teeth.

Suddenly a silver tray of hors d'oeuvres appeared in front of her. Gin bit warily into a vol-au-vent. She could feel the young waitress staring at her as fish mornay squeezed out either side of her mouth. Now her champagne glass was smeared and a caper had fallen into her drink. Should she scoop it out, she wondered, or leave it there?

'Ah, well then ...' Noel's voice appeared from nowhere. 'So you're off to the country tomorrow, eh?' His large freckled hand clamped her shoulder. 'You got on like a house on fire with Attie last time, didn't you?'

Gin fingered her angora bolero. Had her aunt totally forgotten the wedding or was she just running late, as usual? Time and distance meant nothing when you lived in the country. You had to make allowances. People spoke slower. Things often took longer to happen. Those three months that Gin had spent on her aunt's farm now seemed like a dream.

'Nothing like a bit of fresh air.' Noel rocked on his patent leather shoes. 'Got your bags all ready?'

Gin nodded, staring through the heads to avoid his glance. Her eyes lit up. 'Look,' she cried. 'There's Attie!'

'Not before time,' replied Noel wryly, glancing at his watch.

Valerie tottered up to his side and linked her arm in his.

'Apparently she had a puncture.'

'What a darned nuisance.' Noel *titched*. 'I dare say it was those blessed pot-holes on the coast road.'

'Looks like she changed the tyre in her good clothes, if you ask me.' Valerie nodded pointedly across the room. 'Have you ever seen such a sight?' she sniffed.

Attie's silk skirt was crumpled but she appeared unconcerned as she threaded her way across the room to join them.

'We'd have been in a spot of bother if she hadn't arrived at all, now wouldn't we?' Noel laughed, thumbing the pockets of his waistcoat.

Valerie arched her eyebrows at Gin. 'Then who would have looked after you?'

'Sorry, everybody,' said Attie, casually winding stray wisps of hair behind her ears. 'Just been getting myself a beer.' She embraced her niece. 'You look very smart today Gin, I must say.'

Noel briskly clapped his hands and paused, looking at each in turn. 'Well, lass,' he said, 'your mother and I'll be shooting through directly, so we may as well say goodbye now.'

Gin turned suddenly to miss his smoky kiss. Her face felt hot. She breathed in her mother's fragrance as pink lips puckered and lightly touched her cheek.

'See you soon, darling,' Valerie waved. 'Be good for Attie.'

Chapter 1

'Just call me Attie,' she said. 'Aunty Attie sounds absolutely ghastly.'

The blurry blue flame flickered for a moment as she turned down the lamp. A puff of black smoke clouded the glass, expelling a whiff of burnt kerosene.

Gin sat on the iron bed as shadows unfolded around the room. At the foot of the bed was an old Saratoga, a compound of canvas bound by buff leather stays. MISS ADELINE PARTRIDGE, COLOMBO—FREMANTLE was barely decipherable on the P & O stickers.

Gin wanted to cry again. It was the first time she'd ever been away from home, away from her mother. Valerie, by now, was somewhere in the dark Indian Ocean, too far away even to care. Only that morning, they'd stood on Fremantle wharf watching the brown Globite luggage being slung, case by case, into the ship's hold.

I'll only be gone three months. Anyone would think it was a year. You're old enough to be left now. After all, Virginia, you are twelve.

The floorboards were hard and uneven as she knelt beside the Saratoga. Squeezing the corroded latch, Gin carefully eased open the lid, trying to predict the treasures inside. The lining was shabby and mottled with mildew, and drifts of mustiness filled the air as she began to unearth the contents from the shrouding dust. Mostly books, she found, a few toys, and a fat-cheeked doll lying naked on top.

What had she expected? At the very least, Gin had hoped there would be something of value, some small item that might bring her consolation. She wondered what it would be like not to be an only child, not to have to endure the aching loneliness inside her now.

Gin looked again at the destination stickers and tried to picture Miss Adeline Partridge as a child. At least her aunt would have had a brother for company besides that hideous doll. Perhaps it was the pallor of its face or its sleeping eyes that made it look so deathly. But as she picked it up, the cloth body instantly yielded to her touch.

A flush of tenderness came over her and Gin began to cradle the doll, inspecting it carefully as if it were a newborn child. The stained calico was frayed, and flock floated out of the stuffing. A thumb was missing. Chips scarred the composition limbs, but the head was surprisingly intact, and its rosebud mouth still parted in awe. Lids suddenly clicked open. The pair of periwinkle eyes staring back at her seemed so real that, for a second to two, she felt she was nursing a baby brother or sister. Gin knew it was silly but she couldn't resist it. She poked her little finger into the rigid mouth, prising, teasing, to see if the doll would bite. Instantly she heard her mother's last-minute reminder.

Make sure you clean your teeth, Virginia, and don't forget to wash your face and hands thoroughly every night. Field mice might come and nibble at the corners of your mouth when you're asleep.

Even a skerrick of food is enough to attract them.

'Do you really have mice here, Attie?' was the first thing Gin had asked her aunt.

'My word! Last year there was a plague. They ate through the saddles out in the sheds. I dare say that it was the smell of dead sweat they were after. Even got into my handbag after some chocolate and left the silver paper and their nasty little droppings behind. I fixed the blighters, though. Plugged all the cracks in the kitchen cupboards with steel wool.'

Gin sat cross-legged on the patchwork quilt. Little creatures peeped out of the bundle of Beatrix Potter books she had dug out of the chest. Mice, rabbits, hedgehogs, all dressed in aprons and bonnets and smart dress-coats with knickerbockers and stockings, begging to be noticed.

Gin began flipping idly through the illustrations. It was intriguing how the animals transformed. She'd never noticed before. They wore clothes only when they were in their own secret animal kingdom. But when humans were present, they never wore clothes at all. They simply reverted to being animals in a human world. Just like that.

Two distinct worlds, she concluded as she turned off the lamp. That's how it was in life. One for children. One for adults. One for her mother and one for herself, and nothing in between.

*

In the morning the kitchen was warm and smelt of stale cooking odours from the night before.

'Not unusual to get a few late frosts now and then.' Attie bent over the slow combustion stove.

Gin watched her aunt empty the remaining wood-chips into the glowing coals.

The gas stove in her mother's kitchen was clean and modern but it didn't have the life of a wood fire. Breakfasts at home tended to be cold, silent affairs. Even on weekends. Gin pictured the seal of her mother's lips. She could see her now, pressed against the kitchen bench, the jut of her hips over the chrome-trimmed laminex, and her red thumbnail puncturing the foil of a fresh bottle of milk. Valerie never liked talking until she'd eaten. And then it was always something horrible like kedgeree or kippers poached in milk.

A gush of heat whooshed over her as Attie opened the damper. Beads of perspiration suddenly flooded her forehead. Gin felt woozy. Hot one minute and cold the next.

Attie slid the kettle from the black hob. Drips spat on the range as she scooped out two eggs, and poured the remaining boiling water into the empty teapot beside.

'Here,' she said. 'Growing girl like you must be hungry. Eat up your porridge and have one of these.' The eggs looked dirty and smeared against the willow-patterned plate.

Gin lifted the beaded fly net from the jug. She shuddered. A slick of cream was floating on the surface of the milk. She wanted to be sick and her throat was starting to throb again. Her eyes rolled, and from out of the blur came the distant pressure of Dr Buckingham's yellow-tipped index finger on her tongue.

Say Aah and she gagged, overcome by the foul, burning taste of nicotine. Gin tried not to swallow because every time she did, it felt like barbed wire in her throat. *Quinsies,* the word floated back and she gave the most excruciating retch. *Tonsils double the*

normal size, almost touching, they're so big. Full of muck. Covered
in ulcers and pus. Stick a pin in them and there'd be enough to fill
a teacup. Not much use in there poisoning up the system. Give it
another few months, then best we take 'em out.

'That must be cold by now,' said Attie, referring to the half-eaten egg. 'And your tea,' she said, peering down at the anaemic liquid in her cup, 'you haven't touched it. Here, let me make you another one.'

'No thanks, Attie. I'm not feeling very well.'

'Just a little homesick I suspect.' Attie gave her a pat. 'Don't worry, Gin. Your mother was, you know ... homesick, that is.'

Twelve years now since we left England and I need to go back. Dr
Buckingham said it would do me the world of good to have a little
holiday. Good for my nerves.

*

The next afternoon, they sat on the northern side of the veranda protected from the wind. Gin sipped hot lemon tea and occasionally poked her big toe through a hole in the rotting wicker of the chaise-longue. Everything was old and more dilapidated than she'd imagined. There was a strange sense of abandonment about the place, as if life had mysteriously come to a halt.

Through the yellow-berried branches of the Cape lilac tree, Gin could see the remnants of a tennis court—cracked clay crazed with roots and weeds—and the surrounding chicken-wire half-fallen beneath a tangle of purple creeper. Where was the garden her mother had mentioned? Wild oats had worked their way right up to the house. Gin watched them swaying in the breeze. Some of the higher stalks were almost as tall as she was. They looked strange and out of place, their blond spears prickling the fresh-faced hollyhocks. 'Granny had tried to make the garden English,' explained Attie, 'to remind her of home. Only the hollyhocks survived. Year after year they kept self-seeding, reaching out in the oddest of places.' How quaint they looked as they peered down snootily from their pink-frilled bonnets.

'Your mother loathed the farm,' said Attie, draining her cup. She broke off a piece of milk arrowroot biscuit and threw it to the brown dog lying against her feet. 'I can hear her now. *I'm a city girl born and bred.* She couldn't wait. Left as soon as it became obvious that your father wasn't coming home, and never brought you back to Grasswood again.' Suddenly Attie's eyes looked sad and she stood up and walked away.

The dog slunk down beside Gin, yellowy gaze fixed upon the young girl's face. Every now and then she thump-thumped her tail on the veranda. But Gin was oblivious. She sat there staring at the empty paddocks which rolled away into sandiness and a distant forest of gloomy conifers and karri. Down in the valley the pewter waters of the dam stretched out dark against the tarnished reeds. Occasionally she could hear the plaintive *baa* of a sheep from far away or the agonising dry rasps of crows as they swooped down from the purply clouds above. Eventually the dog hung her head and sloped into the shadows. Then the silence began to close in on Gin and she took herself inside.

*

The warped floorboards creaked; they groaned with every footstep. Gin plopped herself down in cushions of faded Indian chintz, immersing herself in the weary patterns around the room.

Most of the knick-knacks and furniture looked as if they had come from another world.

She caressed the intricately carved cedar, fidgeted with the rattan, all the while conscious of each second that ticked loudly and concisely from the grandfather clock in the hall. Every quarter hour, its chimes resonated throughout the house. Soon snakes, peacocks and a myriad of exotic animals began swirling around and around in her mind.

Gin must have been dreaming. When she opened her eyes, she found herself confronted by a pair of green jade elephants either side of the hearth. Behind folded lids, their enigmatic eyes gazed at her, as if remembering secrets from the past.

Now she could feel the shivers coming on. Even the rug, shabby and muted against the brown floorboards, could not conceal the bitter draught that was coming through the cracks. *Watch out for snakes*, Attie had told her. They'd been known to come through a door or a gaping floorboard. Once she'd almost stepped on one stretched out on the bathroom floor.

Gin found herself tiptoeing around in trepidation, wending cautiously around the agapanthus and the dangling wisteria that veiled the outside lav. Only yesterday, peering into that evil-smelling hole in there, she'd screamed on spotting two glassy eyes staring up at her.

Attie had armed herself without any fuss, stabbing the darkness with the handle of a rake. There'd been a loud hiss and suddenly the side hatch flung open with a bang. 'Just that bally tortoiseshell,' she'd laughed, as it scuttled through the grass.

*

'Why don't you go and play the piano?' Attie at last suggested. 'Needs a damned good blast to blow the dust off the dampers.'

Gin's arms still felt heavy, listless. Yet there was something comforting about her aunt's old piano and before long she found herself sitting hour after hour playing everything she'd ever learnt.

At first the burrs in the walnut panels reminded Gin of human faces and the brass candlestick holders gave the instrument a romantic feel unlike their standard rosewood Chappell at home. Even the tone was different. The notes in the upper register sounded warmer, brighter. She often found herself transposing everything an octave higher so the notes sparkled even more.

When she played the piano, Gin felt important, always gathering an imaginary audience close around her.

From the mantelpiece, faces in sepia photographs looked down at her from their silver frames.

'You'd be hard-pressed to tell the difference between us at that age.' Attie was beside her now, pointing out two toddlers standing hand in hand on a garden seat, identically dressed in embroidered Chinese smocks. 'That's your father,' she said, pointing to another photo of an older boy in a white sailor suit and cap in hand. 'Now these two were taken at our twenty-first.' Attie edged the double portrait forward.

'Oh! I didn't realise you were twins,' said Gin in surprise. Yet the similarity was obvious; the symmetry of features, the same mouth and nose and russet-coloured eyes. Even non-identical twins, she knew, were likely to share a special bond. It gave her father a kind of fleeting presence and for a moment something skipped inside her.

*

The following Friday Attie drove the old Rover into town. She led Gin to the upstairs studio of Mr Penworthy, the music teacher, above the haberdashery shop. Up rickety steps hollowed with time and wear, they twisted and turned in the darkness. Gin was disorientated when they reached the top. Looking out of the window she realised where they were. There was the railway station across the road and the tops of the Norfolk pines and the hatted heads down on the footpath below.

The sun was shining through a row of amber Bex bottles assembled on the windowsill before her. They looked strangely empty, Gin observed, and had all lost their caps.

'Hello, young lady.' Now Mr Penworthy was talking to her. 'Well, let's see what you can do.'

The outline of his singlet showed through his pale blue nylon shirt. His cheeks were smooth and fleshy, like pink jelly, which wobbled when he laughed. Tufts of something white and fluffy poked out deep from within his ears. Cottonwool, she suspected, from one of those empty Bex bottles.

'Well, come on then, play me something you know well,' he urged, rubbing his hands together. And then, before she could finish the piece, 'Wrist staccato, my poppet, should be like this.' His brown eyes shone down at her. They had golden flecks and reminded her of tadpoles swimming in a jar of water. Gin could smell Palmolive soap as he bent over her, close, extending a hairless arm to the keyboard to correct her. His pudgy hand pecked at the keys.

'Like a bird picking up seed,' he suggested, and she immediately thought of one of Attie's fat white hens.

His bottom and tummy were now level with her eyes. They were plump like an old woman's, much larger than his narrow shoulders, and his trousers were belted too high, almost to his chest.

'You've a very good ear but, remember, always practise the hard bits first. Build them into really strong bridges so they can't break and let you down.'

*

Gin found it hard to believe that the gramophone hadn't been used since Granny had died, but it still worked when Attie cranked it up. Gin played the records, one after the other, bulky black plates, some thick with dust. Apart from Mendelssohn's Violin Concerto, most of the records featured dancing songs of the twenties and thirties. Gin wondered if Attie had been a flapper, the kind she'd seen in old silent films. Headbands taut over foreheads. Arms crossed in front of bent knees, then flicking from one foot to the other, kicking out in time to the Charleston. As jaunty rhythms and honky-tonk tones played throughout the afternoon, Gin returned again and again to the photo of the twenty-one-year-old woman on the mantelpiece. Hair, short and shingled, was clasped either side of the middle part by diamante clips so that curls licked the sides of her creamy cheeks. Only the softest hues of watercolours had been used to tint the photo. The slippery folds of her silk frock were the shade of mountains far away. And while lipstick cut the shape of her cherry mouth, the tips curled the tiniest bit upwards, just like those of her twin brother beside.

Gin turned around and stole another glance at her aunt. Attie was still at the Davenport, pen poised in her hand. Wisps of hair had fallen about her cheek and neck, and her eyes were downcast in the shadow of her brow. How old was her aunt exactly? The same age her father would have been of course, around forty at a guess. Looking at her now, it was hard to believe Attie had once been so young and beautiful. Why had she never married? Gin wanted to ask her if the gramophone music brought back special memories, but Attie was deep in writing.

*

There was no gas or electricity on the farm. Attie had shown Gin how to light the chip bath-heater. It was now her daily responsibility to collect a bucketful of leafy twigs and larger sticks fallen from the tall gum trees behind the sheds. It soon became one of her favourite chores: every evening, the scrunching up of newspaper, lighting a match and letting the flames draw, breathing in the wonderful aroma as they took hold of the dead gum leaves with crackle and spit. She would then close the small metal door on them with a great sense of satisfaction. And when the water was ready, she would lie back in the bath, enjoying the warmth and the friendly rush of sounds beside it.

Gin also knew how to light the lamps by now as well. After they had washed up, she would go to each in turn, and then sit down at the piano once again. The limited lighting gave the room a special ambience that heightened Gin's imagination. Only an hour earlier, the walnut burrs in the piano cabinetry had transformed into a pair of monkeys, but now under the softer light the knotted swirls had taken on a ghost-like appearance.

'How about you play something for me now, Attie?' Gin slid

herself from the stool.

Her aunt's eyes appeared to fix on the empty filigree of the brass candlestick holders.

'Your father and I used to play duets when we were young,' she murmured. 'Now I couldn't play a note to save my life.'

Lamplight flickered for a moment and, from the whitewashed chimney-breast, Gin caught the glint of silver reflecting from the mounted sword and scabbard. According to family legend, the heirloom had once belonged to a great-great-great grandfather, who died in the Battle of Waterloo, although Attie suspected that was just a story.

Yet there were no family stories of Gin's father. Ever since she could remember, a silence had hung around his name. Whenever she'd asked her mother what had happened to him, she'd always been fobbed off. And even though she knew it was impossible— she was only six weeks old when her father had waved his last goodbye—Gin wanted desperately to remember him. In the back of her mind, there was a man lifting her up to show her how the gramophone worked, and, from this cloudy image, the light tickle of a moustache from a face bent close to hers, and the waft of Californian Poppy. Even the sound of his voice and his words she could hear.

See that big brass arm? Well, there's a diamond in there.

Is it a real one?

Of course, sweetheart, and do you know something?

What?

You are my little diamond.

It must have been her father, for in a flourish he had gathered her up, standing her on his big shiny shoes. With his large hand in a V under her armpit, he had bent over holding her other hand outstretched.

Now we will dance. Just keep your feet on mine. I will take the lead. The man always leads the woman, you know. Wherever my footsteps go, yours will automatically follow, I promise.

'For God's sake, Gin, if you play that wretched piece one more time I'll scream,' called Attie from the kitchen.

'But it's the 'Radetzky March', Attie.'

'I know what it is, and I don't give a flying hoot about Radetzky or Johann Bloody Strauss for that matter. It goes on and on and it's driving me mad. Play something you can sing to, for goodness sake, something lyrical.'

Gin began to play 'My Bonnie Lies over the Ocean'. During the refrain, she found herself swaying her body and luxuriating in the comfort of the simple rocking rhythm. And she could see the ship moving slowly away from the docks. She was entwined in streamers. They began to tighten, pulling her back onto the ship, back to her mother. Suddenly they snapped and she instantly began to cry. Attie was pointing. Through her tears, she could see her mother waving stiffly in the crowd, until everything became blurred, diffusing into the flood of coloured ribbons before her. Then Attie wrapped her arms around her. *There, there,* she said, as Gin buried her face in her shoulder. *Never mind, Pom-pom.*

Chapter 2

They were not as alone as Gin had thought. Far in the distant paddock, she could spot someone working.

'Who's that over there, Attie?'

'That,' her aunt hesitated for a second as if choosing her words with care, 'that is *the German*.' She almost spat the word.

'Hasn't he got a name?'

'Herr Dieter Hasse is his rightful name. He's on a government contract going from farm to farm doing odd jobs.'

'Where's he live?'

'In the old settler's hut over near the state forest.'

She told Gin how she gave him a bed and some pine packing cases when he arrived, a few blankets and some of Jasper's clothes.

'What I don't know doesn't hurt me. He comes over once a week and collects his mail and so forth, whatever's due. I do what I have to.' Then she added, 'But as far as I'm concerned, a German is a German and a dirty Hun, and that's all there is to it.'

'But Attie,' said Gin, 'the war's been over for years.'

'Easy for you to say, Gin. You're too young to remember, but believe me, I won't forget in a hurry.'

*

At the bottom of the Saratoga were a number of *Billabong* books. Judging from the pictures on their covers, the books would have probably been written when Attie was a young girl. Gin carefully turned the yellowing pages to the illustrations. It was hard to imagine her aunt in the funny fashions of the time when here she was getting about in flared shorts and a brightly checked seersucker shirt. Gin looked up to find Attie behind her, rummaging around in the chest of drawers.

'Did you ride when you were young, Attie?'

'Of course, Jasper and I always had horses.' Attie gave a chuckle. 'We'd go like the clappers, downhill, over logs, rabbit-holes and all. Just as well Father couldn't see. Suspect deep down we knew what a horse could and couldn't do. We grew up in hill country, you see, the highlands of Ceylon.'

Gin thought of the rat-eaten saddles and cracked bridles she'd seen hanging in the shed. It must have been years since they'd been used.

'What are you looking for, Attie?'

'Just sorting through some of Jasper's things,' she explained. She held out the garments, smoothing each fold with tenderness. 'Your mother didn't want to keep them but I couldn't bear to throw them out. Look, Jasper's old riding breeches. They must have shrunk as all clothes do with age.'

Gin had to try them on. The camel drill cloth was heavy and coarse, and reeked of camphor. The fly and the leg-slits on the outside of the calves were fiddly. There was obviously a knack in hooking the little bone buttons through their loops. She stood in front of the bevelled mirror, flared thighs fanning out either side like elephant ears. It was strange to think that her father had worn these breeches when he was not much older than her.

Jasper. Jasper. Why couldn't he have had a normal name like everybody else's father, Bill or Bob, Ken, Norm or Bruce? *Jasper.* Attie always seemed to say it softly and swiftly, half under her breath, like it was some kind of secret. Jasper. Jasper? Perhaps it was her accent but the way she said it sounded more like *whisper*.

As the day wore on, it became hotter and hotter.

'You're not actually going to wear that ridiculous clobber, are you?' scoffed her aunt. 'You'll swelter. Anyway, they swim on you. Talking of which, why don't you go down to the dam for a dip? Here, these might fit, and I suppose you better have a hat.' Attie clamped an old pith helmet on Gin's head. 'Why don't you take the dog for company?'

'Arushi!' called Gin. Funny name. Why would you call a dog Arushi? 'A-rushi! A-rushi!'

Arushi soon came trotting along, nose in the air, tongue lolling out the side of her smiling mouth. Apart from the occasional snap at a cricket, the dog kept faithfully by her side.

Gin felt afraid of nothing, not even snakes, listening only to the satisfying sound of her boots crunching over the dried-out stubble. For the moment, she was Norah of Billabong in charge of the property in her father's absence. In a gingham drawstring bag she carried a towel and an old black costume of Attie's. Far too big, but it'd do the trick.

The dog stopped abruptly in front of her, ears pricked forward, front paw poised in the air, staring at the dam. Suddenly, a flurry of wild ducks rose up out of their spatter, heads and necks outstretched and legs tucked under, their bodies in straight planes. The front bird was the leader now. Gin observed how the others soon dropped back to form a perfect V formation, like the beginning of her name. *Wark, wark, waark*, they went, as they disappeared over the dam. How did they form that V? How did they know how to get it so perfect?

From where she stood, Gin could see the green rectangle of kikuyu surrounding the pump-house, flanked by peppermint trees to the water's edge. Further away the grass escaped, long and wild. It tongued its way between the rusty heights of the bulrushes, reaching up to feed off the sun. What did bulrushes have to do with bulls, she wondered, observing that great bulk tearing at the kikuyu? The bull looked up, eyes lolling. You were not meant to eyeball a bull, Gin remembered, even if it did have angelic curls around its pearly-coloured face. There was something comic about the beast; bumbling frame, and its balls, a shiny grey, dangling above the pink-tipped grasses.

Gin tugged at her waistband. Down here everything was calm and peaceful and the water looked inviting. Past the oily shallows, green and gold reflections shimmered, undefined, penetrating the constantly merging brown and silver streaks that stretched across the water. Back and forth above the ripples, metallic dragonflies hovered, then darted, their wings a brilliant blur of blue. And the old wooden dinghy moored in the shallows rocked gently, as if trying to slough off the remainder of its flaking blue paintwork. A diving board of sorts poked out at an angle from the clay bank. The water, Attie had assured her, was so deep that nobody had ever been able to measure it.

Gin pushed on the pump-house door, projecting a sudden chink of sunlight into the darkness. Within its beam, motes of dust floated above a layer of grease. The engine continued pounding away while gossamer threads of cobwebs quivered in the gloom. The air was thick and warm with diesel fumes, and dirty rags and used cans of fuel lay scattered on the floor. Within seconds she was in her bathers and out the door, the dull throb of the engine becoming rapidly absorbed into the silence and rhythms of the outside world.

A blast of gunshots shattered the air. Gin took off. More shots rang out resounding in her ears. Her stomach lurched, dropped suddenly into her bowels, but still she kept running down the track past the bull and, when she reached the cattle-pit, she leapt right over it and skidded into a tangle of saplings, grating her knees on the gravel. *Bang! Bang! Bang!* Gin picked herself up and scurried back to the house.

*

Attie remained unfazed when she found her.

'But who was it, Attie?'

'*The German,* I suspect,' she said, as she gently bathed her grazes.

'But he was shooting at me!'

'Not you, Gin, rabbits, or ducks, more likely. After a bit of fresh meat. He only gets a pension, you know. He's what's called a *displaced person.*'

*

The butcher wiped his hands on his bloodstained apron. His eyes keen with interest.

'You'd have to be Jasper's daughter, eh?' he boomed. Gin nodded eagerly but already he had turned and was speaking to her aunt.

'Well now, Miss Partridge, how can I help you today?'

'Four cutlets, a nice piece of brisket, thank you Sam ... and two sets of kidneys. I rather fancy some kidneys. Do you like kidneys, Gin?'

A boy of about fourteen appeared as the row of carcasses divided. Gin could feel him staring at her. 'I don't think I've ever tried them, Attie,' she said, watching the carcasses swaying on their hooks.

Slivers of glossy white fat fell onto the wooden chopping block as Sam trimmed the cutlets. He transferred them onto greaseproof paper, squaring them together with plate-like hands.

'Bring me some kidneys from out the back, Rodney,' he called, as he brought out a fatty piece of rolled brisket.

Rodney re-emerged from the coolroom and plopped the kidneys down on the counter.

'How do they look, Miss Partridge? Fresh in this morning.'

The purply-pink organs wobbled as Sam wrapped them up. With a flick of his wrist, he knotted the string on each parcel so that each formed a nice little handle.

'There you are, Miss Partridge,' he said, 'and these, young Missie,' he winked at Gin, 'are for you.' He pressed the little parcel containing the kidneys into her hands.

Gin felt her face begin to redden. Once outside, she saw the two of them grinning through the window, grinning at each other and grinning at her.

Suddenly, from out of nowhere, came her mother's voice. *Don't look back, Virginia. Show some poise!*

*

Gravel spun under her slippery leather soles. Grass-seeds tickled her bare toes. Her mother had always insisted on socks with sandals but Attie didn't give a hoot. All around, the air was busy with bees, so thick with pollen it had made her nose begin to prickle. The apple trees looked exquisite, the last of their late white blossoms fluttering like a cloud of butterflies above the fence. And greeting them either side of the entrance to the farm were large flushes of oleander blossom. Something rustled in the bushes. Gin shied, eyeing a cluster of trembling pink flowers. Suddenly a browny-grey bird dived out of the leaves, *chlicka-chlicka-chlicking* as it swooped over her head.

'Just a wattle-bird,' said Attie, explaining that there would be hundreds of them over in the forest, feasting themselves silly on kangaroo paws and bottlebrush blossoms. Near the house they were aggressively territorial. She'd seen them before, dive-bombing wagtails, even magpies, a dog or a cat, or anything in their way.

Attie reached inside the half kerosene tin. Shuffling through the mail, she handed Gin two airmail letters addressed to Herr Dieter Hasse with intriguing-looking stamps.

'Ah! One from your mother, finally! Look, Gin, there's even a postcard for you.'

It was postmarked Ceylon. Gin inspected the stamp, a delicate, pink-edged square framing a greyish print of a woman in a sari tapping rubber. On the other side of the card was a delightful photo of an elephant cow and baby. But it was a struggle to decipher her mother's message.

... there are lots of little monkeys around the temples ...

Attie sliced open the aerogramme with her finger.

Thank God we're about to leave Colombo, she read aloud, while putting on Valerie's oh-so English accent. *What a horrid, dirty hole of a place. Beggars on every corner and I didn't dare drink the water. The traffic chaotic, streets thick with rickshaws dodging pedestrians and bikes. The constant smell of the open sewers is vile and intolerable. I really can't imagine, Adeline, how you remember this place with such affection ...*

'Oh, how interesting,' Attie continued. 'She says here that her bank manager, Noel Wheatley, is on the ship too. Well now ... *isn't that a coincidence?* Fancy him booking a passage on the very same ship. I call it a bloody amazing *coincidence.*'

Already Gin was picturing Noel Wheatley, the Minties and the money box he once gave her. Ever since she could remember there was a kind of oiliness in his voice whenever he came around.

And how're you today, sweetie? Would Mummy be at home? And Mummy's edgy laugh, blades of hair swishing like mudlark wings in her flurry of excitement; then that one-eyed look of hers with fringe dark and blunt against her profile ... *Outside and play, dear. Mr Wheatley and I've some important business to discuss and you're not to interrupt.*

*

Outside there was quite a commotion. Yelping and barking and a whirl of dust rising from the driveway. Gin counted at least a dozen dogs of all shapes and sizes milling around with their ears pricked and tails erect. They kept running around in circles, nipping and snapping and smelling under each other's tails. She ran in to tell Attie.

'Fighting?' Attie hooted at Gin's suggestion. 'Blasted dog's on heat again.' She ratted around in the duster drawer. 'Here, these should keep her out of mischief,' she said, shaking out a tattered pair of bloomers.

'Arushi!' The dog had a stupid guilty look, standing, head bent downwards as Attie slipped Arushi's hind legs into the leg holes and eased her drooping tail through a small incision she'd made in the back of the cloth.

Chapter 3

'Here Gin, this new book will be just the shot,' said Mr Penworthy. 'The pieces may have childish names but they're sometimes fiendishly difficult to play. Ah, but I'm sure you like a challenge. Now, shall we start with the first—it's called 'About Strange Lands and People'. Try to think about somewhere strange, Gin, or somebody foreign so as to get the feeling for the piece.'

Gin had heard the piece before so the notes came easily.

'Don't forget what I said about those intervals, Gin. You mustn't allow your fingers to jump up on the high notes. You must make yourself reach out and embrace your stranger. Don't be afraid; don't be put off by the gap … the distance. I want a yearning quality, a desire to reach out. Now, let's see what you can do.'

Gin played the first section to a round of applause.

'Yes. You've got it alright!' said Mr Penworthy. 'No doubt about that.'

He turned to Attie at the end of the lesson. 'Gin tells me you played your violin last night, is that right, Miss Partridge?'

'Hardly think a bit of scratching around is what you'd call playing.' Attie let out a hoot. 'Rather rusty, I'm afraid. Haven't picked up a fiddle since well before the war.'

'Now, if you ever need an accompanist, I'd be only too happy to oblige. It always sounds so much better, you know, the violin, when it's played with the piano. Otherwise it can sound like a sad lonely voice crying out for help.' Mr Penworthy touched her shoulder. 'I didn't mean that, Miss Partridge. Forgive me. I'm a pianist, you know. We tend to say rude things at times. Do bring your violin next time and after Gin's lesson, you must play me something and I'll see if I can join in.'

*

Within days Gin had learnt the Schumann piece by heart.

'A good memory is a rare gift that should be developed,' remarked Attie. 'Here, I want you to have this as a small reward.' She presented Gin with a tiny carved ebony elephant.

Gin admired the craftsmanship, the noble head and fine white tusks.

'It's from my childhood collection,' Attie smiled. 'Every time I memorised a violin sonata your Grandfather Charlie would present me with another miniature elephant like this. The elephant, of course, is revered in Ceylon. Did you know an elephant has the highest powers of memory in the whole of the animal kingdom? The Hindus even worship a god with an elephant head. Go and look up *Ganesh*,' she said, handing her a book on Eastern mythology.

After Gin had studied the picture of the god's strange animalised face, she turned the page and read.

> *Ganesh, is the most venerated of all the Hindu gods.*
> *He is known as The Remover of Obstacles, the god*
> *of domestic harmony and of success. When Lord*

Shiva was away fighting for the gods, the lady of the house, goddess Parvathi was alone at home. She wanted someone to guard the house while she took a bath. Unable to think of any alternative, she created a son, Ganesh. She instructed him to keep strict vigil on the entrance to the house and not to allow anyone in. Ganesh agreed and stayed on the strictest of vigils. In the meantime Lord Shiva returned happy after a glorious victory for the gods, only to be stopped at the entrance by Ganesh. Ganesh, acting on Parvathi's orders, did not allow Shiva to enter the house. Lord Shiva became enraged beyond control and in a fit of rage cut off Ganesh's head.

Parvathi came out of her bath and was aghast at the scene. She was very very angry at her lordship for what had happened and explained the situation to him. Lord Shiva wanted to make it up to Parvathi and agreed to put life back into Ganesh by replacing his head with that of the first living creature sighted asleep with its head to the north. He sent his soldiers to go in search of the creature. The first creature they saw was an elephant. So Lord Shiva re-created his son with the head of the elephant. Hence the trunk of Lord Ganesh. Parvathi was still not totally happy so Shiva granted Ganesh a boon that before the beginning of any undertaking or task people would worship Lord Ganesh. That is why Hindus worship Ganesh before starting any work.

'Where exactly is Ceylon, Attie?'

'A clever girl like you doesn't know where Ceylon is?' Attie locked her eyebrows in disbelief. She went off and within minutes had returned with an old discoloured globe of the world. 'Well, then,' she asked, 'do you know where India is?'

'Yes.'

'Well, they say that Ceylon hangs like a teardrop from the bottom of India.' Dust lifted in the air as Attie gave the globe a flick. Next to her aunt's pointed finger, Gin could spot a small green island in the blue.

*

At the end of Attie's bed was another Saratoga. A travelling trunk, lined with faded gold satin that had fallen into shreds. The different compartments, Attie explained, were so your clothes always stayed well-pressed while you were travelling.

'Would you believe,' she went on, 'that some of those clothes have been stored in that trunk for nearly twenty-five years and never been worn! Look how beautifully pressed they've stayed. And aren't they just gorgeous? It was 1932. Your grandmother wanted to take us back to the Old Country,' she said, 'back to her roots. Jasper and I were seventeen and had just finished school. We were all prepared. Each of us had a trunk of new clothes beautifully handmade by tailors in Colombo. Then, at the last minute, we couldn't go. Granny was devastated when your grandfather cancelled the tickets.'

Attie unfolded each garment and laid it out on the bed so Gin could see. 'Perhaps there's something here that will fit you. Look at you, growing like a beanstalk!' She held up a white spotted linen tunic belted on the hip. 'Won't come down to your ankles, that's for certain, but it'll do for Christmas Day.'

Gin rubbed her arms as a fresh waft of breeze filtered through the French doors.

'When I was a girl in Ceylon we had servants. Everyone did. *The good old days,* my mother used to call them.' Attie gave a chortle. 'But of course, she couldn't afford a servant when we came here during the Depression. Worked herself to the bone for the first few years trying to maintain colonial standards. Not me. I don't give a brass razoo. These days I rarely iron,' she admitted cheerfully. 'Well, except for Mother's linen. *The finest Irish linen,* she always liked to remind me. When I go to bed, somehow it's like entering another world. I can lie there and black everything out, luxuriate in my childhood.' Attie paused as she held a sheet up and inspected it closely in the light. 'Which reminds me, Gin, don't let that naughty dog sleep in your bed again, especially when she's on heat.'

*

The clean sheets had a sweet smell. It was the scent of the purple-flowered lavender that grew beside the wash-house door, which, after drying, had been bundled into small muslin bags and tucked into drawers.

Gin tried to picture her grandmother lying between these same embroidered sheets. Many times she had studied the ivory-framed photo on the dressing-table showing Granny as young and pretty with translucent skin and thick auburn plaits coiled upon her head. But, as much as she tried, Gin could not reconcile this photo with the vague, grey-haired, bespectacled image of the granny she'd known as a small child. How could that be the same person? Even though Granny had been dead six years she could still recall her presence.

Somewhere in that tumbling haze of events Gin could bring to mind a Saturday morning fending for herself on *Mummy's weekend off*. It was late and Granny was still in bed, having given instructions not to be disturbed. Gin had put her ear to the keyhole and heard the drone of rough male voices coming from the crackly wireless in Granny's room. Very quietly, she'd turned the handle and peeped through a crack in the door. Granny was sitting bolt upright in bed, pondering the punting guide through the bottom of her bifocals. Gin could see straight through her nightie to her bosoms, which lay on the counterpane like a pair of large poached eggs.

Not just now, dear, I'm too busy. Pencil poised, Granny bit the air. *Far too busy for little wanty girls.*

Then Granny began to cough and splutter, eyes watering, her face red and about to explode.

Now look what you've done, you naughty girl. You've started me off coughing again. Quick, fetch me a clean hankie from the top drawer. I'll miss the start of the race if I'm not careful.

It wasn't just Granny's bedroom. Gin could visualise different aspects of their old house in Swanbourne where they'd lived after leaving the farm: the kitchen and the vestibule, garden rambling with every imaginable flower. Granny standing beneath the white-anted rafters of the outside lav; Granny doubled over, clutching the trellis, hacking into the damp evening air; Granny's face, white, tinged with blue, like the moon which lay waiting for night-time to come.

Gin hopped into bed and pulled up the clean scented sheets. For some reason her mind kept harking back to when Granny died; how she'd lain awake for hours like this, tossing and turning, tossing and turning. She remembered shadows on the walls shifting and transforming in the dark; part animal, part human, they entered the strange world of her half-sleep. Once again, the clock chimed. Once again, she'd lost count of time waiting for the next spate of Granny's coughing. A sigh had followed in the wake of a white candlewick dressing-gown as her mother floated back and forth down the hall. Recurrent *brr* patterns of dialling on the telephone and the frantic tones of her mother's voice. For a while Granny's coughing settled, and, as the shadows dissolved, Gin drifted back to sleep once more. The low hum of voices had woken her again. She'd tiptoed into the hall and peeped around the door and caught the glint of a dangling stethoscope. Quickly she'd scampered back to bed and the steady pattering of rain on the tin roof soon lulled her off to sleep again.

The following morning the sun was sparkling like ginger ale through the leadlight windows, casting square coloured patterns on the floor. Magpies started up their *creedle-crawdle* song. From the window-seat in the vestibule, she had watched them stalking across the wet lawn, one eye watchful as they spiked the grass for worms. And, as she passed Granny's room, she'd checked to see whether she was still breathing. Deathly silent, Granny was lying, half-propped by pillows, patchwork quilt pulled up to her chin. She noticed how her closed eyes were almost buried in their sockets, and her face had fallen and exposed the hollow of her mouth. Everything about Granny seemed to have suddenly shrunk. A pink and white swirl had caught her eye. Granny's two sets of false teeth were floating in a glass of water and they looked absolutely huge. It was only later her mother told her that Granny was dead. She had wiped the misty pane with her hand and through the clearing circle had seen Attie outside bending over the open boot of her car. Spots of rain spat into puddles near her feet.

The house had been filled with people and flowers. Gin remembered a man in a pinstriped suit arriving and the sound of lowered voices in the vestibule.

Just the farm, Valerie, Attie had said. *That's all I want.* The man licked his thumb and turned a page. *Sign here.*

The next thing Gin remembered was Attie saying goodbye, gravel spinning under the wheels. She had stood on the running-board, hanging on for grim death—*Look Mummy*—feeling the thrilling sensation of gathering speed, only to jump off at the gate. Looking back now, she recalled how her mother had stood pinch-eyed on the front steps watching Attie driving away.

Kensington SW1
December 8th, 1956

Dearest Virginia,
   Landed at Southampton two days ago feeling on top of the world. Not one single headache to speak of since leaving Australia. As mentioned

Noel Wheatley happened to be travelling on the same ship. I've been busy showing him the sights of London. So much has changed, some areas I would hardly have recognised. Dozens of new housing estates being developed but a lot of war damage still remains to be seen in the old part of the city, especially around St Paul's. We didn't spend much time there as I'm afraid it brought back bad memories of the Blitz.

Winter is well and truly here now. Leaves rotting in the parks and all the trees so bare and ghostly-looking. I'd forgotten how cold it can get. Very glad I remembered to bring my astrakhan overcoat. A bit old-fashioned but with my old lambskin gloves keeps me nice and cosy.

Hope you're being a big help to Attie. Lots of lovely things to do on a farm, aren't there? Well, tomorrow Noel and I will take the train from Charing Cross down to Sidcup to see the family. Fingers crossed for a white Christmas in Kent. I'm looking forward to your letters which I hope are awaiting me there.

Be good, won't you dear.

Love from Mummy
PS I hope you haven't had any more bouts of tonsillitis.

One night, Gin caught her aunt undressing as she passed by her room. Attie's legs were long and shaped rather like her own. A final flounce of frock over the head revealed a bony ribcage pushing out above her diaphragm. Gin watched Attie grope with hooks and eyes. Slipping the brassiere over her arms, Attie tossed it on the chair and suddenly a strange, pointy cone-shaped piece of sponge rubber fell to the floor. Only then did Gin see the scar. White and shiny, it extended from around the underside of her aunt's shoulder through her chest to her stomach. Ooh! She reeled. There was nothing, nothing there at all. Not even a nipple. Attie, by now, was completely naked. As she turned around , one white breast on her other side suddenly swung front-on to face Gin.

'Ooh! I'm sorry Attie ... I didn't mean to ...' Gin blushed, not knowing where to look. She wanted to run away and hide.

Attie continued putting on her nightie. 'It's alright, dear. Don't go,' she said calmly. 'Sit down. There's something you should know.'

Turning away, Attie slowly began to brush her hair.

'After Granny died,' she said, 'I thought it was the build-up of sadness I was feeling. Not realising how seriously ill I was. Then one evening, lying in the bath, I found a lump in my breast. It was a very big operation, Gin. It took a long time for me to recover. The farm went downhill during that time. I had to sell part of it to a neighbour because I couldn't manage all the hard physical work anymore. But, still, I was grateful to be alive. Cam Carter, one of our neighbours, came over to help out for a while. One day he brought me a little puppy from his bitch's new litter. Easy to train, he said. Wasn't sure what I was in for. We'd never kept dogs before. Granny wouldn't have a bar of them. The streets of Ceylon were littered with stray dogs, mangy pariahs considered by the locals as the lowest form of life. But, you know, Gin, that little puppy was just gorgeous. She gave me the strength and energy to get back on my feet. Every morning I'd wake up at first light to hear her scratching at the door, whimpering for attention. That's why I called her Arushi. She was such a delight. Stopped me feeling sorry for myself.'

'But why did you call her Arushi?' asked Gin.

'*Arushi* means dawn or red sky in the early morning. It was partly because of her red cloud colouring and because she was so full of life.'

Then Attie went on to explain how Grandfather Charlie had once taken her and Jasper on their thirteenth birthdays up to the highest mountain in Ceylon. They had started out in the early hours of the morning from the rest house, taking a guide in case of leopards, and there, at over 8,000 feet, on the summit of Pidurutalagala, they had watched the sunrise.

'It was an ordeal for Father, for most of the time he wasn't very well, but he felt it was important. *My life is almost over,* he said to us then, *but yours are only beginning. Look,* he pointed at the glorious vista, *you young ones have the world at your feet. There's nothing you cannot do.* I'll always be grateful to Father for taking the trouble,' said Attie. She told Gin she would never forget that experience of looking down on everything and watching the sunrise, and the pink hills and the valleys struggling out of the golden mist.

*

'Here Gin, Dieter will be over any tick of the clock to pick up his stores. Be a chum and run them down. You can meet him at the shed.'

'Could we give him some eggs, Attie?'

'I suppose we've more than enough for the two of us. There you are then, take those.'

Gin whistled. 'A-rushi!' and the dog came trotting up behind. A billy of milk, fresh from a neighbouring farm, swung by her side. In her other hand Gin clutched the eggs and the brown paper parcels containing Dieter's shopping. No free hand to wave away the flies crawling around her eyes and lips. She hitched her shoulder up to her mouth, blowing them away with her bottom lip.

For goodness' sake, child, close your lips. You look like an imbecile. Nothing looks worse than a slack mouth.

But, Mummy, I can't breathe if I don't open my mouth.

Rubbish. That's what your nose is for.

But I can't breathe through my nose, it's all blocked up.

Nonsense.

Gin shuffled along, kicking up the dust with her sandals. She was trying to imagine what he looked like, when she saw him coming towards the shed, a tall figure, with a rifle slung over his shoulder and boots laced up above his ankle. His head was lowered as if he hadn't noticed her. And there was something in his hand, swinging by his side.

As she approached, the man looked up in surprise and instantly lowered the rifle. He clicked his heels together, as if to attention, and doffing his hat, made a passing bow.

'*Guten Tag, Fräulein.* Hallo.' His eyes were dark. 'I have today here for Miss Partridge ... zis ... zis, how do you say?' He held his arm outstretched. '*Hier, bitte, Fräulein.*'

A rabbit hung from his hand. Its long ears were squeezed into his fist, pink mouth drawn back firmly into pouchy cheeks emphasising the prominence of the two front teeth. A tiny trickle of blood dripped from the tip of the rabbit's tongue, Gin noticed, and its bulging eyes had a fixed, startled expression, as if it had been caught totally unawares.

Gin wanted to stroke and comfort the little animal, feel the softness of its fur and the white downy underside of its belly.

'I'm sorry ... I ...' her words floundered as she began to stutter.

He stood there for a moment and then smiled back as if he understood.

'Your name is ...?'

'Vir-ginia but I prefer Gin.'

'*Ah. Chin. Fräulein,* how many years have you?'

'Twelve.'

'Aah! *Zwölf.* That is *gut!*'

Suddenly his expression changed, became overcast, then he beckoned her.

'*Kommen Sie* to the house. I will the rabbit bring.'

*

Attie was dusting ornaments and had a fine piece of china in her hand. It was a little figurine, a boy in bracer shorts and pale blue blouse, with a tiny fiddle at his chin. 'Ah,' she murmured. 'Dresden. Apparently he comes from Dresden.'

'Where's Dresden, Attie?'

'Dresden, what's left of it, is in Eastern Germany, what's now the communist part. Lucky Dieter got out when he did.'

Gin wondered how the German had escaped from the communists and remembered how at ease he looked with a rifle.

'What are you going to do with the rabbit, Attie?'

'Well, now that it's skinned, I shall cook it, of course. Once they're skinned and lost their pretty fur, I don't think so much of their being animals anymore, they just seem to me to be like any other meat, really, just something that hangs in a butcher shop that you cook and eat. But, anyway, rabbit will certainly make a nice change, won't it? And how'd you like it done, dear, baked or stewed?'

'I don't think I've ever eaten rabbit before, Attie.'

'Haven't you, now? Well, I like it stewed best. Yes, so that's what I'll do, Gin. I'll make a nice rabbit stew. A bit of bacon, a few prunes and carrots, and a drop of port,' she added with a wink.

*

Attie drained the last of her sherry and placed two plates on the table. She sat down beaming at Gin.

'Well, come on then, tuck in,' she said.

Gin picked up her knife and fork and waited for Attie to start. She watched as her aunt cut into the meat with great gusto, then closed her eyes as she chewed the first mouthful. Attie's face took on a dramatic air. She was making slow rotations with her lips. Then she stopped and said, 'Mmm. Beautiful. Simply beautiful. Haven't had rabbit for years. We used to eat a lot of it once. Your mother refused to even look at it when she arrived here. Said she was fed up to the teeth with fricasseed rabbit, it was the only meat she'd had for five bloody years. But what a lovely change it makes from brisket and cutlets. I'll have to ask Dieter to bring me rabbit more often.'

Gin stared at the piece of jointed white meat on her plate. It was surrounded by a pool of thick dark gravy dotted with prunes and carrot wheels. What she was looking at was the breast, she realised, the shoulder and the short little foreleg. Her eyes followed the thickness of the meat down to the darkish sinews which had been cut off at the lower joint, the part which belonged to the soft front paw. Gin tried not to think of it but somehow it reminded her of a cat's leg, and, all of a sudden, she could see Tiddles, Granny's tabby, playing with a ball of wool. She tucked the meat safely under her mashed potato when Attie wasn't looking.

'Attie,' she said, putting her knife and fork together, 'what are we going to be eating for Christmas dinner?'

'Well, I thought we could have one of the older chooks. There're just the two of us and turkey is far too expensive.'

'What do you think Dieter'll be having, Attie?'

Gin listened to the low grind of teeth chewing from the other side of the table. It was interrupted by the sudden gurgle of the kerosene fridge.

'He must be terribly, terribly lonely over there all by himself with no friends or relatives,' she said after a while. 'Do you think we could ask Dieter for Christmas dinner, Attie?'

Attie stopped chewing and held up one finger.

'Shh! Listen!' Through the stillness and the outside dark came the sound of some sort of bird or an animal, *boobook, boobook*, its call lonely and enduring.

'What is it, Attie?'

'It's a mopoke. Have you not heard a mopoke before?'

Chapter 4

It was that time of the afternoon when the sun was hidden low behind the saplings. Every so often, slanted rays would burst between the dappled trunks, dividing the ground into alternate stripes of grey and gold. The effect was to send Gin into a half-jog, leaping breathlessly over the long dark shadows that snaked across the gold. She was trying to avoid the darkness, trying to make her feet land only on the golden sunlit streaks.

She couldn't stop thinking about the bungarra she'd seen earlier that day scuttling up a tree. They always go to the highest point. Attie knew firsthand. Years ago, when she was out riding, one ran up over the top of her. All three feet of it, she said, up the flank of her chestnut mare then right over her head and down the other side again. Even now, she could distinctly remember the creep of its claws and the nasty scratch it left on her cheek.

Gin was glad to reach the relative safety of the cattle-pit and to have the open sunlit paddocks spread out before her. From here the diagonal patterns of the vineyard stood in fresh relief, their vivid colour crisscrossing the pale grey hillside, larger in the beginning and gradually becoming smaller on the rise. The closer she approached, the less defined the terraced rows, appearing before her now as just a small legion of vines, pointy green leaves flapping gaily in the breeze.

Gin half-closed her eyes and put her head to one side. Elves, that's what they reminded her of, hand in hand with their arms thrust upwards in jubilation, a green chorus waving and dancing and laughing and nodding their heads. *Come on*, they seemed to be saying, *come closer and we'll tell you our secrets. Come closer if you dare.*

Without warning, the sun slipped behind a cloud again and the vines soon lost their magic. The dog had already trotted on ahead and was busy sniffing around the kikuyu by the time she reached the pump-house.

Gin scanned the dam, startled by the sound of a heavy splash. Everything appeared to be normal apart from a series of rings spreading outwards across the black water. Then, every few seconds, something would suddenly appear to bob up and down, some kind of water bird she presumed.

She stood enjoying the cool aroma of the peppermint tree and the delicious tickle of its leaves upon her face. Between changing gaps of light, she soon came to realise that the thing bobbing in the water was not a wild duck or a shag but a man, lunging around, duck-diving now with his white bottom rolling through the surface like a porpoise. Yikes! Fancy swimming with nothing on! Dieter wouldn't do a thing like that! Yet, even from this close distance, she wasn't so sure it was Dieter. But if it wasn't Dieter, who was it then?

Eventually, that brown-and-white striped body emerged in full. The man was huddled over, Gin noticed, his hands cupped loosely between his hairy legs as he climbed into a pair of rubber boots before clambering up the bank.

At the top he stood briefly drying himself in the sunshine. In a flash he was respectable in baggy shorts and singlet, and, with his back now turned to her, nothing more than a lonely silhouette making his way off into the shadows of the state forest.

Gin remained in the shadow of the pump-house, flabbergasted. Gingerly she stepped down from the bank into the sludgy shallows. Did it really happen, she kept wondering, or was it just a dream that had slipped away? She shuddered at the slimy brush of weeds and sticks on the bottom and, as mud squelched between her toes, she lunged forward, piercing the ripples. On the surface, the water was warm but underneath, where her legs kicked down into the deep darkness, it was so suddenly cold it took her breath away.

For some time, she lay on her back, swirling her hands through the warmer water to keep herself afloat. What exactly did it look like? she asked the sky. She'd never seen a naked male before! She squeezed her eyes and tried hard to bring it into focus, that thing, to make it clearer and nearer. She had the colour of it, a sort of dirty pink colour, but then it all seemed to vanish into a curly twirl of black.

When Gin opened her eyes again, she noticed the bull drinking in amongst the reeds and suddenly … suddenly she remembered now what it looked like. Yes, that's right, like the mottled teat of a cow's udder, swinging against his hairy thighs.

*

'Attie,' said Gin, 'guess what! There was a strange man swimming in the dam.'

'Oh?' said Attie with little interest. 'I dare say it was Dieter.'

'I don't think so, Attie; didn't really look like Dieter.'

'Well, maybe it was old Fitzy then.'

'Who?' asked Gin.

'Fitzy. That's what they call him. Fellow on a neighbouring property. Bit of an oddball, if you ask me, but he can be well-meaning. He was bragging the other day about the good crop of cherries he's got. Said to come over and help ourselves.'

Attie was bent over the stove, with her back to her, blacking the hotplates.

'I suppose he's entitled to have a swim if he feels inclined,' she said, working the small brush across the hob. 'It's not hurting anyone. There!' she exclaimed, standing back admiringly. 'What do you think of that? Give the old stove a Christmas present.'

'Not long now. Only twelve days to go,' exclaimed Gin, following her out of the room. 'Can we have a tree, Attie? You know, a Christmas tree.'

Attie didn't answer for a while.

'Just look around outside, my dear,' she said with a wide sweep of her hand. 'You can have all the Christmas trees you want. They're in flower now. There're at least six down there in the back paddocks. Absolutely brilliant and all decorated in nature's glory. You'll never see a sight like that in the city, you know.'

Gin could imagine what her mother would say if she were here.

Ghastly orange things. Goodness knows why they're called Christmas trees. I don't find them at all attractive. As far as I'm concerned, the only real Christmas trees are proper fir trees like we have back home.

'Come in Miss Partridge, please,' Mr Penworthy said, offering her a chair. 'Oh, splendid, you've brought your violin.'

'For goodness' sake, Mr Penworthy, please don't call me Miss Partridge. When I was a schoolteacher, I always loathed being Miss Partridge. All day long it was *Yes Miss, no Miss, three bags full Miss.* Just because I'm over forty and unmarried doesn't mean people have to call me Miss.'

'Dear, dear. I didn't mean to offend you.' He produced an airy smile. 'I shall never call you Miss Partridge again. Never again.' His pink cheeks wobbled as he spoke.

'Just call me Attie then,' she said, having settled the issue. 'My mother obviously liked Adeline but I can't say I'm particularly fond of it.'

'Splendid! Attie it is then ... and you must call me Percy. It's my middle name but I like it, it's different. My mother knew Mr Grainger, you know. Well then, Attie, what are you going to play for me? 'Ah, *Humoresque,*' he said, noticing the score. 'Just play it once through if you like and then I'll join in. What key are you in? I'll just put in a few chords here and there to get myself acquainted. Righty-o then, would you like an A?' he asked, as Attie lifted the violin up to her chin and raised her bow. Together they played. Mr Penworthy was right. The violin sounded so much better when it was accompanied by the piano. And the liveliness of the tune made Gin want to dance.

'Well done, Attie,' said Mr Penworthy. 'Let's play it again,' he said with a chuckle. 'Yes, play it again.'

*

'What have you there?' said Attie, peering down. 'Ah ... Christmas beetles.'

Gin gently nudged the insects, trying unsuccessfully to contain them in an ashtray.

'Is that what they're called?' It intrigued her how the beetles kept trying to climb the china ridge, only to fall upside-down, legs wriggling helplessly in the air. She righted them with a match, noting the deeply coloured burnish of their humps.

'Think you only find them in the bush,' said Attie.

Gin was fascinated. They refused to be put off-course. It looked as if they were on a very important mission, marching around with their enormous loads.

*

From the opened French doors, Gin could see Dieter coming towards the house. He appeared to be dragging something through the gravel.

'Ah, *guten Tag, Fräulein,*' he called as she rushed up to meet him.

There beside him was a baby Norfolk pine tree, fresh and spiky and smelling of resin.

'For you,' he said, nodding to the tree. '*Tannenbaum.*'

His brown eyes looked kind.

'Come,' he said, as he dragged it to the house.

Later Attie brought in the Christmas tree and sat it in a tin bucket filled with sand.

'What about decorations, Attie?'

Together they collected some bulrushes and cut them into thin lengths and made chains, and some purple native creeper which wilted as soon as they draped it about the tree. 'Gum-nuts,' Attie said, 'we'll silverfrost some gum-nuts and tie them on with string.'

'Look Attie!' cried Gin. 'It's a real Christmas tree, isn't it?'

But the fairy, she whispered inside. Suddenly Gin knew that she didn't care about the fairy anymore. Suddenly she realised she was twelve and it had actually been quite some time since she'd believed in fairies.

Chapter 5

There was something satisfying about gathering eggs. Every day, the chooks' constant racket could be heard drifting from the stale-aired pen. On and on they went, mostly, it seemed, about nothing. Would they ever stop to draw breath, Gin often wondered. But then, as soon as her fossicking fingers had grasped each smooth warm oval shape in turn from the nests, she knew she was being rewarded by their efforts. Funny creatures, chooks. So fastidious the way they picked up their scaly feet from in amongst the dust and the food-scraps.

'Attie, have you invited Dieter yet to come for Christmas dinner?' she asked, handing her the basket of eggs.

Attie was pretending again she hadn't heard, so Gin went on.

'Mr Penworthy said he was going to spend Christmas day at the Federal Hotel. They do a nice turkey dinner there, he said, with all the trimmings.'

*

The air was hot and dry but it was cooler out than in. Patterns of afternoon shade flitted across her face as she lay staring up through the stillness into the fern-like foliage of the jacaranda tree. Patches of purple flowers shifted and merged overhead into the fuming blue heat of the overhead sky. Gin picked up one of the fragile lilac bells that had fallen on her face. How perfect it seemed until the damp bruise of her fingers imprinted on its side.

'Well,' announced Attie, as she drained her cup of tea. 'I think the time of reckoning has finally arrived. Come on, Gin, I need a hand. Chop chop!'

'What are we going to do now, Attie?'

'Ask no questions, tell no lies,' she says. 'Just follow me.'

Attie grabbed two hessian bags and the scrap bucket from the back veranda and headed towards the shed, humming the first part of the little Chopin waltz Gin had been playing earlier in the day.

Bees hovered around the scrappy grapevine and the rest of the corrugated iron lean-to. Most of the chooks were lying in the shade, half-buried in dust bowls, their dirty feathers fluffed and their eyes half-closed. They had almost stopped their racket, hoarse no doubt from their constant gasping and all that *bock-bock-bocking*. They lifted their heads and frowned, beaks gaping open and wings held out in exasperation.

'See that black speckled one over there,' Attie pointed, 'that's the one. Now, Gin, you're quicker than I am. You stand in there and, when I throw the food scraps in, run over and throw this bag over and hold her down.'

The other chooks squawked and scattered as Gin zipped here and there in chase. At last, the one in question was caught and bagged, but, in the raucous struggle, two hoary, crusted feet emerged kicking out in protest.

'Right,' said Attie, grabbing them still. 'Now, quick, see that piece of raffia twine there, tie them together as tight as you can.'

Over at the wood heap, Attie straightened the chopping block. She laid the flapping, cackling bird on its side. Gin caught the glint of axe poised above her aunt's head and quickly covered her eyes. There was a thump, and the squawking stopped once and for all.

'Blast and bugger it!' shouted Attie. 'Now look what I've done!'

Gin took a peep through parted fingers. The bird remained on the block, wings flapping in desperation, although its head still appeared to be intact. Blood oozed from around its fat lidded eyes and suddenly—the beak—the whole beak was missing. Ergh! There it is with that piece of red rubbery comb. Gin blocked her eyes to the awful blur that was Attie's second swipe. Thump! Gin shrieked as the headless body made its escape. But it soon stopped short in a black and crimson swirl. Only its wings were alive, futile circles sweeping up the dust.

'We have to let it hang,' explained Attie, attaching the scaly legs to a big metal hook. 'To let the blood drain out. That way the meat is sure to be nice and tender. There's nothing I dislike more than tough poultry.'

Under the cool of the tank-stand and its rampant creepers, it hung inside one of Attie's freshly laundered pillowcases to protect it from the flies. Gin stood by for a moment as bloodstains began to emerge across the fold marks of clean white cloth. Soon the fragrance of the creamy honeysuckle began to overpower her and she felt quite sick and had to walk away.

'Well,' said Attie, washing her hands thoroughly in the wash-house with a piece of yellow soap. 'That's that!'

*

It was a very long carol but Gin had committed herself to singing and playing all twelve verses without a break. But on the second verse she couldn't resist calling out:

'Hey, Attie, what are turtledoves?'

Hearing no answer, she continued ... *and a par-tri-dge in a pear tree* ... only to notice her aunt standing in the doorway.

'Yes!' Attie's eyes were bright. Gin thought she was going to make some joke about the word 'partridge' and how they were Partridges as well.

But instead she said, 'Of course, why didn't I think of that before. Apricots! Thanks for reminding me, Gin. Apricots we shall have! Let's go down to the orchard and see what we can find. They're always beautiful straight off the tree.'

Attie explained how these days she didn't bother sending stone fruit off to market. The trees were old and neglected; the fruit too much trouble. Bruised easily and what the birds didn't spoil wasn't worth her while. After Christmas, they would preserve some in Vacola bottles and maybe make some jam for her to take back to Perth.

Once in the orchard they found that silver-eyes had already punctured some of the riper apricots on the lower branches.

'But look at that crop of apples,' said Attie, pointing to the tiny unformed fruit. 'What a bumper. Not many windfalls so far. Your father grafted those trees back before the war. Now they're in their prime. I'm certainly going to have my work cut out for me in another couple of months. Might have to ask Dieter to come and give me a hand. Go on, up you go, Gin. You're younger than I am,' called Attie. 'Higher. There'll be plenty on the top.'

Gin scrambled over the craggy branches carefully passing

each ripe apricot down to her aunt. She stopped to bite into one, stunned by its sweet intensity.

'Plums,' said Attie, scanning the rows. 'Some plums would be nice to go with the cherries, what we have of them.'

Back at the house, Attie lifted the basket onto the table and sat herself down.

'You know Gin,' she sighed. 'I've got used to not making Christmas puddings. It's funny, I don't actually miss them. Anyway, what could be nicer than all this beautiful fresh fruit?'

'I don't like Christmas pudding, Attie. It's too rich. I reckon the only good thing about Christmas pudding is the thruppences and sixpences.'

Gin carefully arranged the fruit in a large white china bowl. She liked the contrast between the cold blue translucence of the ruby plums and the warm ripeness of the sun-flecked apricots. She found an orange and a lemon and two pairs of cherries and laid them on top. Then she drew an imaginary frame with her eyes. Yes, a painting, that's what it looked like, a painting.

*

'Hallo ... o! Hallo ... o!' It was Dieter. Gin could see him waving from behind the flywire door. She opened it to find him holding out two damp, limp ducks.

'Good morning, Miss Partridge.' He was observing Attie from under his brow. 'I have today for you ...'

After he had left, Attie stood looking out the kitchen window with her arms wrapped across her chest.

'Just like a wild duck, that's what it must have been like.'

'What do you mean, Attie?'

'For a bomber pilot. Most of them probably didn't stand a chance. I often think of that, whenever I hear gunshots.'

'What about rabbits?'

'Rabbits are different,' replied Attie. 'They are shy, silent little creatures, and they blend easily into the landscape and tend to run away and hide deep inside their burrows. Ducks are noisy and give themselves away. They must fly in order to escape, yet when airborne they are even more exposed. Some would argue that, with ducks, the shooter can send in a retriever. A dog would know exactly where a duck has fallen, bring it back and drop it at his master's feet. At least with ducks I suppose you know they're dead. But it's dreadful never to know for certain, Gin, it's simply dreadful.'

'What happened to Dad, Attie? Tell me.'

'His Lancaster was shot down, poor darling. He and his crew, lost presumably, but the rest we will never know, Gin, the rest we will never know.'

*

Gin's face was grave as she gathered strength and passion to her voice.

O Tannenbaum, she sang.

O Tannenbaum, she sang even louder.

How true you stand unchanging.

Gin pressed out the chords, on and on she went, filling the room with all her emotions.

'Is Dieter coming to Christmas dinner, Attie?' she enquired when she'd finished the third and final verse.

'He doesn't understand much English, Gin ... it's all too hard,' she muttered.

As the day wore on it became hotter and hotter. Gin noticed that Attie had taken off what her mother would call *foundation garments*. She was wearing a strappy sundress with a shirred elastic bodice.

'Hey Attie,' she reminded, 'your bosom's slipped again.'

It looked very strange, sitting all neat and perky on one side of her ribcage.

'Oh dear,' said Attie with a laugh, and, cupping it with her hand, whipped it around in line with the other, the soft and rounded one.

'Now I've got two again,' she pulled a face.

Later, they sat on the veranda, reading in the last of the light. Gin put down her book. It was hard to believe it was only two more days till Christmas. The *fowl*, as Attie called it, was in the process of being *dressed*. It was now in the fridge, its sticky pimpled breast covered securely with a tea-towel. Beside it were the ducks, now jointed and marinating in parsley, peppercorns and cider, waiting to be *jugged*, whatever that meant.

Gin curled herself up in the comfortable curve of the sea-grass chair and, closing her eyes, replayed the afternoon's preparations in her head. There was Attie dunking the birds into a pot of boiling water. That reek of hot dank feathers lingered in her nose. She could still smell it on her hands, though she'd just had a bath and washed her hair. Those quick little snatches as Attie stripped the bodies bare. How it clung to her fingers as she flicked the fluff away. *Achk!*—rubbing her itchy nose with her arm—*your turn*, and how the hilarity had erupted. Flecked down floating all over the kitchen, in the air, in her hair, all over her. Shrieking, reaching out and grabbing and losing a button off her shirt in the process!

Before going to bed that night, Gin stood inspecting herself in front of the long bevelled mirror. With the yoke of her nightie pulling against her chest she knew she would definitely be out of it before the year was out.

She slipped the garment over her shoulders and with her body open to the cool night air began trailing her fingertips lightly over her skin. She stood this way and that, even looking over her shoulder out of the corner of one eye. Then turned sideways. She found there was more to be seen in profile. *Goosebumps, that's all they are.* It was what her mother had called them just before she left. *Two little goosebumps, my pet.*

*

'What's that you're putting in there?' Gin asked, as Attie extracted her hand from the carcass.

'Everything,' she replied. 'Breadcrumbs, bacon, onion and sage, a beaten egg and some of those lovely plums and apricots we picked. And, of course, these,' she said, waving the wet, slimy giblets in front of Gin's nose.

'Don't!' Gin squealed and drew away. What she really wanted to know was who would be joining them for Christmas dinner, but somehow Attie always managed to avoid the question.

Gin returned to peeling potatoes. It was fun to see how long the strip of peel could last. Suddenly, the knife slipped and lifted her skin.

'Quick, Attie, I'm bleeding!'

Redheads are bleeders! What utter rot! Just an old wives' tale, Mr Wheatley's voice sprang from out of nowhere. *Dear, oh dear, Valerie ... you really must stop worrying. Sooner or later the child will have to have her tonsils out, and that's all there is to it.* Then came her mother's voice rising out in protest. *But Mrs Robinson said she once knew of a little redhead who had her tonsils out. She kept vomiting up black clots soon after the operation and the poor little mite bled to death in a matter of hours.*

But her hair wasn't red at all, Attie was quick to reassure her. It was actually auburn, just like Granny's used to be.

'What time is it in England now?' Gin asked, as Attie bound her finger up.

*

It was late but Gin could still hear Attie pottering about in the kitchen. She reopened the *Billabong* book she'd been reading earlier in the day. It was about Norah's soldier brother, Captain Jim, who was fighting in the muddy battlefields of Flanders. Gin turned the page to find Norah has just received a telegram advising of his death. Gin's nose began to prickle. Like Norah, she too was crying now but the pain she felt was welcome.

Gin read on and on, sniffing and swallowing down hard on the lump in her throat. Many pages later, her weary eyes widened when Jim suddenly returns home one day, alive and unannounced, just in time for Christmas. *I'm in a dream*, he tells his sister. *All those months have been the dream—and you can wake up now.*

Gin wanted to hold the story still, there and then, just where it was on the page. She pictured Attie and her mother and Granny, now, holding out their arms to Jasper, to find his absence too had only been a dream. Gin held the image for as long as she could until finally it merged into her own dream. She was dreaming she was standing on the edge of the dam. *Coo-ee!* she called. *Coo-*

ee! As the echoes rang across the water, floating ducks began to scatter. Now the ducks were changing into humans and bore her father's quirky smile. Gin could see him hovering in full service uniform. Suddenly the braids on his uniform began to expand and wave, transforming into huge golden wings. She called out to him but he didn't seem to hear her. Just kept sailing up away and into the clouds.

*

'Happy Christmas, Gin darling.' Attie hugged her extra hard. 'Here you are,' she said, handing her a brown paper parcel. 'Do hope they fit.'

'Ooh, Attie! Bathers, thank you. Just what I need!' She held them out. Jansen. XSSW. A shiny green colour with tiny little cups.

'And, here's a parcel from your mother.'

Gin ripped open the paper wrapping. A tall doll stood captive behind the cellophane window of a long rectangular box.

> *My dearest Virginia,*
>
> *It's hard to know what to give a girl your age but I didn't think you'd be too old for this. Isn't she just beautiful and rather special at that? A collector's item, one might say. We found her in Dickens and Jones. You just can't get things like this in Australia ...*

Arushi lay on the veranda stretched out asleep. Her tummy twitched and she gave little whimpers every now and then. Perhaps dogs, too, had dreams, thought Gin, and her own dream came to mind. She sat on the steps, her head against the chocolate warmth of the dog. Part red cloud kelpie, so Attie said. Gin held out a strand of her hair against her fur to compare the colour. A fly landed on the dog's rusty nose. Up she jumped, snapping at all the flies.

'Hey, Arushi, come ... come ... here Rushi.' The dog checked her over through golden eyes. Her blond brows softened now, ears no longer cocked. Then she sniffed Gin's hand and licked it until it made her squirm.

Worms! Did you hear me? You'll end up with hydatids. Don't touch that filthy, disgusting dog. At least cats are clean and keep their tongues to themselves. Now, for goodness' sake, child, go and wash your hands. Do you hear, Virginia? At once!

'Down,' said Gin firmly, and the dog flopped onto her foot, tongue searching for the salty sweat between her toes. 'C'mon! Off, Arushi! I want to try my new bathers on.' As Gin slipped down her bloomers, her eyes caught the browny red stain on the crotch. 'Attie,' she shrieked. 'Atteeee! Quick! I need you! Now!'

*

There was no time to ask any questions. Gin quickly helped Attie assemble the trestle table under the shade of the Cape lilac tree. Fallen yellow berries squashed between her toes as she went around the table carefully smoothing the white damask cloth flat so that the edges were touching the tips of the thousands of baby Cape lilac trees sprouting through the lawn.

'Be a chum and go and turn the potatoes for me please, Gin,' called Attie.

Barely had she done so when Arushi suddenly leapt up. The dog nosed open the door and let it close with a bang. Quick as a whistle, she was out on the lawn barking her head off.

Behind all the fuss and drawing of breath, Gin could faintly hear the spin of gravel and the soft crunch of tyres on the driveway. Who on earth could it be? For a moment she couldn't help thinking of Captain Jim.

'Attie! It's a baby Austin,' she called from the doorway. 'Who do you know owns a white baby Austin?'

A plump bottom emerged from the door of the car.

'Happy Christmas everyone,' called Mr Penworthy with his Panama pressed to his heart.

'Oh my goodness,' she said out loud, 'and now ...' as she saw Dieter coming up the driveway.

Gin had never felt so flustered.

Dieter produced a rather formal bow. His suntanned hand had hold of Mr Penworthy's chubby white one and was pumping it up and down. Strands of wet hair neatly separated across his head and Gin couldn't help but notice how his face, warm and brown against his white shirt, was riddled with deep worry lines like the walnut she was holding in her hand. He reminded her of someone in a film, but who the devil was it now? An older Humphrey Bogart, perhaps? And with Attie sneaking sly looks his way Gin couldn't help but wonder if she thought the same.

Gin stood to one side, the other three nodding and smiling and chatting to each other. She caught half-sentences and jerks of conversation as she bobbed back and forth from the bathroom to check on her spotting.

Attie's eyes were flashing, her face made fresh by the flush in her cheeks. In the heat and excitement, damp wisps of hair had curled against her forehead giving her a pretty, girlish look.

'More beer,' she prompted, pointing the bottle at Dieter. 'Please!'

'*Prost!*' He raised his glass and, leaning towards Attie, asked in his deep dark voice, 'In English, how do you say?'

'Cheers!' she blurted, 'or *chin-chin* as my mother used to say.'

'Bottoms up!' boomed Mr Penworthy.

He leant back on his chair, tweaking his spotted bow-tie while Attie carved, then served the fowl.

'Oh, I bags the parson's nose,' he chortled.

'Whose nose is zis?' frowned Dieter.

'Oh, and do try some of your duck,' said Attie, offering him the platter. 'My mother's good old English recipe,' she said proudly.

Mr Penworthy was holding a drumstick poised with his little finger delicately outstretched.

'Mmm, *wunderbar!*' he rolled his eyes at Dieter.

'*Ja, wunderbar!*' replied Dieter. '*Alles in der Welt ist wunderbar.*'

*

'So, Dieter,' said Mr Penworthy, opening the bottle of wine he'd brought, 'tell me, where are you from?'

'Chermany.'

'Yes, my friend, but which city?'

'Dresden.'

'And, Dieter, have you any family here in Australia?'

'No.' His voice began to crack a little as he went on. 'My wife and my baby, all my family killed in the bombings.'

'I am so sorry, Dieter,' said Mr Penworthy. 'Dreadfully sorry.'

Dieter shrugged his shoulders and held out his hands.

'For twelve years I have no home, no family,' he said, 'but still I have something special—I have my life.'

Everyone was quiet for a few seconds.

'Then we must celebrate your life and ours together with music,' cried Mr Penworthy. He instantly rose and went and sat down at the piano. 'Do you know this song?' he asked and he started playing the first few chords of 'Joy to the World'. He chuckled. 'My friend Mr Handel wrote this—he was a German.'

But Dieter didn't know the words in English so Mr Penworthy suggested they sing 'Dona Nobis Pacem' instead. He played it through once. The words were Latin for 'give us peace', he explained, and because those three words were the only words in the song, it would be easy, and they could sing it in rounds while he added chords.

'I wonder if we can do it,' he said, 'you first, Gin, then Attie, then you come in last, Dieter.'

Their voices rang throughout the house in harmony. It was glorious. Who would have thought that just three words and three voices could sound so beautiful sung all together?

'Well, that'll knock the dust from the rafters,' laughed Attie.

'Bravo!' exclaimed Mr Penworthy. 'Well done! And what a splendid voice you have, Dieter. You must give us some *Lieder* now! A little Schubert or Schumann, perhaps?'

Mr Penworthy leant back from the piano, elbows rotating passionately with sweeps and flourishes as he played the introduction. Head tilted back, mouth gaping slightly and eyebrows raised in anticipation of Dieter's opening entry. And then the German's tenor voice came through, as sweet, rich and smooth as the *Liebfraumilch* that they were drinking.

Was that a little smile on Attie's face as she dusted the resin from her fiddle with an old silk scarf? As her aunt began to play, Gin followed the movements of her arm swirling elegantly backwards and forwards, over and across, each time exposing the fine golden curls which tufted like baby's hair from the delicate shadows of her armpit. Dieter became thoughtful and solemn, his thumb to his mouth. His eyes had not once left Attie, and Gin knew he was watching the sweet ache that had flooded her face.

'Your turn, Gin,' said Attie, restoring her smile.

Gin wriggled and twisted as she stared blankly at the keys.

'Carols will do,' someone said.

Somehow her fingers managed to find the keys though she had no idea of what she was rattling off. All she could think of was that awful thick wadding between her legs and the hard piano stool.

*

When the two men had left, and they had cleaned up, Attie turned on the wireless.

This is the BBC, came the clipped voice from the latticed gauze. *Here is the news ... Overnight snowfalls throughout most of the south-east of England have provided a White Christmas ... Stay tuned for the Queen's Christmas message ...*

Gin squeezed her eyes and for the first time today thought of her mother. She tried to picture her rugged up against the cold, an open fire blazing against the outside whiteness. All she could see was the apple-cheeked child from her Christmas card, pawing a snowman with fur-cuffed mittens.

'Oh, sorry, Gin. In all the rush today I forgot to tell you about the telegram,' said Attie, flapping a piece of paper in her hand. 'The operator phoned it through late last night.'

Happy Christmas stop celebrations all around stop Noel and I engaged stop wedding May stop earliest depart Southampton 14 Jan stop love mummy

'Quick, Gin, take a look at the sky,' said Attie, 'before it goes.'

Gin sprang out onto the veranda. The sky was burning behind the redgums. The dusty paddocks had almost been swallowed up by their shadows, but, far away in the distance, she could faintly see the golden orange of the Christmas trees melting into the horizon.

Part 2

Chapter 6
JANUARY 1945

Valerie felt the swell subsiding as they slipped through the heads. It was less than half an hour ago when she'd heard that they were coming into port. She'd quickly climbed the steps to the upper deck and stood in disbelief at the miles and miles of white uninterrupted coastline emerging before her, watched the silos and the row of pine trees become clearer by the minute.

Only now, safely inside the Fremantle moles, did she realise just how lucky they were to arrive at all. Blackened port holes at night, escort boats and detours to escape German U-boats had made the journey difficult and dangerous. Almost surreal at times.

Yes, she was here at last but now the reality was rather daunting. During the long weeks on board, Valerie often dreamt of her reunion with Jasper. Every day she paced the decks, anxiously scanning the horizon from under her wide-brimmed hat. At nights, after the baby had fallen asleep in her hammock, Valerie leant over the railings and stared out into the galaxies pondering her future life over the other side of the world. Jasper had tried to reassure her before she left.

At least you'll be safe over there, darling. No chance of the Japs invading that little corner of Western Australia. Anyway, I've been given the word. I'll be home by Easter. Bit of luck, I might even be there to meet you.

Seemed so long ago that she'd met him at a party in the mess. It was the first time that she'd ever seen an Aussie. Next thing he was standing before her, tall and tanned, in his dark blue uniform, asking her to dance. One minute he was twirling her around and then the next, she couldn't quite remember, for everything seemed to happen in such a whirl. But Jasper didn't think twice about it. They were married quickly and quietly, without ceremony. Hush-hush. Not even her parents had known she was four months gone.

Now she could feel the warmth of the baby against her breast as she lifted the shawl gently from her face. But the tiny undeveloped features were of no help at all. The further she sailed away from England, the more difficult it was for her to imagine Jasper, the touch of his body or even the sound of his voice. Everything now seemed so remote, so uncertain.

Valerie wrapped the baby tighter, protecting her head from the fresh ocean wind. Down below, swirling water pummelled against the rusty hull while tugboats nudged it closer and closer towards the quay.

But really, when all was said and done, what could a girl expect? She'd barely had a chance to get to know him. His leave was always brief. When they saw each other it was a few days snatched here and there. The future was only vaguely discussed for there was no point when everyone knew that tomorrow might never come.

The wind dropped a little. Valerie lifted her head to see pine trees slowly sliding behind a street façade of Victorian buildings. Then a long row of weatherboard sheds loomed from nowhere.

She leant over the salt-crusted railing, looking down at the swarms of people on the tarmac below. Voices cheered. Names rang out as a hat or hand waved in the air. Suddenly, the haunting blast of a horn echoed through the bright morning light.

She grasped at her billowing skirt in the wind. She gathered her small frame as tall as she could and began searching the crowded heads for his face. What was it he'd said? *Don't bank on it, love.* No, of course, she'd not really expected him to be there. But, now, as she stepped down the gangway into the throng she felt cheated. Abandoned. Where was the bunting? Where was the band?

*

'There!' Attie closed the boot with a bang.

Valerie felt faint. She waited, fox-fur draped over her white arm as Attie cranked the motor car. It had taken all morning for the luggage to be cleared and now the midday sun beat down against her turban-scarfed head. She sighed and wiped her brow. It was so unbelievably hot that she could feel the tarmac sticking to her thin-soled courts.

'Poor Jasper. Shame he won't be coming home for Easter now,' Attie said as they drove along the Esplanade. 'He's long due for some R & R.'

Valerie didn't say much on the trip down. She just held the baby and stared hard at the grey road. It wasn't fair. She should have been informed of Jasper's movements before anybody else. Surely a wife's rights came first. Weren't they more important than a mother's or a sister's? Hardly her fault she'd been out of contact for months on end.

Valerie stole a glance at her sister-in-law beside her. There was an uncanny likeness; almost the same shaped lips as Jasper's, even the tilt of the nose and golden complexion. But just who did she think she was sitting behind the steering wheel looking so damned self-assured? If only she could see all those dirty flies sitting on her shoulder.

Valerie wrinkled her brow. The putrid smell of drying sheep skins suddenly filled the car as they passed the fellmongers and the Robbs Jetty meatworks.

Attie looked across at Valerie. '*Boronia Valley*, they call it,' she laughed, winding up the window. 'Sorry about that, Valerie. It'll pass.'

Attie slowed down a little as they approached Woodman's Point and nodded to the right. Behind the high barbed-wire fence, clustered in the shrubbery, were giant mounds of earth, each one marked by a wooden door. Goodness me, thought Valerie, was this the way some people lived?

'We're pretty isolated over here,' said Attie observing Valerie's puzzled face, 'but it's a darn sight reassuring when you think what's stored away in each of those.'

'Sorry?'

'Ammunition dump,' Attie whispered loudly.

Valerie closed her eyes. What an idiot she was beginning to feel.

'Now, can you see Garden Island?' Attie said, pointing her finger towards the wedge of blue. 'Just on the left of there you'll see the top of an American submarine.'

The last thing Valerie wanted to talk about was ships. The rocking hadn't left her yet. Perhaps if she had some idea of where they were going, it might help. Up ahead, she saw a lighthouse on a hill. There'd always been something comforting about a winking light in the dark, but now she could barely look at the approaching tower, stark and bleached and dazzling against the bright metallic sky. Waves of seediness churned inside with that floating sensation that came and went. Maybe if she'd eaten that disgusting sandwich at the tea-rooms after all.

Valerie looked over at the keepers' cottages standing desolate amongst the pines. Perhaps she should try and think of the future now and the house where she would live. But houses seemed few and far between.

'Well,' said Attie, 'at least it must be a relief to be on dry land again.'

'Yes, of course,' replied Valerie, although the land still looked decidedly barren. She sat silently absorbing the changing Australian landscape. For a while, the rise and fall of the sand dunes offered glimpses of the ocean through the low-lying scrub. Salt lakes appeared through the trees and shrubs. Bloody hell, she thought, and closed her eyes again.

Suddenly a fishing town emerged. There was something pleasantly nostalgic about the squeals of silver gulls, the fishing boats and wide estuary waters slapping against the limestone wall that reminded Valerie of seaside holidays as a child in Kent. But it was only fleeting.

As they drove over the wooden causeway, Attie pointed over the pylons to the mud flats below.

'Look,' she cried, 'an albatross!' Valerie craned her neck. She'd never seen one before. It appeared almost mythical, with its white wings outstretched, ready to take off in flight. Suddenly they started flapping, colossal arms working harder and faster, until it rose, soaring above the sea-green water. Magnificent. Then it was gone. Out of sight. Behind them. Valerie would have given anything at that moment, if only it could have plucked her out of this wretched car and carried her on its back, back home to England.

'The inland road's normally in better condition. But seeing you're a newcomer we'll take the scenic route instead,' announced Attie.

As they followed the meandering course of the estuary southwards, the land soon flattened out. Long stretches of the Coast Road remained unsealed and riddled with potholes and corrugations. Valerie braced herself against the vibrations and held the lace of her handkerchief to her nose as dust floated from the soft leather upholstery. Miles of khaki bush swept past. Flashes of irritatingly bright sunlight darted between the overhanging branches of the trees, blinding her to the nuances of the passing landscape. Condemned to a headache, she closed her eyes and, to avoid conversation, pretended she was asleep like the baby in her arms.

*

It was dark when they arrived at the farm. Her new mother-in-law greeted her as best she could.

'I must say, dear,' remarked Audrey, holding her at arm's length, 'you look different from in those lovely wedding photos Jasper sent us. Lost a bit of weight, have we? Suspect you've been fretting. And the baby? Here, let's have a look,' she said, poking her finger into the flannel swaddling. 'Aah ... what a little speck, hey? Not much of her, is there?'

'I had to wean her,' explained Valerie. 'My milk dried up.' Her voice was strained and beginning to crack. 'We were twelve to a cabin and I was sick as a dog most of the time.'

'Never mind, dear, put the little one down and come and have a drink.' She took her elbow and ushered her into the kitchen. 'This is the last of the gin, I'm afraid. Bloody rations. Damn shame,' she said. 'Well then ... *chin-chin*,' she clinked her glass against Valerie's.

Attie opened a tin of Sunshine milk and whisked up some powder and water. 'A cup of tea is my first priority,' she said pouring the kettle. 'There you are, Valerie, there's some milk made up ready for the bottles.'

'Well.' Audrey leant back, drawing on the last of her cigarette. She held out her glass again, searching for a toast. 'What can I say? Welcome my dear ... yes, welcome to ... another ruddy war, I suppose. As if one in progress isn't enough,' she added, stubbing out her cigarette. 'Our poor darlings. Goodness knows now how long this island campaign's going to drag on for.'

'Never mind,' said Attie. 'Fingers crossed. Won't be long before Jasper's home.'

'But I couldn't bear it if he had to go away again,' quavered Valerie.

'Trouble is,' said Attie, 'if they all stay over there fighting for Churchill, they won't have an Australia to come home to, will they? It'll belong to the Japs.'

*

Attie sighed in irritation. Eavesdropping was a habit she despised in others. But there was not a thing she could do about the drift of her mother's conversation spilling through the open window.

'I know exactly what you're going through, Valerie dear.' Audrey's voice was soft and clear. It had lightened, taken on a dulcet creamy tone, her words rippling like that endless string of pearls she used to wear. Many times as a small child, Attie had climbed into her mother's lap, scooped the long ropes falling against the folds of muslin and sat fondling the beads one by one in her little hand. *Infinity Pearls,* they called them back in the twenties, but these days nobody seemed to wear them anymore.

Attie knew that any moment now Valerie would feel the light touch of Audrey's hand on her shoulder as the two women sat side by side outside. Audrey was trying to comfort her, going on and on about her own run of misfortunes over the years, for hadn't she herself once been a war bride all alone in a new country? In 1914 she'd barely arrived in Colombo before Charles whisked her off to the hill country. The culture shock at first was bad enough. Then, not long after he'd sailed for Egypt, she discovered she was pregnant with the twins. For seven months she scarcely lifted her head from under the mosquito net. She remembered only too well the isolation, the unrelenting heat and humidity. She'd nearly died of dengue. That constant worry of tropical diseases was such a drain ... what with the babies growing up, and then when Charlie finally returned from war, he was a different man entirely. Bouts of malaria compounded the ongoing effects of shell shock, leaving him weakened in body and in spirit. She'd had years of living alone only to be left with the burden of living with an invalid. Then Wall Street and the Depression. My God! That was about as much as she could take.

Oh, but that lovely couple they'd met off a boat, a professor by the name of Park and his wife, from Perth on their way up to Dambulla and the ancient cities. The fellow gave them a bundle of Australian newspapers to keep. Charlie read her an article about 'a gentle life in a gentle climate not far from the sea', and because the land was cheap as chips, he bought it unseen. A retirement property, he'd been looking for. Something to pass on to young Jasper. The only dream he had left. But, my goodness, how Jasper had lapped it up once they'd arrived. Within a year, they increased the freehold by buying up land partly cleared then abandoned by group settlers. Of course, they knew nothing of farm animals and labour-intensive dairying. Tropical plantations had been their lot. Tea and rubber and the jungle. But at least he knew they'd be able to grow something. Paddy fields, if the worst came to the worst. But Jasper was always full of new ideas.

Attie could hear Audrey's voice quicken as she spoke of Jasper's youth and enthusiasm. Well, the first thing he did was to sell off the English milkers that had come with the land and buy a few shorthorns just for breeding. But in his heart he knew he was really a grower. He planted new fruit trees and experimented with grafting onto existing root stock. He even started a vineyard. Cuttings he bought from a Slav chappie up in the Swan Valley. Not content with that, he felled the ring-barked trees in the half-cleared paddocks and blasted the remaining stumps with gelignite. He'd return in the evenings, hands black and blistered, face lobster-red. Then he set to damming the creek with sandbags, working like a coolie. She had to laugh. All those hours he'd spent as a child playing with bits of bamboo beneath the falls, while she sewed patiently in the shade. He could tell you all about the ancient tanks and the waterways. It was only natural he'd know a thing or two about irrigation. Now, looking back, it was unbelievable what Jasper had achieved in that short time. Of course, Charlie sometimes helped him (if he was having one of his good days). But within five years of arriving in Western Australia Charlie was dead. And she remembered the horror, the unbearable horror of thinking what was to happen now, with Europe on the brink of another war?

*

Attie slapped the journal shut. It was no use trying to balance a set of figures with this going on. From the cedar table where she was sitting she could see their tilted heads, black and grey, nodding in front of the sitting-room window. How much longer would Valerie put up with it? Attie wished they'd take a walk or move somewhere else to chat. It was hard adding up a year's expenditure when her mother kept blathering on about the past. Look at all these unpaid accounts piling up. Little she cared about the farm or if they were in the red.

Attie remembered only too well the fuss when Jasper had enlisted and her mother's dismay that her only daughter had resigned from teaching to come back and look after the farm.

She had arrived home only a few days before he was due to leave.

'There's no reason why a woman can't do the work until you get back,' Attie had announced. 'There's the fruit of course, but I could always keep on a few breeding stock, plant some potatoes and tomatoes, or even some flax for that matter.'

Jasper said nothing. He spat and continued polishing his black air force boots.

'No, Adeline, no dear.' Audrey shook her head, turning her back on her. 'I won't have it!'

'Flax? Why not, Mother? I've seen it over at the Roberts', cut in sheaves and stooked. It's easy enough to grow. So are potatoes and tomatoes. I'm strong and healthy. Anyway, somebody needs to keep the farms going,' she persisted. 'Someone needs to help feed the troops. Give me one good reason, Mother.'

'Because I'm too old,' she sighed. 'And you, my dear, can't possibly manage on your own.' Attie remembered the tears in her mother's eyes.

'Sheer madness.' Audrey looked away and shook her head again. 'No, Jasper. Don't listen. We'll lease the farm, move up to Perth.'

Wasn't that exactly what her mother had been wanting ever since her father died? A little bit of social life was all she asked for. Attie bit her bottom lip. She admired Jasper for the calm way in which he'd intervened. She knew her mother would always defer to her *favourite* son, as she jokingly liked to call him.

'Let her be, Mother,' he'd said quietly. 'It's Attie's decision. I think you should respect that.'

Well, thought Attie, as she opened the cheque book. I can only blame myself. I finally got my way and now I have to live with it.

In some ways, though, Attie felt a sense of failure. She'd not been able to do half the things she'd wanted, battling these last years, virtually on her own. She hadn't banked on the war dragging on for so damn long. Now, it seemed she had another hiccup to contend with, as she turned to see Valerie coming down the hall.

*

Valerie's headache had almost gone. She'd been lying down most of the afternoon with the cold flannel soaked in lavender, which Audrey had given her to put over her forehead.

'I know how you feel, dear.' Audrey had tiptoed in and placed an enamel bowl of ice-blocks by the bed. If the silly goose said that one more time Valerie would scream. 'But summer won't last forever,' added Audrey. 'I dare say you'll feel so much better when Jasper comes home.'

Home? How could she feel at home when everything around her was so damned foreign? All this Asian memorabilia, Valerie sighed. That frightful furniture, ornately carved with lions' heads and cobras, and those ghastly jade elephants on either side of the fireplace. She loathed the stuff. Sometimes when she was half-asleep she dreamt they were coming to get her in the dark. And that peculiar smell that she'd noticed when she first arrived at the house. Sandalwood or whatever it was. She couldn't smell it now, but only, she supposed, because her sinuses were so blocked up from the grass-seeds and the hay.

Outside on the veranda, Valerie placed the tray on the wicker table, and sat down and poured herself a cup of tea. She remembered Jasper teasing her.

You'll have to remember to stir your tea the other way around when you get to Australia otherwise the sugar won't dissolve and that other one about the bathwater going down the plughole.

Yet, funnily enough, everything actually was back to front, she'd found. Summer for Valerie meant weekends driving through the Kent lanes in the countryside, winding through apple orchards and bright green and yellow fields. Picking strawberries and hearing the buzzing of bees in the hedges and the white-blossomed hawthorn trees. Here in Australia, everything looked drab. There was no life or colour in the bush. It even smelt different. *Wait till the wattle comes out next spring*, said Audrey. Wattle, or mimosa as Valerie called it, had a tendency to droop, and it had been so damned hot lately she'd seen bubbles of red sap oozing out of those dreary looking gums. As far as she was concerned, the sight of the Australian bush did no more than bring tears to her eyes.

Valerie was willing to make one exception. The thousands of white lilies she'd seen reaching out along the riverbanks as they crossed the bridge going into town. Now that was something beautiful, almost comforting at times. She'd remarked on the lilies to Audrey and discovered they'd been introduced by pioneers and now ran rampant in the wooded valleys around the creeks and riverbeds.

Lily. She said it out loud. *Lily*. That was what Jasper sometimes called her in his letters. *Lily of the Valerie*. It was such a silly name but she quite liked it now and then.

My one and only darling Lily,

You've no idea how much I've missed you ...

And was she still missing Jasper? She twisted the ring on her finger. Even though it was barely a year, there were times now when she almost forgot she was married.

Valerie stood up and looked out at the paddocks again. A cluster of sheep huddled in the shade. Further down, she could see the dam, a long grey slit gleaming in the sun.

Jasper's *three hundred acres* had sounded impressive. *And a vineyard, planted with my own hands*, he'd said eagerly holding them up. *Mark my words. There'll be grapes on it by the time you get there, Lil.* She'd immediately pictured something resembling the *Côtes de Bordeaux* where she'd always dreamed of going for a holiday. Now, she stood up, lifting the binoculars. Close up, she could see the outline of a rectangle. A fence. She focused on the few rows of curling vines. Barely a leaf could be seen above the wild oats and the dying deadly nightshade.

Hah! *Grasswood* they call the place. She lit one of Audrey's cigarettes and let out a puff. *I can't wait to take you down to Grasswood,* Jasper had said after they were married. *You'll love it at Grasswood.* It had sounded plush. Romantic even. *Grasswood.* But where was the grass, pray tell? The paddocks as far as she could see were dry and bare. And the wood? Endless clusters of dirty blue-grey in the distance. What fool had called this place Grasswood?

Chapter 7

The temperature had dropped but there was no sign of movement as Attie came inside. It was the time of the day she most treasured, when all the lengthening shadows began to close in on the paddocks, the time when she could finally sit down and relax.

Through the kitchen window she could see Audrey's silhouette winding through the redgums, the curve of her widow's hump and her plump arm swaying in balance as she carried the scrap bucket over to the chooks. Attie took a look at the grandfather clock. It was getting on for five. No sound of the baby yet. Valerie would still be lying down, as she did most afternoons, waiting for the heat to go away. Attie could guarantee it. Any minute now, Valerie would arise, then she'd lock herself in the bathroom and lie back, sluicing her body in the tin bath for half an hour. It never occurred to her that the baby would be waking soon, would need changing and feeding. She never seemed to hear her cries. That wasn't quite normal for a mother.

Ice-blocks clinked in the glass as Attie poured herself an iced tea from the jug. She sat down at the kitchen table. There was pleasure in savouring the tranquillity of this time of the evening when the smallest sounds around her became heightened and definable. This was her special time, when she could momentarily put aside her worries.

Attie wound a curling wing of hair behind her ear and sipped her tea. The *tick-tock* of the grandfather clock echoed in the hall. The kero refrigerator began to gurgle across the room. The occasional sound of the tin roof contracting seemed so loud at times she thought the house would crack. If she listened very carefully, she could even hear the creaking of the Cape lilac branches above the roof and the leaves rustling faintly as the late afternoon breeze filtered through the farm. From the redgums it carried the dying chuckle of a kookaburra, which suddenly erupted now into open throttle, breaking the evening peace.

Perhaps she was being hard on Valerie. It was only natural she would be feeling homesick. But, it was war-time and she was in Australia now, and she'd better hurry up and change. That superior air of hers didn't go down well in a small country town. All the locals thought she was uppity as she sauntered down the main street in her hat and gloves. *La-de-dah*, they whispered behind their hands. Just the other day when Attie had taken her into the Co-op to find some summer clothes, there was that unnecessary rudeness to Mrs Myers.

'Goodness me,' Valerie had said, sifting through the racks. She'd held out a dropped-waist frock. 'How old is the stock? Must be years since I've seen one of these,' she'd scoffed.

'I think it's time we went, Val.' Attie had taken her by the arm.

Mrs Myers was not amused. 'Pommie cow,' she muttered as they walked out the door.

What did Valerie expect in war-time? She knew that clothes were hard to get. That trunk-load of English suits she'd brought with her was most unsuitable, silk and cashmere and God knows what. Why couldn't she make do with some of the sensible things which she'd been offered—drill slacks and skirts and cotton blouses—that's all you needed on a farm. But Valerie had huffed. Turned her nose up at them and said they made her look like a Shetland pony. It had taken the last of Audrey's rations to eventually buy some peace.

Attie had never met such a fuss-pot. Didn't like this and didn't like that. Would never get her hands dirty. *I'm terribly sorry, Adeline, I can't possibly do that. Not now, Adeline, I'm afraid I have a headache.*

Valerie wouldn't even light the kero iron, let alone a chip bath-heater or the copper. She might iron under sufferance, do the dishes or sweep the veranda sometimes. But, most of the time, she seemed in another world. Yesterday she'd spent the morning out on the veranda beside the pram staring blankly out at the paddocks.

The bathroom door clicked. Attie could hear the sound of running water. That was another thing. Valerie always used far too much water. She'd told her time and time again about it but it didn't seem to make any difference.

The wireless hissed and crackled as Attie turned the knob. The news music rose to a cadence. *This is the ABC.* Just then, the baby began to cry, softly at first, a kind of whimpering sound. How selfish. Why couldn't Valerie have her bath a little later, at least wait until she'd settled the baby down?

Within minutes, the crying had become angry. Urgent. Attie peered out on the shadowy veranda. The cane pram was rocking. Beneath the white gauze, she could see the baby's face, red and wild, legs and arms entangled in the net.

Attie looked around for Audrey. She was still over near the

sheds shooing the chooks back into their pen. This time of the year she let them range till dark. It was a funny sight, her aproned mother shuffling after the hens, arms flailing in a cloud of dust. All that noise. What a kerfuffle. *Her babies*, she called them. *I'm just going to pop my babies to bed before I have a drink. I wouldn't want the foxes to get them would I?* Attie had to laugh. Babies? For as long as she could remember, Audrey had never been the least maternal. It was Padmah, the *ayah*, who spoon-fed Attie and Jasper, rocked them to sleep in her lap when either was ill.

On the few occasions her mother had held Virginia, she'd done so awkwardly, reluctantly.

Oh dear, what have I done now. She's started crying again. Doesn't seem to like me. Not much good with babies, I'm afraid. I'm either too old or I've forgotten. Here Adeline, Valerie's busy. You take her for a while.

It wasn't that difficult holding a baby, thought Attie. All you had to do was imagine you were holding a puppy.

Anyway, Audrey would be ages chattering to those silly hens, fussing around, gathering eggs and cleaning out their enamel water bowl with fresh water. Better over there than in the house. Audrey's constant prattle nearly drove her mad.

Blast! There was no other option. Attie carried the baby's tin bathtub from the wash-house and put it on the kitchen table with some towels. She hesitated as she poured in some lukewarm water from the kettle. Surely it wasn't that difficult a task. Every day in Ceylon, hundreds of mothers could be seen washing their children and babies in the shallows of the streams. For years she'd unconsciously watched them. It was a simple daily ritual, as simple and as natural to the women as cleansing their own bodies, which they did so artfully and elegantly beneath their clinging wet saris.

Attie unbuttoned the woollen pilchers and flung the sodden nappy in the bucket.

'Oops-a-daisy,' she said, immersing the baby's hot body slowly in the water. Sliding the palm of her hand under her back, she could feel the softness of skin and the rapid heaving of her tummy. Soon the pattern of involuntary sobs was subsiding. Gradually the little fists unclenched, the body relaxed and the frowning brow returned again to innocence.

Babies were babies as far as Attie was concerned. They all cried and they all looked the same. But this wasn't a puppy or a fledgling that had lost its nest. This was Jasper's baby she was holding. Part of her blood as well.

'Feeling better now, Virginia?'

It was the first time she'd used the baby's name. It was hard to think of the baby as a real person and Virginia was such a grown-up, formal-sounding name. But there, she'd said it.

Oh dear! There was a rash around the baby's bottom and the thighs. It was obvious that Valerie, despite her airs and graces, wasn't coping very well. Attie gently patted the tender skin dry, paying special attention to the creases with a smear of Vaseline. Not her place to draw it to Valerie's attention. Better off saying nothing, she thought, as she pinned the nappy into place. Not her place to tell her what to do.

There you are, *Ginnypin*. She bounced the freshly dressed child on her knee, looking for some response. The baby blinked and continued gnawing on her fist. Attie started singing a little rhyme, swaying her body from side to side. She was surprised at the sudden rush of affection she felt, washing and dressing the baby, holding her close to her body and now singing to her.

She knew as a teacher that she had a way with children but, oh no, that didn't mean she'd ever wanted one of her own. God forbid. There were enough children in the world not receiving the care they deserved, ones without mothers, and increasing numbers these days without fathers.

She remembered the ragged urchins in Colombo, little beggars running alongside, their black hands rapping on the window of the car. *Please missie, please missie.* Only one in a hundred might end up in a starched white tunic behind the walls of a mission orphanage, like the one of which her mother had been a patron.

Here in the land of opportunity children still grew up without their parents. She'd heard about little half-caste children being taken from their Aboriginal mothers by state authorities and placed into mission schools or Sister Kate's Home up in Perth.

And, what about the hundreds of children who'd grown up victims of the Depression? She thought of those freckled-faced tots she'd encountered in her classrooms before the war, little barefooted mites who buried their runny noses into the fallen hems of their mothers' skirts, who were dulled by constant hunger and cold before they even arrived in the classroom. There was a futility about these bush schools that still upset her. How could children learn in such an environment, with dirt floors and four to a bed and nothing to eat at home but bread and dripping?

How could she change the shape of their lives when there was no course to change her own? Teaching was a worthy vocation, despite her father's disapproval. Yet it was hardly one that gave a woman any power or independence. Given the same work and conditions, she'd earned only a fraction of the salary of her male equivalents. For five years she'd been relegated to the social isolation of dreary little mill towns, always been at the mercy of a local billet and strict departmental constraints. Forget about romance. For a woman teacher, marriage was a crime that was rewarded by dismissal.

Of course, since she'd given up teaching, she'd missed her little charges. She could still see their ragged line marching as she played *The Colonel Bogey*.

'But that's enough of that,' she said, looking down at Virginia.

She sat the sweet-smelling child down on an old quilt on the floor, supporting her back with some cushions. Then, finding a crust of bread, Attie bent down to give it to her.

'Don't give her that,' screeched Valerie, coming into the room in a waft of fresh scent. 'She'll choke,' she said, snatching it away.

'She needs something to chew on.'

'I don't care. She's my baby.'

January 15th, 1945

Dear Mother and Father,

We eventually arrived at Fremantle safely. The constant heat was the first shock but since then each day has been hotter and dryer than the one before. I honestly feel I've come to the end of the earth. The farm is nothing like I imagined. Rather primitive in fact. Everything is so drab and old-fashioned. No hot

running water. No inside lavatory. Just a backyard
'dunny' they call it, dark and dangerous and lurking
with spiders and snakes.

  We're miles from anywhere. There's all the land in
the world over here, more space than anyone could
possibly want, yet I've never felt so miserable and
claustrophobic in all my life. You've no idea how
beastly it gets with three women on top of each other
all the time. Baby cries night and day and doesn't
give me a break. To tell you the truth I'm fed up to
the teeth with it all. As soon as Jasper comes back
I'm getting the next boat home to England.

  Your loving daughter,
  Valerie

Valerie licked the envelope. Through the kitchen window, she could see Attie kicking off sods of earth from her boots against the fence railing. She'd said she was going down to the dam to try and fix the pump.

Good God! If only that woman knew how hideous she looked in those appalling bib-fronted dungarees, hair sticking out like a scarecrow. Too busy being bossy, no doubt. Trying to make her feel inferior by running the show, telling her to do this and to do that.

Valerie's heels clicked across the brown lino. Well, she too could have done something important, far more important than wretched farm work, where these days you didn't see a man from one day to the next. The short time she was at the base, she'd certainly made an impression. All that excitement and action, yes, she'd had a proper job. She'd really been part of the war machine. Too smart for radio work, she'd eventually been posted to Bomber Command to work in a top job interpreting aerial photographs. If she'd stayed on, she would have been up for a commission.

'Baby's crying again, Valerie dear.'

'I don't know what to do with her.' Valerie sighed, stubbing out her cigarette. 'Night after night, she doesn't stop,' she said. 'I can't get any sleep and it's really getting me down, Audrey. It was every couple of hours last night.'

'I don't hear a thing I'm afraid, dear. Couple of drinks and I'm out like a light.'

'No matter what I do,' continued Valerie, pacing around the floor, 'she's constantly unsettled.'

The flywire door banged. Attie stepped inside in her socks.

'Oh. By the way, Adeline, when are you going to the village next?'

'You mean town?' laughed Attie. 'Well, Friday's the usual day, Val. Why? What is it you need?'

Valerie turned her back on her and stared at the flaking kalsomine wall. It had recently been stained by oily black fumes from the fridge.

'Some more aspirin,' she said slowly, 'and something to make me sleep.'

After Attie had washed her hands, she went in and picked up the crying baby. She put her finger in the child's mouth, rubbing the tiny gums.

'Mite's probably teething,' she said.

'Of course. Why didn't I think of that,' said Audrey. 'Ah, now that you mention *teething*, I think I remember giving you and Jasper ivory rings to bite on back when you were that age. I'm sure there's one tucked away in the Saratoga.'

'Either that, Mother, or she needs something more to eat. Why don't you try her on some rice water, Val, or a spoon of egg custard, something to line her little tum?'

Chapter 8

Valerie ducked her head under the line. She stood back, shielding her eyes against the white glare of the washing. There was something depressing about the Australian light, so bright and strong that it showed up every stain and flaw. It wasn't just the napkins, which had been boiled thoroughly in the copper under her sweating brow. Everything about Grasswood looked dirty and tattered, especially this time of day.

Valerie thinned her lips. She glanced at the flaking paintwork on the veranda and the ragged canvas blind. Here, standing in the backyard, she had the feeling that things were closing in on her. Leaves tumbled from the craggy branches of a mulberry tree whose trunk leant sideways, propped against the wash-house roof. Wasted berries lay in the shady dust like dead grubs. And, in the hot air, she could smell the sickly scent of honeysuckle from the cascading tendrils winding their way from the rusty tank-stand into Audrey's vegetable patch. All that remained were a few corn shucks and shrivelled-up beanstalks. Everything strangled. Here and there, fanning out between the runners of kikuyu, were flurries of nasturtiums.

'Can't we get rid of them,' Valerie complained, 'and this blasted bougainvillea,' she said, unhooking a thorny arm from the washing, 'needs a jolly good prune.'

'I suspect so. But I do like a bit of random colour,' said Audrey, handing her the last of the pegs. 'Anyway, dear, the back garden is the least of our worries. Things can't be perfect on a farm,' she said, heaving the other wooden prop under the line. 'Give me a bit of jungle and I always feel at home,' she laughed.

Scarlet and ginger-faced nasturtiums laughed back between the flapping lines of nappies. Valerie frowned. Flaming weeds. Their clash of colour looked positively common next to the purple bougainvillea. There was no reason why they should be able to trail unchecked up the lattice-work and over the corrugations of the red tin roof. She'd have ripped them out long ago, if it were up to her.

*

Valerie decided it was too hot to do anything other than lie on the front veranda waiting for the breeze to come. The baby had finally gone to sleep, thank God. If she craned her neck she could see her little body stretched out on her back in the pram, arms curled above the lace-edged pillow. She couldn't believe it. The child was growing before her eyes. In another month or so she'd be too big for the pram. Before she knew it, Virginia would be crawling and then how would she keep her clean.

Valerie could hear the soft *click-clack* of the lawnmower blades going around and around. She opened her eyes again and saw Attie pushing the mower backwards and forwards across the grass. Damn! She could have sworn it was Jasper coming through the jacaranda shadows. Valerie sighed. She supposed it was another man's job that had to be done. Well, she could mow for all she cared, mow to her heart's content.

Corks on strings swayed from the brim of Attie's straw hat to keep the flies away. Valerie could see the swell of muscle beneath her seersucker shorts and the flaps of her long-sleeved shirt. From where she was lying on the chaise-longue, Valerie could even make out the muscles in the backs of Attie's calves, contracting into faint upside-down hearts from the pressure of her strides. Sweat gleamed on her honey-coloured skin. Not many women looked as good in shorts. Valerie pulled her skirt down over her dumpy knees. If only she had legs like that.

Clippings spat out from the turning blades. Through half-closed eyes, Valerie followed the mowing patterns forming and reforming across the lawn. Squares and rectangles disappeared into circular tracks as Attie edged around the date palm, folding the long grass into the blades. White butterflies flitted above the crumbling fence railings. Beyond, Valerie could see the tennis court which Jasper had built. It was hardly a proper court. Just another piece of dirt. The lines had long since gone and, the last time she had looked, the damn thing was riddled with anthills. Red dust drifted off it daily with the wind, continually settling throughout the house. You could trail your fingers through it, morning, noon and night.

Valerie closed her eyes again and tried to picture the *wonderful tennis parties* which Audrey had told her about. Only recently, she'd come across a number of old racquets in their wooden presses in Jasper's cupboard and quickly closed the door. The stale smell of rubber and dust from the beaten-up balls and sandshoes was more than she cared to know. On occasions she'd fingered the tarnished silver cups clustered on top of the bookshelf, whose engravings told of Jasper Partridge as champion of men's singles, doubles and mixed doubles at the Kandy Tennis Club. Valerie wondered about the mixed doubles. What was Jasper really like as a partner? She had no idea. Glancing again at the tennis court, Valerie tried to picture them playing together, Jasper in white flannels, bronzed arms reaching up to serve while she stood, knees flexed, waiting at the net. Waiting ... waiting ...

When Valerie opened her eyes again, the mowing had stopped. Garden beds had suddenly come into definition. Attie had nearly finished raking the clippings into piles. Valerie sat up. Ah! She was feeling a little better now. Sweet and sour. There was nothing like the smell of freshly cut grass to restore her sense of order.

*

'Come, dear, I'll give you a *Cook's Tour*.' Audrey took Valerie by the arm, nattering non-stop, as she showed her this or that. Audrey's romantic attempts at gardening seemed futile. Valerie observed the way her mother-in-law pottered about, crumbling dead blooms she'd broken off in her hand before absent-mindedly casting them to the wind. Fat wrens no doubt fed off them. 'But,' Audrey explained, 'those seeds that hadn't withered or been taken, might still be waiting in the soil for their time to ripen.'

As the days went by, Valerie found herself looking for little patches of Englishness that occasionally appeared between the weeds. The surprise of finding another familiar perennial, self-sown in the most unusual place, brightened her day. She treasured the pink and white spotted bells of the solitary foxglove she found, and the clusters of day lilies, whose trumpet-shaped flowers rejoiced for a few weeks in the sandy shade.

Old-fashioned tea roses, grown from stocks which Audrey had

shipped out from Ceylon in wet hessian, rambled freely over a broken wooden trellis. Now, another bloom was out.

'Valerie dear, I want to show you something,' Audrey's voice drifted through the hot, dry air.

'Yes, I won't be a minute.' Valerie needed to savour the perfume of 'Lady Hillingdon' one more time. Soon, before they wilted in the heat, she would cut a few opening buds and put them in a glass of water in her room. Maybe later in the afternoon when it was cooler she might try and pull some weeds.

'I've been at it for five years,' said Audrey, smoothing out the half-finished quilt over the cedar table. 'Scraps of the past,' she laughed. 'Don't ask how I do it. The pattern is all in my head.'

The quilt seemed to be taking an awfully long time, thought Valerie. Goodness knows how Audrey remembered what was what. There were discarded hems which she'd had cut off old cotton print aprons and silk cocktail dresses to make the garments more in keeping with the time; pieces of ribbon and satin and old Liberty scarves, and folded remnants which had never been touched.

'And you should see what I've just found,' said Audrey, opening an old hat box. 'All Charlie's.' Her eyes brightened as a tangle of silk slipped out: ties, scarves and cravats. She spread them out on the other end of the table, stroking them one by one. They came in an assortment of patterns: paisley, geometrics, spots and stripes, blobs on blobs, some plain with embroidered insignias. 'I couldn't throw them out. I knew I'd find a use for them one day.' Then suddenly Audrey became wistful.

For a few seconds, Valerie thought she saw teardrops in her eyes.

'Oh dear. Now I'm not sure if I could bear to cut them,' Audrey said, putting down the pinking shears. 'Do you know, Valerie, I could still tell you every single occasion when dear Charlie wore this or that, all the wonderful times we had together. In some ways, cutting them is going to be like cutting into my own heart.'

*

Valerie unclipped the secateurs. It was pathetic, watching Audrey fluffing around all those musty rags. She leant forward and snipped the stem of another newly opened rose. She'd only ever seen Jasper in an air force tie, even on their wedding day. How could anyone be so sentimental about a tie?

'Here, Audrey, smell this.' She offered her the soft apricot-coloured rose bloom she'd picked.

'It's exquisite, isn't it?' said Audrey, going back to her quilt.

'By the way, Audrey, I presume none of those are Jasper's ties.'

'Of course not, dear. I wouldn't dream of it. Jasper's ties are exactly where he left them. Come.' Audrey took Valerie and showed her where they were hanging in the lowboy.

'See, there.' Audrey began rummaging in the chest of drawers. 'Ah, here it is,' she said, taking a small velvet box from the top drawer. 'Look, this was what Charlie and I gave Jasper for his twenty-first birthday. He looked so handsome all dressed up.'

Valerie fondled the set of pearl studs and cufflinks set in gold. It was hard to picture Jasper in anything other than a blue uniform. She held the white piqué bow-tie and waistcoat to her nose. She wanted to remember the smell of his body. Audrey was right. When Valerie thought about it, there was something rather intimate about this part of a man's attire, especially the tie. She closed her eyes. Just imagine stroking a silky tie flat over a man's buttoned shirt, then watching him taking it off. Then, of course, there were the secrets it concealed.

How vulnerable Jasper had looked that first time. Suddenly she caught an image of him standing before the hand-basin without his tie, rolling back his sleeves and pulling open his shirt from his chest. She was back in that second-rate room at the Strand Palace Hotel, her fingers lightly tracing the rise and fall of his Adam's apple and the hairs curling in the hollows beneath … They were drunk at the time but now parts of it were coming back. She'd helped him with the buttons and seen his naked body standing pumped and proud as he carefully pinched the pleats of his fallen air force trousers so they wouldn't crease.

The next morning, she'd watched like a sleepy cat from the double bed as he dressed back into his uniform and carefully tied his Windsor knot. Before he left, he'd lifted her up gently by her wrists to the window where they'd kissed again in the early morning light. Their goodbyes became a ritual. A habit. There were so many of them and she never knew if he'd be coming back. *Just a minute, darling.* She'd hold him there on some pretext, picking at imaginary specks of lint on his blue uniform. Then standing on tiptoes, she'd reach up and finally straighten his tie. *There!*

'It's all looking rather grand, Valerie,' Audrey's voice floated down the hallway. 'Come and tell me what you think, dear.' Audrey had positioned the cut-up pieces of ties around the quilt in accordance with their colour.

'Such beautiful fabrics we wore then, don't you think? And men's ties were so sleek and elegant. Not like those frightful wide belly-warmers you see men wearing nowadays.'

*

Valerie bent over the hollyhock with gloved hands, plucking the spent leaves from the stalk. Tomorrow, all going well, she would stake them to stop them blowing over in the wind. She unravelled the hose and smiled as she watered the weeded bed. Those few clusters of forget-me-nots Audrey had shown her had finally opened, like tiny eyes, the colour of Wedgwood blue. *Forget-me-not.* She tried to picture Jasper's eyes looking deeply into hers. But they were not blue like the shade of his uniform. They were brown like his sister's, weren't they? And yet she desperately wanted to think of Jasper. After all, wasn't it the 14th today, St Valentine's Day?

Bab-ba. Ba-ba. Virginia was happily knocking pegs together on the shaded tartan rug. She glanced up. In this light, her eyes looked a murky grey. But, what did it really matter? The child lifted the peg to her mouth, rubbing it against her gums. She slept less now during the day, but at least she seemed contented.

Footsteps scuffed against the gravel drive. Valerie could hear someone humming 'The Red Red Robin'. Out of the corner of her eye she caught Attie's shadow slowly moving past her. Damn, she thought, turning around. Attie had beaten her to it again and gone and got the mail. Anyone would think it was some sort of daily competition.

'Sorry Val,' Attie called out. 'Nothing for you today, I'm afraid.' She bent down over the rug to cluck over Virginia.

'Hello Ginnypin,' she chuckled and held out her finger.

Valerie pulled harder on the hose. What a cheek. She had a damned good mind to spray her down.

Alyssum and babies tears tumbled from cracks in the wet

gravel near her toes. It was funny how some things survived where nothing else would grow.

Attie had stopped. Valerie could see her checkered bottom bent over the coiled hose.

'Damn and blast! Why hasn't someone told me this ruddy tap needs a new washer?' Attie's face was red as she flicked back errant locks of hair. 'Just look at that waste, Valerie,' she pointed at the wet gravel. 'How many times must I tell you that we can't afford the water?'

Go to blazes, thought Valerie. She couldn't understand what all the fuss was about. Silly woman was always getting her knickers in a twist about water. What a sight she looked, a right *Wreck of the Hesperus*. Why didn't she do something with that hair of hers? It was so unfashionable.

'By the way, Adeline, it's Friday tomorrow,' called Valerie, without looking up. 'Why don't you treat yourself to a good trim and one of Beryl's new perms?'

'My hair is my own concern, not yours, thank you very much, Valerie,' Attie said tartly. 'What's more, I don't give a bloody toss about it,' she snapped, twisting it up in a bun. 'There are more important things to worry about around here, like saving water.'

*

You could have cut the air with a knife, thought Valerie, as they sat at the lunch table eating Audrey's boiled brisket and potatoes. Scraping back her chair from the table, Attie went and turned on the wireless.

British and US bombers have dropped hundreds of thousands of explosives on the German city of Dresden ...

They all stopped eating and listened.

Last night, 800 RAF Bomber Command planes let loose 650,000 incendiaries. As soon as one part of the city was alight, the bombers went for another until the whole of Dresden was ablaze. The city is devastated. RAF crew reported smoke rising to a height of 15,000 feet. 'I could still see the fires hundreds of miles away from Dresden,' recounted one pilot. The bombing has been followed by further daylight attacks by 311 US heavy bombers.

A map of lines gathered across Audrey's forehead. 'Would it be likely Jasper took part in that raid, Valerie?' she asked.

'Shouldn't think so,' she replied, not wanting to alarm Audrey. 'After all the hours he's done.' Valerie used to be able to tell when Jasper was on an operation. After she'd left the base, she'd ring up of an evening and they'd say she couldn't speak to him and she'd know why at once. But, in all probability, Jasper and his RAAF Squadron mates, being part of the RAF Bomber Command, would have been on that raid. With 800 planes taking part, how could he not have been? 'Well, anyway,' she added, 'doesn't sound like there was much resistance.'

Attie was horrified at the bombings.

'Imagine all those innocent civilians,' she said. 'I know they're bloody Huns but there'd have to be thousands and thousands of civilian casualties. What's Churchill think he's doing? It's sickening.'

Innocent civilians? Well, thought Valerie, what about the Blitz? You never had to live through that day in, day out, with innocent civilians being killed all around. All very well when you were safe on a farm on the other side of the world. But if you're going to talk about innocent civilians, what about the poor Jews in the cattle trucks and the gas chambers? Valerie didn't say that. But she knew she wouldn't have stood a chance if she'd lived in Germany, or Europe for that matter, with a maiden name like Lesser.

Jasper said once that he thanked God he was flying Lancasters, that he wasn't some poor bugger in a Spitfire. The only reason he could do what he was doing was that it didn't seem real. At night, that black background, he said, with its sprinkling of pretty white lights down below was just a target. From the height he was at, you couldn't see anything else, let alone the human casualties. He pitied all those other poor blokes, having to watch the whites of eyes rolling in their enemy's blazing faces.

Chapter 9

Attie tried not to think about it. The repeated bombings, the papers said, were aimed at whittling away the German public morale, cutting off relief supplies to the eastern front and giving support to the approaching Soviet armies. Besides, there was a closer enemy at hand. The Japs. And the best thing she could do was to get on with the job of helping feed the troops.

Attie wheeled the barrow of pine cases she had made over to the orchard, smelling the apples as soon as she opened the gate, an old summer variety called Baths that nobody bothered to grow any more. To test the sharpness of flavour, she took a bite, watching the red skin bleed into the white flesh. Normally she'd have needed help to pick the fruit but this year it wouldn't take her long. Five minutes of hail in a freak storm last December had pitted the young apples. Rotten luck, or an *act of God*, the insurance companies liked to call it. With the leather bag strung from her neck and the help of a ladder, Attie began stripping the trees, a soft twist until each apple gave way, ripe and free, in the palm of the hand. At first she counted the picked apples to add interest to her work. At one hundred she would stop, unhook the bag and release the tumbling contents into one of the cases.

It gave Attie immense pleasure having gradually filled the bag, then to feel its fullness hanging across her stomach like a massive pregnancy. But it was hard work. By lunchtime the muscles in her neck and shoulders ached and bruises had risen where the apples bumped against her thighs.

She thought of the dozens of tea-pickers who had worked from morning to dusk, week in, week out. The Tamils, in their brightly coloured saris, were part of her childhood landscape. Every day, she had seen them working with their baskets on their backs. From a distance, they looked like giant locusts munching their way across the green terraced hillsides. Attie winced. It horrified her now recalling this childhood image, innocent though it was. The very young always delight in make believe. It is their instinct to personify or objectify almost everything they see. Yet still it stung her adult conscience that she could possibly have thought of the Tamils as anything other than human beings. These were men and women who rose at dawn to trudge two or three hours over the sloping terrain before starting their long day's work.

And exactly what would these women think if they could see the daughter of their former master working on the land like them? She stopped for a minute to adjust the buckles of the bag. The leather straps were cutting into her shoulders. She'd only counted to fifty. Half-way point. There was no way she would allow herself to empty the bag yet. Heavens, she thought. On market days there would be hundreds of women, laden with sheaves of corn and baskets of fruit on their backs, trudging miles and miles along the dusty roads into town. Even pregnancy would not exempt them from carrying such heavy loads. But then, wasn't pregnancy a sickness designed for educated western women like herself?

Attie drew her shoulders back again. The weight was excruciating. For a few seconds it became part of her, straining every joint in her body. A giant pregnancy, indeed, she snorted. How could she entertain such a thought? Any day that little mite Virginia would be crawling and then where would they be? One baby in the house was enough, thank you very much.

*

A few rows of ripening Golden Delicious and Granny Smiths were all that remained when she had finished. The whole process took less time than she thought. As a rule, she picked during the cooler part of the day. Before she stopped for lunch, she wheeled the full cases in twos back to the shed. Under the shade of the high-pitched roof, she then graded the apples by sight. Some of the fruit would be taken under the government's Apple and Pear Scheme for a few shillings a case. Any day now, a couple of girls from the Women's Land Army would come in a truck and take them away to the cannery to be made into juice for the troops.

The remainder Attie wrapped meticulously in waxed paper, packing each apple, cell-like, as Jasper used to do, into cases lined with corrugated cardboard. The most rewarding part came next. Wielding the hammer, she nailed the boards on top, feeling the satisfaction of at last sealing the apples in their boxes. Now, all she had to do was to label the boxes with the Grasswood stencil. Then that was that. Good old Cam Carter had once again offered to come over in his utility and take the boxes to the siding to send off by rail to market.

*

Valerie noticed that the garden and lawn had lost body and colour since she'd arrived. The nasturtiums had gone. All that remained of the backyard was a tangle of dried grasses. Gold, brown, silver. Everything half-dead, drab, blurring into the landscape. The forest in the distance was simply a smudge quivering against the grey paddocks and the blue haze of coastal plain seemed to have almost disappeared into the sky. Beyond the fading bougainvillea and the barbed-wire fence, as far as Valerie could see, was the shimmering emptiness of late summer.

And that was exactly how she felt as she sat in the shade of the Cape lilac helping cut up seed potatoes. It was as if the sun had sucked every ounce of energy out of her. At times, she wondered if she was hallucinating. If she'd had her compact in her apron pocket, as she usually did, she could have checked her face to see whether she was seeing straight. Perhaps she was a little dehydrated. Valerie unhooked the canvas water bottle from under the tank-stand and took a few gulps. The water had a ropey taste and didn't quench her thirst. What she really wanted was a decent cup of tea.

Birds flittered in the branches above. Occasionally, a cluster of yellow berries fell onto the burnt lawn. But no one spoke much for they could barely breathe around the dusty hessian bags. It wasn't hard work, just dirty and repetitive, yet Valerie didn't dare complain again. At times there was even a rhythm to it, she supposed, selecting the sprouts, slicing the rubbery potato and tossing the quarters into the bag. Maybe it was that which had reduced her to her almost trance-like state.

What's that? Valerie stopped and listened. The air was still and thick with the electric *zicking* of cicadas. Something twitched near her feet. She jumped. *Go away!* It was one of those nasty little hoppers again. Within seconds it had disappeared into the ghostly silver-greyness.

Would there ever be a time, she wondered, when she would blend into the landscape like an insect or a bird? Be Australian, that's what they all expected, didn't they? But up to now, she'd been proud, hadn't wanted to let her standards go. Standards? Her face felt flushed and moist with perspiration. Dark tendrils of hair clung to her cheeks and drips ran down between her breasts. Tears suddenly started overflowing, like they often did, but she no longer cared about the smudges on her cheeks.

Would Jasper think she'd changed when he came home? It was Easter, over six months since she'd seen him last. What would it be like if he suddenly arrived home as he'd originally promised and found her looking like … like God knows what? Would he think less of her? She tried to imagine him, the railway bus having dropped him off, trudging unseen up the driveway with a small kitbag slung over his shoulder. As she closed her eyes, she thought she could hear the waft of a whistle and his black air force boots crunching along the gravel.

Coo-ee! he would cry that ridiculous greeting of his.

All three women would stand there stunned, unbelieving, each unsure of who should first embrace him. Letters were bad enough, what few there were. There was always that battle of ownership rights. What did it matter, she would tell herself, he was home at last. Wasn't that enough? But wouldn't she feel angry? Surely, Jasper, you could have telegrammed to let me know. Then I could have been prepared. Had a bath and washed my hair. Instead of that, I'm covered in filth, almost expiring in this wretched heat.

No time even to wash my hands or powder my nose.

Valerie opened her eyes and clenched her fists. Oh, how she hated it here. If only he would come and take her out of this bloody hole, away from it all. *A bit of dirt doesn't matter one iota*, he would say, wrapping his arms around her. *I still love you, Lil. To me, you're the most beautiful woman in the world.* With her face in his hands, he would look at her long and hard and then kiss her lips and she would breathe in the dampness of his sweat and the rough serge pressed against her dirty cheek. Only after he'd released her would he hold out either arm to the other two women. Valerie had forgotten about baby rocking on her knees on the tartan rug. Virginia was only six weeks old when he'd cradled her last, her head so tiny against the palm of his hand. Of course, he would hardly recognise the tot in her new smock and bonnet. *Look, Jasper, she's crawling now.*

He would probably boost her high in the air, play with her, and then what would he say?

Sorry, I've only got a few days, Lil, like he always did with his eyes directed somewhere else. Then perhaps he would add something like, *You see, Lil, I have to be back.*

Where are you going then?

I'm afraid they don't tell you much.

And, later that night, after they'd made love, he would sleep fitfully, despite being safely back in Australia. That awful habit he had of lashing out at times with his feet at the end of the bed. Lying in his arms, she would plead with him to take her away from the farm.

But where are you going this time, Jasper? He would put his finger to her lips.

Sorry, darling, I'm sworn to secrecy. It was what he'd always said every time he was on leave from Wickerton.

She threw the wrinkled potato she was holding into the agapanthus.

It's just not fair, she sobbed inside. How long is it all going to go on for? How long do I have to wait? I think I'll die if I have to stay here much longer.

*

Sometimes in the evening when the south-westerly had died down, the three of them sat out on the veranda waiting for the sun to set. A mob of kangaroos from the state forest often came lolloping across the paddocks to graze down near the water. Attie picked up the binoculars.

'Bally pests,' she complained. 'Beautifully unique but so damned destructive.' She'd been brought up surrounded by wildlife in Ceylon. Monkeys, squirrels and mongooses. As a child she'd spent hours watching them eating in the jackfruit trees or skittering across the veranda roof. They were delightful little creatures, she remembered, but her mother loathed them with a vengeance because they piddled and they stank. Even monkeys, she warned, were disease-ridden, vicious little sods. As a lad Jasper might have teased them now and then with his sling. Often, he would call out to come and look at a mongoose which had a snake pinned down by its neck. They were all bally pests for that matter. But you didn't destroy them. You left them alone and they left you alone as well.

Attie watched now as the sun slid further into the forest and the darkening colours of the paddocks began merging into one. The kangaroos must have slipped away without her even noticing. She peered again. No. They were still there, their grey outlines almost absorbed into the colour of the earth. They stopped nibbling. Paused. Then sniffed the air and stared at her.

A shotgun'd do the trick, had been Cam Carter's advice. Yet Attie had never been one for guns. Back in Ceylon she'd always avoided the deer and leopard hunts when she was a girl. She'd have a go at most things but not guns. She couldn't see the sense.

Some years ago she'd asked Cam to come over and put old Troy down. The Clydesdale was sick and getting on, poor devil. He'd done all the hard work for them. Pulling out stumps, helping clear the land and carting fruit. They'd bought him soon after they arrived.

Twenty pounds from Smiley's Bazaar, Jasper had boasted with a grin. The horse had been sent down by train and she remembered her brother walking him home from the siding. Troy had served them well. Even now Attie was saddened by the memory of his death. She'd watched Cam quietly leading him by a halter up into the state forest with the rifle tucked under his arm. It was as if the useless animal felt her shame too as he plodded, head down and back to the weather.

She knew the exact spot where that horse had died. Last November, when she'd taken Audrey walking to look for wildflowers, she had accidentally come across his bones scattered in a clearing. They were half-hidden beneath a flurry of spider orchids which Audrey was clambering to pick. The conspicuousness of their long white streaky petals and red tongues had camouflaged the broken carcass and a glimpse of metal in the sand. Attie stooped to salvage one of the horse-shoes. She started shivering uncontrollably as she spotted the black hole in the animal's skull.

Attie supposed guns were a necessary evil. These days, Jasper's guns were locked securely in the closet, thank God. They were all there: a twelve-gauge shotgun along with a three-oh-three, a twenty-two rifle, boxes of bullets and cartridges, the works. She pictured her brother cleaning the guns, as he had on a number of occasions, over sheets of newspaper spread out on the kitchen table, oiling the barrels and paying meticulous attention to the breech and bolt. Sometimes he'd go over to the dam duck-shooting with his cartridge belt slung low on his hip. She'd accompanied him only once, against her will.

It's quite simple really, he'd said, holding up the shotgun. *Here, just watch.* He pressed the release, then broke it open with a crack, loaded in two cartridges and snapped it shut with an air of resolution. He raised it, packing the butt firmly into his shoulder, closed his left eye and lowered his other gradually down towards the sight. Standing behind him, Attie followed the waving barrels of the gun as he tracked his target in the greying light. She plugged her fingers in her ears, heart thumping against her ribs as she waited for that deafening sound to come. *Bang!* Then, the after-ring of its echo in her ears, and, all around, the lingering smell of shot.

Her father rarely spoke about the war. Once, when they were children, Charlie instructed them to always treat their ponies kindly. A man was nothing without his horse. A horse was a friend who could save your life. During the war, her father said, fellow cavalrymen had shot their injured horses for fresh meat.

How could they do it, Daddy? she'd asked him at the time.

That's nothing, Jasper had piped up cheerily. *The French eat horse-meat every day.*

Charlie had smiled gently. *Well, maybe if you had bully beef for months on end, my pet, you might do it too.* He didn't tell them that the horses were dying or that, when you've killed a man, putting an animal out of its misery becomes a relatively easy thing to do. She'd only found that out recently when she'd come across his bloodstained pocket diary, a war memento that had fallen out of the bundle of old letters Audrey had been poring over.

Attie wondered how many people Jasper had killed since he'd been away. Flight Lieutenant Jasper Partridge couldn't say what operations he was on, not even what sort of aircraft he flew. *Bomber Command,* Valerie had intimated, possibly Wickerton where they'd met, but these days even she was in the dark. All Attie knew was that he was one of the *Brylcreem Boys.* The elite. They were all basically an educated bunch, according to Jasper, sportsmen, prefects, school captains, that sort of thing. After all, he said, a pilot had to be a leader.

Attie thought of Jasper often. His five-year absence. She missed her brother, more than she would ever have imagined.

'Poor Jasper.' It came out little more than a whisper.

'Yes,' said Audrey. 'Our darling Jasper. Well, let's hope it's not too long before he comes home and takes over from where he left off,' she said with a sigh, 'and you, my dear, can start looking for a husband.'

'Like a hole in the head,' muttered Attie. There, she'd said it, and she was glad, if only to annoy her mother. But within seconds she regretted her words for, in her mind, she could still see the black hole in the horse's skull.

The more Attie tried to put the horse out of her mind, the more Troy kept re-appearing for she knew a horse was essential to the farm. Only this morning she had spoken to Cam about whether it was worthwhile growing potatoes. She had always thought of it as sheer hard work. But because demand for production had grown over the last few years, it was now an essential occupation. The government was even offering incentives and she'd be able to get a good price per ton. There'd be a problem with harvesting, when the time came, but Cam explained they'd be responsible for providing her with a labour troop of Italian internees. If she could sow an early crop in June, it might just be ready for Jasper to harvest when he came home, in which case there might not be a need for bringing in extra manpower. That was all very well. But, how would she manage to plant her crop without a horse?

'You look worried, dear. Penny for your thoughts.'

'Actually, I was thinking about how I'm going to plant those darned potatoes.'

'Perhaps you could ask Cam to come over and give a hand.'

'Stubborn old sod,' muttered Attie to herself.

'Shame on you for saying such a thing,' said Audrey. 'He's been very kind over the years. And don't you forget that.'

Attie said nothing more. She couldn't stop thinking of the draught-horse. If he didn't want to do something, then, by Jove, there was nothing you could do to make him. It made her smile as she remembered Troy's sudden attempt at galloping backwards just to prove a point, with Jasper running along behind hanging onto the reins in vain.

'We could always get the Land Army in,' suggested Valerie as an afterthought.

'What, city girls with perms and rubber boots?' laughed Attie. 'What we really need around here is an iron horse.'

'An iron horse?'

'Otherwise known as a tractor, Val,' she replied. 'One of those new Fordsons that I saw advertised a few weeks back would be just the shot.'

*

'Poor Valerie,' said Audrey, giving her a little pat. 'What can we do to brighten you up? I know, let's have a party.'

'It might be one way to make it rain,' laughed Attie.

Over the next few days, Valerie watched the house come alive. Audrey, invigorated, bustled around making curries, fried rice and pavlovas, inviting neighbours and those who had befriended them over the years.

The French doors of the sitting room were opened onto the veranda. Together, she and Audrey assembled a trestle table outside for supper, covering it with a white damask cloth. Extra kerosene lamps were hung in the branches and, despite Attie's protest about starting bushfires, a brazier was lit on the lawn, flames curling up from a forty-four gallon drum in case anyone felt cold.

Valerie was introduced to guests as they arrived armed with bottles of hops beer and homemade lemonade. She felt awkward, conscious that she was being judged as *that new English wife of Jasper's*. The women clustered around her in the kitchen, but, after asking a few hasty questions, turned to local topics from which she felt excluded. Valerie, looking for an escape from the dreariness of kitchen conversation, peered hopefully into the sitting room at the untidy group of men.

Audrey was bent over the cabinet rifling through records.

'Here, Chip,' she said, eyeing one of the younger men, 'be a dear, would you, and pop this on for me?'

Valerie hoped the music would bring some life to the party. She smiled in anticipation at Chip as he began to crank the handle. But the records were outdated, mostly from the twenties and early thirties. It was the music of her parents' youth, the lyrics corny and irrelevant in a modern world at war.

'How about tinkling the old ivories for us, Attie?' said Cam Carter, after the records had run their course.

'I'll do my best,' she laughed. 'It's been years, I must say.'

'Rubbish!' said Audrey. 'Don't believe a word she says. She's just like her brother. Only needs to hear a song once and she can play it on the piano picking out a bass.'

The piano was a little out of tune but no one seemed to mind. Everyone gathered around, singing and calling out requests. Valerie wanted to join in. She had a good voice but something made her hold back.

'Shh. Can you tone it down a bit,' she complained. 'You'll wake the baby.'

'Don't fret, Val. A few precious hours won't make any difference to her,' Attie replied. 'Let her stay up. What's wrong with the tot experiencing a little joy in the world for once?'

'So, Valerie,' said Chip, 'when's young Jasper due back? I've heard some of the other chaps are already heading home.'

'Nothing definite, really. Should be getting his release any day now I expect.'

'Come on, Cam, give us a poem, mate,' said Bruce Sutherland.

'Something patriotic for us old war heroes, and something to remember our boys by. Here's to them coming home shortly,' he said, raising his glass. Cam hobbled from the corner, picking his way through the crowd with his walking stick. The room filled with hilarity as the men bunked him up on the dining table. Valerie watched the old man as he launched into a poem. As the verses flowed his face grew more florid and his cheeks began to tremble.

Drunken Australians. Nothing she hadn't seen before. She'd been to some of the informal parties at the mess and knew how quickly things got out of hand. *Getting on the piss*, they called it. Numerous stories had done the rounds. One minute our blue heroes would be quietly playing snooker and the next minute an aborted mission would be announced and all hell would break loose. Suddenly there'd be acrobatics on the snooker table, someone would let fly with a football, or you'd hear the roar of a motorbike down the corridor.

Tonight's display was mild by comparison. But what on earth was this fool reciting? A lot of nonsense, as far as she was concerned. Look! Any minute he could overbalance. Cam paced the length of the table and turned, waving his stick at his audience. At the end of the first verse he whacked it down on the end of the table. Everyone jumped. Suddenly his voice changed, became milder, more controlled.

> *And one was there, a stripling on a small and weedy beast,*
> *He was something like a racehorse undersized ...*

There was hardly a falter throughout the whole poem. It was a passionate display, but the words left Valerie in confusion. The room filled with hearty applause as Cam was helped down from the table.

'Wonderful!' Audrey pecked him on the cheek. 'You are clever, darling.' Her words were slurred, as she linked her arm in his, and there was a lilt in her voice. 'Do you know, Cam, that poem reminds me of the races we went to when Charlie was alive ... never missed one if we could help it ... I adore horses, I absolutely adore them. It must be the Irish in my blood.'

Half-shickered, thought Valerie, like the rest of them. Even the gramophone sounded drunk, warbling through the crackles. Chip was now dancing with his wife, Patsy. Together they looked a little cumbersome; there was no unity or rhythm as far as she could see, no bodily communication as they tried to do the foxtrot. Their shuffling looked so staid, boring. Valerie craved the swing and bounciness of the jitterbug, which was now all the rage in London, its give and take, where a woman could take an active part in it all. Valerie looked in disdain at Patsy's hips wobbling towards her, the momentum of her backwards movement disrupted by the sudden catching of her hip against the corner of her chair.

'Awfully sorry, Val,' said Chip, looking down at her over the diamond shapes of his sleeveless sweater. It had never occurred to her until now, as she followed the clumsy shambling action of his body, that there was any remarkable difference between Australian men and English men. It wasn't only the crinkly eyes and toughened complexions that made them stand out, it was the shape of their bodies, she realised, more sturdily built from the waist down to the buttocks and thighs. Perhaps it was the daily horse-riding. She blushed, trying hard to disguise her thoughts of Chip and Patsy as man and wife, and the burden of her own overwhelming loneliness. In an effort to get away from the absurdity of their coupling, Valerie began gathering up empty glasses only to find Audrey had cornered Cam in the kitchen. Valerie wasn't sure what had happened. She supposed it was the drink. No one seemed to notice the tears trickling down the wrinkles in his face.

*

The next afternoon Chip came over. He had ridden across the hills for it was quicker, he said, than driving the back road through town.

'Where's young Attie?' he asked.

'You've just missed her, I'm afraid,' said Audrey. 'She's just popped over to see Cam.'

At first Valerie didn't recognise him as he came down the drive with his felt hat tilted across his face. But now, as he stood beside her, hat in hand, he looked for a few seconds almost boyish and embarrassed.

There was a freshness to his brown face, as he spoke to her; his creases more like expressions of caring concern for her than damage from the sun.

'Fancy coming for a walk, Valerie?' he asked, when he'd finished his cup of tea. 'Attie's asked me to have a look at those cattle of hers. The feed's pretty low.'

They found them in the lower paddock, clustered under a peppermint tree. As they passed, the animals stared blankly at them, chewing their cuds and sighing out their chaffy breaths. Suddenly one moved forward and then the others began to follow, plodding along and nodding their heads in imitation.

'Sorry, my poor old darlings,' he said, holding out his empty hands.

Valerie flinched as they came towards the fence.

'Don't worry. They think we've got some hay for them. Funny blighters, aren't they? You know, Valerie, Attie's been doing a sterling job. They're not in bad knick considering how low the pasture is.'

They sat down under the willow tree by the dam. Chip turned his weathered neck and looked at her.

'Good party last night, Val. Golly, old Cam's a card, isn't he?'

'Well, he certainly went on and on, that's for sure,' she said, waving away the flies with a switch. 'But I couldn't understand a word of that poem. I felt so left out,' she grumbled. 'All I wanted to do was get the next boat home.'

He patted her arm.

'Oh, don't feel like that, love,' he said, 'You see, it's an old ballad about an Australian hero. A fellow called Banjo Paterson wrote it. That poem's almost folklore, really.' He bent down to pick some grass-seeds out of his socks. 'All about bush-men and their mates. Don't fret, Val,' he smiled, and leaned over and touched her cheek. 'You're just a pommie sheila who's waiting for her bloke. You'll understand when you've been here a little longer.'

My dearest Mother and Attie,

Received your most welcome cake last week.

Special thanks to the Grasswood cook, meaning

you dear mother. The food here leaves a lot to be
desired. Even so, the quality is better than what
most civilians can procure. So, I really appreciated
having something homemade for once. The last few
slices, I might add, were quickly polished off by a
couple of my squadron mates who said it was the
best boiled fruit cake they'd ever tasted. Must have
been that extra pinch of spice you added. I have to
confess that every bite of that cake made me hungry
for news of home. It's a while since I had a letter
from Valerie. I do hope she and baby are settling
in now. She sounded rather down in the last letter
and hadn't been sleeping well. Please let me know
how my precious girl is going? I know you'll both be
giving her all the love and attention she needs.

I gather from your last letter that you've been
having a bit of a drought down there. Rather ironic
when you think how it rains here nearly every single
day of the year. The rest of the feed should last you
out the summer. But, I'd say it's better to sell those
cattle early, Attie, than hang on too long waiting
for prices to rise. And how are the vines? Are there
many grapes this year? I can't wait to get home to
have a look.

I was very sorry to hear about Keith Williams.
Pass on my condolences to his parents. I didn't know
him well but he seemed a decent young bloke. A
cobber in my squadron suffered a similar fate last
week. Doesn't help a chap to dwell on these things

otherwise he might go barmy. Better to keep his wits about him and spirits high because we all know it's the beginning of the end for old Fritz. Remember I'm thinking of you both. Have faith that I'll be home soon. Word is, that by the end of the year, it'll definitely be curtains for the Nips as well.

Hoping this letter finds you as it leaves me, in the Pink.

Your loving son and brother
Jasper

'My darling boy, my precious *Blue Orchid*. Bless his soul.' Audrey looked over her bifocals and smiled wistfully. 'We won't recognise him when he gets home. With all his *mates* and *cobbers*, he's sounding more Australian by the day.'

Blue Orchid. Attie looked at the sepia photograph, trying to picture the blue of his uniform. It was nearly five years since Attie last saw Jasper. How could he not have changed? He hadn't wanted any fuss when they'd gone up to Perth to send him off. He said he could easily catch the train. But she'd insisted. After all, it was only right to give him a proper farewell. No one had said much on the way up. From time to time, she'd glanced around at her mother to find her eyes closed, head lolling against the back seat. Audrey had protested at first, had wanted to stay behind because she couldn't bear to see him go. But in the end Attie had convinced her to come. 'After all, Mother,' she said, 'he is your only son.' Attie kept looking across at Jasper during the four-hour drive. His profile was angled, eyes staring ahead at the road in concentration. I bet he's a damn good pilot, she'd thought, with a fine sense of direction. Suntanned hands spread out over the polished walnut wheel, and that air of determination around his jaw. He looked so proficient, inspired such confidence, and yet there was also an edginess about him she'd observed, quirky hesitations when he spoke. Every now and then, a little tic hammered in his cheek. His stammer had returned, ever so slightly. He'd had it as a child when he'd first gone away to school. She hadn't noticed it for years and then, suddenly, there it was back again, just like that.

War changed men. It had taken her these five years to find that out. It changed them from men back into little boys who liked nothing better than the comfort of their mother's boiled fruit cake. But war changed everyone, didn't it? God knows, hadn't they learnt that from the previous one?

*

Attie and Jasper were four years old by the time they met their father. Only Audrey saw him stagger off the ship in Colombo in 1919, thin and bedraggled, and not knowing where he was. Attie's first memory was of him being helped up the veranda steps to the bungalow. She and Jasper had stood gawking at him, knee-high, not knowing what to do. No one expected Charlie would hug his children for he was far too weak. In any case how can you hug someone you don't even know? Instead he sat down slowly on the chaise-longue and started emptying his pockets. It obviously registered that he should at least make some token offering. The golden fob watch with Arabic numerals he gave to Jasper. And for Attie, a little leather-bound volume of Wordsworth he had kept close to his heart. Sensing the gifts were not quite equal, he salvaged an English penny from his pocket and pressed that into her hand as well. Attie was too young to read but she was delighted with the penny. Rolling it round in her fingers, she examined the King's head on the one side and the *tails* on the other. *Which was the right side of the coin?* she'd asked. *There is no right side or wrong side,* Charlie had tried to explain ... *You'll find out, my love, life takes care of that.* For hours she sat on the Indian rug spinning the coin to see which way it would fall.

As weeks went by, she discovered that her father was like the penny, which, by a simple flip of the wrist, could fall one way or the other. Half the time, Charlie woke up *heads* in the morning and half the time he woke up *tails.* On the *heads* days, he would be up at the crack of dawn, freshly dressed in khaki drills. He would twitch his moustache, clamp his pith helmet on top of his slicked-down hair and go off cantering across the hills. By midday he would have returned, showered and changed. After tiffin, he would rest, then work, quietly shuffling papers on his desk.

Mother often tried to manipulate his life. She said that what he needed most was to be with people to keep his mind from dwelling on the war. She was forever dragging him off to the racecourse and luncheon parties or to make up games of whist. And on the *heads* days, he could manage these things. If he felt up to it, he might challenge either of the twins to a game of tennis or take them out riding on their ponies.

Then there were the *tails* days, when he could barely get himself out of bed. Attie could sense it in the air, like the clouds which brooded overhead. Many mornings she had stood outside the shutters, too frightened to go into his darkened room. If she plucked up enough courage, she would tiptoe in and find him still curled up, exactly where he'd been the day before. She would stand looking at him. *Daddy?* She'd whispered ... *Daddy?* He wouldn't move. His eyes blank, just like he was dead. Even when she patted his striped cotton pyjamas, and whispered loudly *Daddy?* he still didn't answer, just kept staring at the rotting wall. Mother would come in, take her by the arm and whisper *later, dear. He's resting now.* For years Attie thought that *resting* was what everyone's father did.

*

Attie folded Jasper's letter, and glanced across at her mother. Audrey's grey head was tilted sideways, as it often was, like a bird looking for some seed.

Mornings were not a problem for Attie. Perhaps it was their gentle symphony annunciating the first few rays of light. She would lie listening to the birds, their music gathering in the darkness as the pale pink sky began to unfold. Then again, waking early was a habit instilled from childhood. Every day she had risen to the call of *Allaaaahu Akbar! Allaaaahu Akbar!* the muezzin's drone hovering over the rooftops wherever she happened to be. Only the sick and waning could not be summoned to witness the rising of the sun.

Opening the shutters of her bedroom, Attie had, on occasions, seen her mother padding around the lawn in her bare feet and white embroidered nightie, collecting the first fallen flowers of the frangipani. Sometimes she would reach down to the glassy surface of the fish pond and take one of the opening blossoms of pink lotus to put by Charlie's bed. Other times she left them as offerings to the carved wooden Buddha in her room.

Attie remembered coming home for school holidays and finding her mother on the veranda sipping her usual gin and tonic.

Where's Daddy? she asked.

He's gone into hospital for a little holiday. Nothing serious, she said, gently knocking the ash off her cigarette. Then there were her father's recurrent bouts of malaria which were serious. Sometimes the fever was so bad Attie could hear the brass bed rattling in his room. As she sat on the chaise-longue outside, her little fingers anxiously threading their way through the wicker, she thought he would die.

When someone once asked Audrey how she had coped all those years with Charlie's chronic illness, she replied that the worst ordeal of her life was when she was a *grass widow* stuck in a foreign country, having twins with no relatives around for support. Of course, the doctor had given her a whiff of chloroform but it was too soon, and she remembered how Adeline arrived bellowing and hadn't stopped being difficult since. *Jasper, as you'd expect, was no trouble at all, he followed five minutes later, sweet as a dream.*

All their lives it had been like that. One standard for little boys and one for little girls. Her mother would say *you wicked child, Adeline,* when she caught her working a pecan nut through a hole she'd found in the damask upholstery. She'd never say *you wicked boy, Jasper,* when she saw him up in the tamarind tree slinging shots at a harmless bird or squirrel.

Chapter 10

Valerie soon noticed the shortness of the autumn days, followed by the first of the nightly frosts. The house was old and draughty, not built for the cold like English dwellings.

'My back's killing me,' groaned Audrey, 'I'm too old for properties and plantations. Too old to be helping run a farm.'

'We could lease it,' suggested Valerie. 'Move up to Perth until Jasper comes home.'

'Damn silly thing to say, Val,' Attie hooted. 'I wonder who put those ideas in your head,' she said, giving Audrey a sideways look. 'Fat chance we'd have leasing a farm at a time like this.'

'Well, the government might if we approached them. They could bring in the Women's Land Army.'

'You could always get a teaching job up in the city, easy as pie,' said Audrey. 'There's such a shortage, you know, with all our men away.'

'Oh really,' said Attie, ignoring her mother, 'and what precisely would you do in the city, Valerie?'

'Well, I could get a job for a start,' she snapped, 'if that's what you're implying. Don't worry,' she added, tossing her head, 'shouldn't think I'd have any problems with all my service training.'

*

It was now late April, just over twelve months since Valerie had been dismissed from the base. *Medically unfit for service* was the term they chose to use when they punished you for pregnancy. Valerie adored being in a predominantly male environment. She prided herself as much on her physical appearance as she did on her disciplined approach to work, her nimble fingers and eye for detail. Her training in the various technical aspects of telecommunications drew on those qualities. It also provided her with important skills she would otherwise not have learnt, skills which she would retain for the rest of her life.

Now, Valerie pined for her work. Frequently, when she was reading war correspondence in the paper, she found herself unconsciously transcribing words into Morse code in her head. On the hour, as they sat listening to the latest news from the ABC, Valerie had to quash an impulse to call out *Alpha Bravo Charlie, can you hear me,* otherwise Audrey would come trotting in and say, *What was that, dear?*

Many times Valerie dreamt she was back at the Wickerton barracks, unencumbered with husband or with child. But it was a strange dream and always the same. She was getting dressed, standing in front of a mirror. Sleek and immaculate she looked, neat as a pin, as if the uniform was designed for her alone. But whether it was a shoe or a hat, there was always some item of clothing that had gone missing and was nowhere to be found. The panic and embarrassment of not being able to report for duty without it always made her wake up, heart pounding and in a frightful sweat.

Valerie had thrived on regimental life. Yet, what sort of life had she here in Australia? The daily tedium, the never-ending dirt and chaos. Audrey had told her to be patient. She had tried to explain that there was an order to farming, the order which lay in the practice of performing tasks as they rotationally fell due, or as the weather dictated. That was all very well, thought Valerie, but how could she understand what was what when she'd experienced barely more than a season at Grasswood?

She felt a little guilty at times for not doing her fair share. Inadequate. But even the simplest of chores could send her into a panic. It was silly really. She now baulked at lighting the chip bath-heater. The damn thing played tricks on her, she found, and the horrific noises inside it were something quite alarming. Hearing nothing once, she had opened the door to take a look, and the mighty great whoosh had knocked her sideways and sent her flying out of the room.

Valerie was a city girl. And that, in itself, was another thing. The farm's isolation nearly drove her mad. She knew that their worst worries of invasion were over now, but she desperately needed the touch, or at least the protective presence, of a man. Every now and then she thought of Chip Johnson, the feel of his toughened hand on her cheek. Had he forgotten so quickly? Many times since their walk together she had looked out at the empty hills in the hope that she might see him riding towards her on his horse. Surely he would want to escape from that silly chit of a wife of his, if only for an hour or two. Valerie wondered if Attie had seen Chip and herself together down at the dam that time. Had she had words with him? Perhaps that's why he hadn't come back.

Every Friday morning when they left the farm to go into town,

Valerie, adjusting her hatpin, would pray for some excitement. There was nowhere to go, nothing to see, but you never know, she thought, perhaps Chip, or even some American servicemen, might just happen to be in town. Every Friday when she went shopping in the main street, Valerie's hopes subsided. And, as she walked past the public bar of the Commercial Hotel, she would have to endure the same foul smell, that mixture of stale urine and beer, from men who had once been, but were now too old or frail, to go to war. There were often times when she would like to have sat up at a bar, in a civilised way as she had in many English pubs, and ordered herself a drink. But she knew it was forbidden. Audrey had told her, in no uncertain terms, that women weren't allowed in public bars here in Australia. They could only drink in the Lounge Bar, chaperoned by a man.

Valerie had to swallow her resentment. She had no option other than to hold her head high, pretend not to notice the leers and drunken winks, and settle for the tea-rooms down the street. Sipping her tea, she would look glumly out the window at the pine trees and the railway station across the road while Attie paid the bills. People stopped and stared at her. She wanted to scream out, tell them that she was bored, bored, bored! Bloody fed up to the teeth with nothing to look forward to but more of the same old thing week in, week out.

*

Not many itinerants called at Grasswood, for the surrounding hills were steep and the farm was well tucked away from the road. But the occasional knock at the back door from a hawker or a travelling salesman sent Valerie into a frenzy. It was ridiculous to think that she'd rushed to run a comb through her hair and line her mouth with lipstick when the *Watkins Man* arrived earlier this morning. Admittedly he was a handsome man, dark and thickset, sporting the build of a county cricketer. But it did not occur to Valerie how obvious it was that they had both stood looking at each other for longer than was polite or necessary.

Finally he opened the case and set out his wares. Valerie felt the rush of blood as his hand brushed hers passing a bottle of cochineal. He was so close she could feel his breath on her face as he spoke, his manly smell.

'Not every day of the week I come across such a pretty face, if you don't mind me saying.' His voice was smooth, and his grey eyes sparkled like sugar frosting as they roved the length of her body. 'Face like that don't come from these parts of the world, I'll warrant. City girl, eh? I can tell by your skin ...'

'I don't think we need anything today, thank you very much,' said Attie, quickly taking command of the situation.

'What about some vanilla, Madam?' he persisted, catching Valerie's eye again.

Attie clicked her tongue. 'Have to cut down on puddings and sweets, rations like they are.'

'Oh, but I do like a piece of cake,' Valerie protested. 'It doesn't feel quite right having a cup of tea without something sweet with it.'

What right had Attie to deprive her of a little conversation? What's more, she was annoyed that the decision had already been made. Only yesterday she'd been gently reminded *that we usually have jam or butter, one or the other, dear, but not both.* For years she had gone without the smallest luxuries. Now it was getting her down. She remembered her excuse of a wedding cake, a plain sponge, and its grand façade of icing her mother had made out of plaster-of-Paris on cardboard. As a teenager, she had always imagined the traditional iced tier would be kept for the christening of her first child. But there had not even been token slices in tins for their absent guests, let alone a christening. Their wedding cake had to be eaten in the first few days so it didn't go stale.

'Don't worry, Valerie, dear,' said Audrey. 'You can still have your cakes. We'll just have to make do with more dried fruit and honey instead of sugar,' she said.

'Thank you, Mr Ridgeway,' said Attie, passing the *Watkins Man* back his miniature bottles of essences. 'We won't be needing any.'

Audrey was distracted. She held out a bottle of green oil to Attie. 'Well,' she said. 'What about some more of that liniment for my poor old back?'

'You and your snake oil,' Attie smiled wryly. 'Yes, have some, Mother, for what it's worth.'

'Snake oil? Ooh! How revolting,' Valerie shuddered. 'Is that honestly what it is?'

*

The following day there was another knock at the back door. Valerie jumped. Attie had gone to check the cattle and Audrey was lying down. Despite her thirst for excitement, Valerie didn't like opening the door when she was alone. Through the flywire she could see a swarthy looking fellow, with a check cloth around his head. She took one look at his beard and the sallow darkness of his skin and cried out 'Audrey!'

'It's all right, Valerie,' said Audrey, hurrying down the hallway. 'I'm coming. Ah, good morning, Mr Singh,' she laughed excitedly. 'We know you well, don't we? How nice to see you again! I'm so glad you've come. Well, now, show us what you have this year and we'll make you a nice cup of tea.'

From the driveway came the sound of jingling harness and the stamp of hooves. Two Clydesdales stood before a covered wagon, flicking flies from their drooping lips. Valerie could smell a mixture of spices as the man unfolded a rug onto the lawn and spread out his wares. Grinning appreciatively, he accepted the black tea and boiled fruit cake which Audrey brought out on a silver tray. Beneath her green parasol, she looked flushed and breathless, almost girlish. She tilted her head, bright-eyed like a bird.

'Mr Singh's wares always remind me of when I was a young bride in Ceylon.' She twirled her parasol.

Valerie wanted to walk away. Any minute Audrey would start waffling on again about Charlie ... Bravo bloody Charlie. But she knew that for the moment Audrey's worry lines had gone. She was back in another world fingering through boxes of needles, cottons, scissors, buttons and toiletries, candles and rolls of exotic silk.

My dearest darling Lily,

I've haven't had a letter from you for such a long time. Is something wrong? I do miss my family, especially you my darling. I hope baby is settling down now. Take care of yourself, dear. I know it's

hard on you but I promise it won't be for long.
I've had a few close shaves over the past few weeks
and thought of you so often during those difficult
moments. I wanted you to know dear that I got a
letter today from Kodak House. There's a chance I'll
get my release sooner than expected. Apparently it's
a case of first in first out. Most of the chaps though
will have to wait for the long haul. But with a bit of
string-pulling I'll try to get home the quickest way
I can. Kangaroo-hopping if you get the gist of it.
Then it might be a case of waiting for a black cat.
Tell Mother there's a chance I might be holed up
in Ceylon for a while. Old Dumbo can only take a
couple of extras. My darling, it's a pity there's not
more a chap can say on paper. Seems a wealth of
material is lost with the limitations they place on
the written word. Makes you think there's nothing
left to write home about sometimes. But the one
thing I can say, my darling girl, is that I love you
more than you can imagine and can't wait to be
back in your arms.

Yours for ever,
Jasper

Valerie could only imagine the things that Jasper concealed. She pictured him in London on a six-day leave pass. After coming out of Kodak House, he'd be off to the pictures or dropping in to the Boomerang Club or Codger's Bar. And who would he be with, she wondered? Would he have a woman on his arm? Valerie often wondered if he'd slept with anyone since she'd left. There was a kind of numbness she felt, conscious as she was of the enormous pressures he faced daily just to stay alive. How could she expect him not to be like many of the other airmen who used women or booze as a release to block out what they did yesterday, today and what they'd have to do tomorrow?

Last year, Jasper had told her morale was bad. Some of the Aussies were kicking up an awful stink about wanting to return to fight on their own home front. Why shouldn't they fight for Australia, he said. Mature pilots like himself were being retained for their skill and experience even though there were many newly trained recruits to replace them. The odds of dying in the air were horrific. Jasper said that when they started their pre-operational training in England, they were told they had a fifty-fifty chance of surviving their first operation. But, after initiation, the odds of being among the missing rose with each operation until it became more probable than not. Even Valerie knew that. From her work at Wickerton, she couldn't help but be aware of the loss rate, exactly which pilots flew out of the base and which ones never came back. She knew damn well that the longer Jasper remained in England, the lower his chances of survival.

*

Valerie lit the lamp with fumbling hands. She crept over and peered into the safe-cot. In the half-light she could see Virginia's baby profile, the open lips and the curve of her plump cheek resting on the pillowcase. She lifted the lamp closer. Within seconds she could see the rise and fall of the quilt against the white sheet and the faint snuffle as the baby breathed. It was hard to believe that it was the first night that Virginia had slept through without a bottle.

It wasn't fair. She had woken and an hour later here she was still unable to get back to sleep. Something else must have disturbed her tonight. At first she thought she'd woken to hear the sound of a car engine coming up the drive. But now she realised it must have been that recurring dream she'd been having, the one about Jasper coming home. The thought began to make her feel uneasy again. She searched for the comforting sound of Jasper's voice and from nowhere it came in a song. *So ... what's the use of worrying, it never was worthwhile.* But soon the voice that had once charmed her had vanished and now the canned jauntiness of melody and words began to irritate her, spiralling around like a stuck record in her head. *Pack up your troubles in your old kit bag and smile, smile, smile ...* She'd long since been tired of smiling, being bright and breezy and making out that nothing ever worried her. God knows how she'd managed to put up such a front in London, making a good impression in her work. Wasn't hard to be brave, though, when you had heroes around you all the time, chaps like Jasper who'd been through hell on earth, some arriving back from sorties bloodstained, with trousers wet or browned, limbs and half their faces blown away. But here, a smile was as good as useless. Here, nothing happened to make you grateful to be alive. Often it seemed as if she was broken off from reality, like she was acting in a play or a film. Putting on airs and graces, she knew that's how it probably appeared—*Lady Muck* attitudes, hamming it up—but it made her feel in control, offered her some sort of authority, protection even, in her sense of isolation.

Now, alone in bed in little more than a cotton nightie, Valerie felt at once terribly cold and exposed. Slipping on her candlewick gown, she crept out to the kitchen with the lamp. She drew the glowing coals together and stoked the stove, then pulled out the damper. The room was light and warm as she slid a small saucepan of milk on the hob to heat. She stood in the doorway rubbing her hands, looking at the shadows down the hall. Suddenly two large circles of light rose like haloes on the sitting room wall. Audrey, silly old goat, must have fallen asleep with an empty glass in her hand, and left the lamp on.

Valerie crept in tentatively. The beams now were still but the room was cold and bare. Perhaps there was a full moon, she thought, drawing back the curtains. A pair of headlights shone from the gate on high-beam. She froze, shielding her eyes. Suddenly the sizzle of milk spilling over on the stove brought her running back to the kitchen. She was shaking uncontrollably when she sat down. Hot cocoa slopped on the kitchen table every time she tried to lift the cup to her lips.

Valerie hesitated. She didn't want to wake the others. Instead, she crept back to her room, worried she might have been hallucinating again. Lately she'd been having the strangest sort of dreams. Now, without warning, she was back in the London Blitz in the height of it all, alone and petrified, reliving what she'd tried so hard to forget. She squeezed her eyes more tightly to block it out but the deluge of horror kept spilling into the blackness behind. *No! Please God, no!* Any second the baby would wake and then how would she cope? Already her heart was up to its old scared-rabbit antics, jump-jump-jumping wildly against her rib-cage looking for an escape route; her breath rapid and huffing in the cold air. Now the old ache in her throat was back, growing ever so hard, contracting, her chest heaving, everything closing in on her, suffocating. She pounded her fists again and again into the pillow, shaking her head and gasping. Gasping trying to free herself from the kaleidoscope of images swirling around in her head. But the swinging cone of searchlights kept bearing down on her; the grind of engines, waves of angry pulsation like bees buzzing in blind fury. And as she ran through the fires searching frantically for the shadowed spaces in the streets, she could hear sirens wailing in the distance ... the thunderous *boom-booms* around her followed seconds later by the sounds of buildings crumpling, that revolting smell ... and all the time she was running faster, faster through the flames with her hanky to her nose, but every time she hid the lights would find her out.

*

'I'm afraid I didn't hear a thing, dear. Usually I'm out like a light. Did you hear anything, Adeline?' Audrey was busy looking through a bundle of old postcards and letters which Charlie had sent her when he was away at war. 'Here, listen to this, Valerie, Charlie wrote me the sweetest letters.'

> *My darling,*
> *I miss you so much. Every day I pray for you to be*
> *by my side. I would gain such comfort, such strength,*
> *just to be able to hold you close to my heart, running*

my fingers through your glorious hair.

    I do hope the twins are thriving, Audrey darling,
and not still getting you down. I long to see them
and cuddle them in my arms. I get so lonely, you
know, being away from everything I hold dear.
But a soldier has no choice as to the company he
keeps here in the trenches. He quickly learns to
befriend those he depends upon. I must say, though,
I'm rather impressed with the young Australians
I've met over here. They're such good sports. One of
them saved my life yesterday ... pulled me down in
the trench when a shell came scuttling overhead ...

Valerie was only half-listening. *Charlie, Charlie, Charlie ...* She could feel one of her headaches coming on again. Perhaps she should ask Audrey for some of the special green liniment to put on her temples. It had seemed to work once before, but now that Valerie knew it was snake oil she really wasn't quite sure.

'How lovely, Audrey. But, I think I'll have to go and lie down. I'm not feeling very well.'

Later, Valerie woke to the sound of the gramophone. It was one of those awful Irish–American songs winding into tune. Yesterday it had been *Daisy, Daisy, give me your answer, do.* Now it was that one about the 'Old Green River'. That whining voice was driving Valerie mad.

    Danny smiled, like a child, but his
    wife she grew awful wild.
    'Where have you been all night long?' she cried

And this is what Danny replied
'I've been floating down that
Old Green River
On the good ship Rock and Rye
But I floated too far — I got stuck on a bar
There was I all alone, wishing that I was home.
The ship got wrecked with the captain and crew
And there was only one thing left to do —
So I had to drink that Old Green River dry
To come back home to you-u-u-u-u-u.'

There was Audrey lounging back in the wireless-chair, drink in her hand, eyes closed, with that ridiculous smile spread over her face. A fire was burning in the grate. Sitting opposite was Attie with Virginia on her knee. She was swaying the child backwards and forwards and making stupid sound effects to the music. She would puff her cheeks out over her forefinger and then suddenly *POP!* it out, like a cork coming out of a bottle. There was nothing remotely funny about it, but, every time she did it, the child would chuckle, waving her arms for a repeat performance.

*

Valerie woke in the early hours around the same time as the night before. Virginia was sleeping peacefully in her cot. Again Valerie crept into the sitting room and peered out through the windows. Again she saw a set of headlights shining into the house. She closed the curtains immediately and pinched herself to make sure she wasn't dreaming. She even looked in the mirror. For the rest of the night, she sat there in her dressing gown, shivering and immobilised by fear. The fire had long since died, and bitter draughts rose constantly through cracks in the sloping floorboards. Valerie tried to cry out for help. Each time she opened her mouth, her dry tongue froze. Someone, she knew, was out to get her.

*

It was early the next morning, before the sun had risen, when Attie found Valerie asleep on the sofa.

'What on earth's wrong, Valerie?' she asked, touching her lightly on the shoulder. 'Why aren't you in bed?'

Valerie tried to explain what had happened. She felt stupid.

'Oh don't worry,' Attie smiled wryly. 'Most likely it's old Fitzy. No one knows his real name, Fitzpatrick, Fitzharding, Fitzgerald … but he lives by himself a mile or so down the track. One could say he's eccentric, to say the least. He's done this before, you know. Probably heard Jasper's wife's in town. But, don't worry; I'm sure he's really quite harmless.' Attie made them both a cup of tea and they stood warming themselves by the stove.

Valerie nearly fainted when Attie told her how Fitzy would kill a calf for its carcass, and then leave the hide to dry on a fence in the mother's paddock. More than once, she had heard what she thought was the lowing of a stray beast and gone over to the boundary to see what was wrong. It distressed her to find the poor cow, berserk with misery, sniffing constantly and mooing at her baby's hide.

'It's not worthwhile wondering what motivates him to do such strange things,' said Attie, keeping her eyes lowered. 'It was an evil thing to do to an animal and he has no right to be on our property, but maybe he is lonely. Who are we to judge?' She pondered on whether or not to tell Valerie the story she had heard about the man's miserable start in life. How when Fitzy's father was killed in the Boer war, his mother went hysterical and abandoned her infant son. Fitzy was found wrapped up in swaddling on clean straw in a chicken coop on a neighbouring property. They searched everywhere for his mother, then eventually found her, drowned in her own water tank, with a rock tied to her foot.

*

A few days later the three women stood on the veranda watching the rapid swell of smoke darken against the haziness of the state forest, clusters upon clusters billowing up higher and higher into the blue above. Valerie had thought it was a rain cloud at first, but now she was overwhelmed by the acrid smell of smoke, its grittiness filling the air around her. Blinking, she reached in her pocket for her handkerchief.

'Where do you think it's coming from?' Already there was a panicky edge to her voice and her body was beginning to tremble.

'Over Fitzy's way, by the looks of it,' replied Attie. 'Bloody fool of a man,' she grumbled. 'What's he think he's doing?' She grabbed the car keys. 'It's obviously got away. Only one thing for it. We'll have to go over and give him a hand.'

Valerie froze. 'No!' she shrieked. 'No!' Nothing would induce her to go anywhere near the fire or Fitzy. Nothing! And as she ran inside, she felt it all come flashing back, the swinging cone of searchlights and the smell of burning flesh.

'I'm sorry Adeline, I can't possibly leave the poor girl on her own,' said Audrey, 'she's too distressed. Can't you see the state she's in?'

'Suit yourselves, if that's the risk you want to take. I'll come back and fetch you all if I think it's really out of hand.'

Audrey did her best to reassure Valerie while tending to the baby.

'Don't worry dear. Fires are a regular occurrence in the bush and neighbours have a duty to help each other.'

Audrey was calm as she poured the tea from the teapot.

'Here dear, sit down and have a cup. It'll settle you down.'

But Valerie could not stop shuddering. Jasper had told her about the horrific bushfires he'd experienced. Houses, forest and stock, all reduced to ashes. Farmers sent to ruin as a result of one little match. A neighbouring family of settlers he'd known boiled alive in their rain-water tank trying to escape. It's the gum in the trees, he'd explained, it's like adding extra fuel to the fire.

Tea slopped on Valerie's apron; china chinked against her teeth. She could barely hold the cup.

Audrey patted her gently on the shoulder.

'Don't worry dear, we can always go and stand in the dam, if the worst comes to the worst.'

But their fears were allayed when Attie returned a few hours later.

'All under control,' she said. 'Silly man, said he'd had to burn a dead beast that was full of maggots. Should have let the crows have their fill and be done with it. Now he's lost what little feed he had.'

Chapter 11

Attie gathered the remaining hay from the shed and bundled it into the wheelbarrow. She ducked as a swallow flew down from above. Looking up, she could see the head of its mate in the clay nest between the rafters. Standing in a shaft of sunlight, she watched the bird performing broad sweeps backwards and forwards over the paddock. There was something fascinating about migratory birds, the way they appeared suddenly, having travelled thousands of miles while eating, sleeping and mating on the wing. Her spirits began to lift. Perhaps the swallow was a good sign. She recalled an old saying she'd been told by a Dutch birdwatcher back in Ceylon: whenever you see a swallow flying low over the ground it will be sure to rain the next day.

Yet, as she watched the swallow's effortless aerobatics, she knew its manic activity might only be a gesture of defence. The elegance of its movements and its boomerang shape reminded her of tiny, black palm swifts she'd seen as a girl, sweeping low over the swampy rice fields to chase away their prey.

This April there had been such little rain. Every now and then over the past few weeks, Attie had felt an isolated spot fall heavy on her bare arm, but that was all. They'd never had a problem with water in the hill country of Ceylon. In her mind she could still see the rivers winding their way through the green valleys, smell the warm rain and the dripping humidity of tropical vegetation. In the wet season, the rain was fine and steady, hanging over the hills in what her mother would call something akin to a *Scotch mist*. And, in the dry season, when the rain was less frequent, they knew they could always rely on the ancient waterways for irrigation.

Twigs and stubble snapped as Attie pushed the iron-wheeled barrow. She noticed how black the cattle looked against the sandy-coloured paddock. Poor things, she thought, as they huddled in the shade. Their *mooing* was enough to make her cry. They'd lost so much condition over the last few months. Even from this distance, she could see the hollows in their flanks as they began to lumber towards her, tossing their weary heads. It was a heartbreaking task feeding them. Within minutes of reaching her, they had demolished the hay and were pawing at the powdery paddock.

Every night Attie prayed for rain. Long after they had gone to bed, she would lie awake, waiting for the empty clunk of the windmill. The tank was low and the well beneath had almost dried up too. In the past, there'd always been enough water to cover domestic needs.

Of course, Valerie had been mortified when Attie had told her again to ease off on the bathwater and not to use the hose. Attie tossed and turned. Even in the darkness, she could picture her mother's garden which was withering daily against the brown lawn. But it was the least of her worries. She tried to tell herself it was simply a test of endurance. If the worst came to the worst, she would sell the stock. But, in the back of her mind, she knew that when the last of their water had gone, they would have no choice but to bail it by bucket from the dam.

Now, as she looked down the valley, Attie could see herons poking furtively in the reeds. She left the empty barrow where it was and walked slowly along the dried-up creek bed. The water-level of the dam had never been so low. Dozens of marron holes lay exposed in the cracked clay banks. What water remained had lost its shine. Still and murky, it rested around the blackened snags and logs with a film of algae on the top.

*

When the storm eventually hit, it was so ferocious no one could sleep. Thunder boomed and flashes of lightning forked through the darkness of the rooms. Lamps flickered as the howling wind rose up through cracks in the floor. Soon the canvas blind was thumping outside on the veranda post. Attie got up to tie it down. The front door nearly slammed on her hand. Then something started banging on the roof, louder and louder. Valerie pulled the eiderdown over her head, muffling her screams. The baby woke and started crying too. Snatching Virginia from her cot, Valerie ran into the kitchen. 'What are we going to do?' she cried, cowering in the corner. 'What are we going to do?'

There was little that Attie could say to reassure her. At one stage she was so frightened herself she thought the roof was going to blow off.

Then, at last, the rains came, lashing through the night. The women huddled together in the kitchen sipping hot cups of cocoa with a splash of Audrey's brandy.

At first light, Attie put on an oilskin coat and went out to inspect the damage. Standing on a ladder, she looked out across at the paddocks. A few branches had fallen on the lawn, otherwise there was little damage that she could see. The first thing she noticed was the tennis court, a sheet of water so deep and still, it gave reflections of pearly clouds parting into blue. Apart from a length of flashing which had lifted off from the gable, the roof was intact. Attie stood there a minute, breathing in the thick wet air. She nearly fell off the ladder, she was so giddy with elation. The gargoyle, she noted, was overflowing, and in the clogged-up gutters, blue wrens stood pecking the sodden leaves.

*

With the rains came the grass. Valerie watched in amazement as the rolling hills quickly changed from grey to green. One day, early in May, Cam came over with a bottle of whisky under his arm.

'I've just heard that the bloody Huns have surrendered. Come on, everyone, let's celebrate.' They sat down together around the wireless with their tumblers, listening to the special BBC broadcast of Churchill's speech to the nation. Valerie closed her eyes. She could quite easily see that bald bulldog of a man in his greatcoat standing thickset on one of the Cabinet balconies in Whitehall, addressing the crowds below.

This is your victory! he called out, gloved hands clutching the wrought iron railings.

No, it is your victory! the crowd roared back. She pictured the streamers and the Union Jacks flying high, and behind the cheers and the whistles she could hear the bells of Big Ben pealing, once bold and courageous, as she remembered them during the Blitz, glorious now in celebration. She wanted to be there to join in. After all, wasn't it her city as well? She could see it all now. The crowds would be so thick around Whitehall and Horse Guards Parade, they'd be milling around The Mall, Birdcage Walk, and spilling out into St James's Park right up to Buckingham Palace.

'Here's to our boys in blue,' said Cam. 'Cheers! To all our troops and may they come home quickly and safely.'

'Yes, *chin-chin*,' said Audrey. 'Here's to our darling boys. Here's to our precious Jasper.' They all raised their glasses.

Audrey made a tuna casserole and Cam stayed for dinner. Later, the BBC broadcast a message from the King, and they sat, all ears to the wireless, as his tired voice stuttered through the crackles.

But Valerie felt cheated. Not unlike how she'd felt when she'd found out she was pregnant. It was Christmas time then, she remembered, a year ago last December. She and Jasper were in Simpsons buying presents for each other. Jasper was suddenly overcome. All that central heating. Said he was suffocating in his uniform, needed to get some fresh air. So they'd walked down Regent Street into St James's Park. And that was where they'd stood, cold and numb, after she'd found the courage to tell him she was pregnant. She was shivering. There were no flowers, just the frozen lake and the trees, bare with a mantle of white, for it was snowing ever so lightly. Jasper was silent. She didn't dare look at him. Her eyes remained lowered. She stood watching a tiny squirrel shimmy up a tree. Her bones were aching by the time the words eventually came out. That wretched stutter again ... *O-Of course, V-Valerie, we'll get m-married as soon as we can.*

*

The next morning, Valerie could still hear Churchill's words, slow and slurred, telling her that every man and woman had done their best. Behind the cheering crowds she could hear the victory music of the brass band playing and the Horse Guards clopping along, and in the park she could see the buds bursting on the trees and the bleak English sun suddenly breaking through a cloud. How desperately she wanted to be there now to celebrate.

Something moved against the frosted kitchen window. Wiping a circle, Valerie saw a robin redbreast. It hopped along, eyeing her with quick movements of its head. It was so close she could've reached out and touched it had it not been for the pane. It was strange, for she never usually noticed birds. That was Attie's interest. But the robin was as English as apple dumplings. Often on sunny weekends driving through country lanes, Valerie had seen robins darting in and out of the hedgerows.

Cheeky little thing. Its splash of colour was an instant joy. Inside her head, Valerie could hear that silly Al Jolson song that Jasper had played on her mother's piano that time they'd all stood with their arms around each other, singing about the 'Red Red Robin'. What was it? *Get up, get out of it*, she'd even joined in as a lark. She could hear them belting it out as Jasper's hands bounced around the keys. She found herself unconsciously humming the tune, and for the rest of the day it hung around her head.

Now, as an experiment, Valerie broke half a stale crust of bread, spreading out the crumbs on the window sill outside. Soon, the robin was back again, bobbing up and down as it pecked up the crumbs. A little later, it returned again, tap-tapping at the window with its beak. After that, Valerie put crumbs out every morning and the bird always returned. Like a miniature Guard, in its red, white and black uniform, checking on me to see if I'm all right. She smiled. Aah, isn't it sweet! She would keep it a secret. It was one thing she didn't have to share.

*

When the first May mist settled in the valley, Audrey remarked to Valerie how the countryside reminded her a little of Wales where she was born.

'The first thing I did when we arrived here was plant those two silver birch trees,' said Audrey, raking the fallen leaves towards Attie's intended bonfire. 'Do you know, Valerie, I hadn't seen a tree change colour for over twenty years, ever since I left the old country. I'd almost forgotten about the seasons. Up in Ceylon, you see, there are no real changes to remind you.'

She was telling Valerie how Ceylon was a paradise, an island of contrasts with both dry and wet seasons, including two monsoons in a year. Inland, there were areas that were hot and dry, yet around the coast the humidity could be so high it almost drove you potty. But where they lived, up in the hill country, the climate was much milder, more like a cool perpetual spring.

Attie lit the fire and stood back as the twigs began to crackle. Never had the silver birches looked more exquisite, their autumn colours like those of the fire deepening in the dull light. She tossed some apple prunings onto the fire. Perhaps it was something she had read, about how an English settler consoles himself with the constant hope that something will turn up to alter the certainty of his exile. He rarely plants a fruit tree, because he is drawn by continual thoughts of his return. Yet, she thought, the Partridges were an exception to this rule. Hadn't her mother and father sown their roots in Australia from the day that they had arrived?

It was twelve years since then. In that time, the apple trees had flourished. Those silver birch saplings had grown higher than the roof. She remembered how Jasper had dug two holes for Audrey, then helped steady the slender trunks as she planted them. Now, glancing up, Attie could see how the two trees had grown differently. The leaves of one were more prolific and intense, the trunk more upright. The other tree had been blown slightly sideways by the wind. Its last dozen or so leaves, blood-red hearts trembling tenuously in the branches.

When was the last time that Jasper had written? He never seemed to give them any news. His letters were sporadic and when they came it was always something jolly and stockstandard like, *Don't worry! I'm safe and sound. This might sound odd but I know where I am but I can't say where!*

'Come on, Valerie,' cried Audrey. 'Let's stoke it up. I always think it makes you feel better, don't you think so? It's not just the warmth. It's also a good way of getting rid of all sorts of rubbish.'

But Valerie was not even looking. She was backing away and hiding her face in her hands.

Audrey continued gathering bundles of sticks and small branches and piled them onto the crackling flames. 'Throw on your worries and let them go.' Her eyes were smarting and it took all her energy to smother her wheeze. Smoke seeped out of the damp leaves as she raked them onto the fire.

For some reason, the smoke always seemed to curl and follow Valerie no matter how many times she changed direction. 'Look, it's chasing me,' she wailed, 'I can't bear it another second.'

She's so damned jumpy, observed Attie, as she watched her take off and run inside. 'Worry doesn't do you any good,' Audrey coughed, holding her handkerchief to her nose. 'All I want in this world is to see Jasper come home alive and well.'

It was what they were all wanting.

*

'I'm going into town to a CWA meeting with Betty Williams,' said Audrey. 'New faces are always welcome you know, Valerie. You can bring Virginia too. There are always a few young lasses like yourself.'

Poor Betty was still suffering, but her friendship with Audrey had grown considerably over the past six months. Audrey had taken a ginger cake over to comfort Betty after she'd received a telegram saying her son, Keith, had been killed in action.

Betty had gone grey almost overnight. A parent's worst nightmare, thought Attie, the reality of having to outlive her own child. Yet parents all over the world, including her mother, had to live with the terrible daily expectation of that knock on the door, or of a telegram informing them that their son had died in action. Attie wondered if it would be worse to see your own child killed before your eyes.

Not long before they left Ceylon, Attie had witnessed the death of a child. They had motored down from Kandy for a New Year's Eve party in Colombo. The traffic was more chaotic than usual. Galle Road was thronging with people beneath the spangled decorations and brightly coloured lights. It was hard to say how it happened. But a child's life was snuffed out, as quickly as a snap of the fingers. Attie had seen a swirl of dust in front of the car ahead, and something white flying through the air. Someone cried out. A figure in pyjamas flashed onto the road. Their driver didn't stop, just looked straight ahead, tooting and weaving the Rover between the rickshaws. Music continued blaring from the market stalls. Audrey fluttered her fan a little faster as a waft of incense drifted through the hot, humid air. Attie sat rigid. Craning her neck, she peered out of the back window. She would never forget the horror in that man's eyes as he ran, arms outstretched, to the child's lifeless body lying in the gutter. No one spoke for a while. She couldn't eat or drink all night because she had such a sick feeling in her stomach.

We could have stopped.

But it wasn't our fault, Adeline. We didn't hit him.

No, it wasn't our fault, Mother. But we still could have stopped. Comforted the child's family in their grief. At least given them money for a decent funeral.

If we'd stopped, Adeline, they would have all descended on us and we'd never have heard the end of it.

If we had stopped, Mother, we would have been late for the party, more to the point. And weren't we late enough as it was?

I don't think you understand dear, but then again you're only seventeen …

*

'Gee! My knee's a bit dicky today,' said Cam apologetically. He stood beside his bullocks. 'It's this blasted weather we've been having. It tends to play up with the cold. If you want to get those spuds in, girl, then I'm afraid you'll have to do the driving. Reckon you can handle my boys by yourself?' He drew in his belt.

'They'll make light work of it, you'll see.'

'I'll give it a go, Cam,' said Attie, overjoyed.

'Goodo.'

They hitched the plough to the bullocks' yoke. Attie took the whip tentatively and clucked the beasts forward. For years she had ridden horses, had even driven a pony-trap. But driving bullocks was somewhat new. There were no reins to hold, so how would she manage to guide them?

After the first row, Attie felt totally in control. It was almost as if these animals knew instinctively what to do. But why was Cam standing in the middle of the paddock, waving his walking stick in the air? What a card he looked, pot belly hanging over his trousers. What on earth was he bellowing?

She smiled. It was good to watch the capeweed folding into the newly turned earth, and to breathe in the aroma rising from the dark and pungent furrows. And, then, as each row formed, the pleasure of planting the seed potatoes with a sprinkle of blood and bone along the bottom. Ploughing and planting. One of the next furrows would cover the seeded one, and the other would create a new one. It was not difficult, just hard physical work. Simply a matter of repeating this procedure over and over until the crop was in.

At first, Attie enlisted the other two women to help with the seeding. After the first few rows, Audrey's back gave way, and then Valerie stopped in sympathy. Throughout the next few days, it was up to Attie to complete the task. And as she trudged, half-stooped, with a sugar bag of seed hanging from her neck, she realised that she'd been overly optimistic.

'I hear *Lady Powder Finger*'s had the bomb,' whispered Cam, when he came back with his scarifier so that she could mound the soil.

Attie laughed as she recalled Valerie's gloved hands delicately dispensing the sprouting pieces into the furrows.

Cam looked at the sky. 'Looks like rain. You'll need to go like the dickens to get this finished. Giddy-up!' He tapped one of the bullocks with his walking stick. 'You don't want to be traipsing through a bloody quagmire.'

Willy wagtails darted in and out of the bullocks. One fidgeted, poking its beak into the bullock's ear. Attie flipped the whip in the air. Little meat-eaters. They reminded her of the white cattle egrets back in Ceylon. They were always hovering around the hill farmers as they ploughed. Sometimes she'd see them standing on the backs of water buffalo. *Look Daddy, look Daddy, that white bird's having a ride.*

And plucking lice, more likely, I'd say.

What would her father say now if he could see her driving the bullocks? Her hands, once white and smooth, were now blistered and ingrained with soil. He'd be shocked. Say it wasn't a woman's job. Well, he hadn't liked her teaching in those bush schools either, miles from anywhere. Wasn't good enough for a daughter of his. She'd been stuck out in the Wheatbelt when he'd collapsed suddenly in her mother's arms. Attie still felt a sense of guilt that she hadn't been around when he died. Her mother was devastated, of course, almost inconsolable. Over the weeks Cam had come over to see if he could be of help. He understood, he said. His Edna had died of cancer only the year before. He knew what Audrey was going through.

The wind was crying when they stopped for lunch. Cam

limped over and together he and Attie lifted off the bullocks' harness. Within half an hour, they were sitting in the warmth of the kitchen eating the shepherd's pie which Audrey had made from the remainder of yesterday's leg of mutton.

'Crop should be ready before Christmas,' he said, putting down his knife and fork. 'It's damn good soil, you know. When Jasper comes back I reckon he'll need a bloody workforce to get the blighters out.'

When Cam had gone, Attie stood admiring her work. It looked like a brown corduroy patch had been sewn into the rolling green pasture. She was grateful for Cam's help and the loan of his bullocks. He was a good chap, *such a dear man*, as her Mother would say. Attie smiled. What a wag. She could still hear the roar of his voice in the wind. It followed her for the rest of the day. She only later realised, when she laid her head against the cold pillow, that it was his commands those beasts were following, not hers, that her power was only an illusion.

*

Thieving sods. Attie adjusted the focus of the lens. The shags were perched on logs in the shallows, drying their outstretched wings in the sunshine. It upset Attie to think that they'd taken most of the marron and the trout that Jasper had bred in the dam. There'd be none left now when he came home.

In between the reeds, a couple of ibis stalked, poking the curve of their beaks in and out of the spongy creek bed. Further over, on the black waters of the dam, she could see a pelican. Unusual, Attie thought, to see one in this part of the world. It was floating languidly. Alone. No chicks. She wondered where its mate might be. For a second she felt that stab of loneliness that hit her every now and then. There were times when she was glad she was unattached. That way, she'd have to bear no loss. She knew only too well the sadness of separation.

When the ship had sailed from Colombo twelve years ago, she knew she'd left something of herself behind. Sometimes, when she least expected it, thoughts of Tony de Souza came into her head. She pictured him waving goodbye from the wharf. She was still haunted by the memory of his figure growing smaller and darker as the ship drew away into the white-frilled waves. Even now, if she let herself go, she could feel the lightness of his hand resting between her shoulder blades and his palm squeezing hers as they danced together on the terrace of the Galle Face Hotel. He held her close. She could smell pomade through the salt air, and as he kissed her she felt nothing could ever come between them, not even the breakers dashing against the limestone wall.

Mother was relieved, of course, when they left. Couldn't get her on the ship quick enough, to find her *someone more their own kind*, as she put it. Audrey's constant hovering and prompted introductions. All that chit-chat over deck quoits, after-dinner strolls and the fancy dress ball had been so utterly boring. Chaps as insipid as sago pudding, Attie remembered. Bland as a bloody blancmange.

Aussie men hadn't been much chop either. At least, not the ones she'd met. They hadn't known how to talk to her. Thought she was superior, and preferred drinking with their mates. Then suddenly she found she was twenty-four and the best ones were either married or else away at war.

Well, these days, Perth was alive with men. There were

hundreds of American servicemen—'overpaid, oversexed and over here'—stealing Australian women from their men. Often, during a short stay in Perth, she had seen them strutting along with a woman wrapped on either arm. Every night there'd be hordes of them out in the bars, or jitterbugging at the Embassy. It wasn't just their boyish crew cuts. They treated women differently, she'd heard, although perhaps it was just the words of money.

She thought of the chances she'd had over the years. Lads she'd met at country dances. Farmers' sons, who'd left school at twelve. She recalled how they'd stood grinning and nudging each other as they looked in her direction. Occasionally, one would brace his shoulders and approach her full of bravado ... *Dance please, Miss?* Red hands outstretched, he would shyly take her onto the sawdust-floor, breathing beer instead of speaking. One day, she had stood in the main street looking over at the station and watched these same young men going off to war. There had been railway carriages full of them leaning out of the windows, waving. It was strange how they all looked the same in their uniforms.

But Attie had been searching for someone different. She thought of Tony de Souza. She'd never felt like that again, or had never let herself, truth be known. And now, here she was, thirty and alone.

But she was being maudlin. She should spare a thought for all the lovers and the war widows she knew who'd been left behind. Love was one thing, an ideal, a pie in the sky, but when you lost it, well then, that was life, and the sadness you had to accept. Look at Mother, she thought. Fifty last birthday. My God, she'd gone downhill since Father died. But two wars and twenty years in the tropics were enough to drive anyone to drink, although the rations had certainly slowed her down. Now Audrey spent most of her days bent over her quilting or knitting socks. It was pathetic; the sad fall of the faded bob, the smeary bifocals, and the lines growing daily on her mother's face. There had been such pride and beauty in that long auburn hair. The daily rituals of washing, brushing and parting, the plaiting and pinning of braids into shiny coils on either side of her head were the basis of Attie's earliest memories of her mother. She could picture it back in Ceylon, her mother sitting outside on the veranda, brushing the sunshine through her long wet hair. Attie was always wanting to pat and stroke it. *Not just now dear ...*

Attie remembered once, during her father's long absence, running to her mother's room after being awoken by a tropical storm. She had stood peeping through the long wooden shutters. Her mother was undressing behind the cane screen. Tiptoeing into the room, Attie had lifted the mosquito net and slipped into the four-poster bed. It seemed as if her mother pretended not to notice, turning down the lamp instead. But within seconds Attie felt her mother's presence, sitting upright beside her. Close yet not close, for it was a very hot, humid night. Attie could tell her mother was crying, silently, and she lay there beside her and watched the movements of her body cutting through the darkness. Grown-ups didn't cry. She wouldn't tell Jasper. And although the sobs were soundless, she could still make out her mother's heaving shoulders and the white wings of a handkerchief waving over her nose. Sheets rustled. Hairpins clinked as they fell one by one into the china dish beside the bed. When the plaits were freed, her mother began to whisper, swishing the brush in long even strokes, and looping it back until her long hair fell into a curtain across her face. And all along, Attie lay there waiting. She held her breath, straining to hear her mother's murmurs long after they'd been absorbed into the shadows. Then, suddenly, Attie noticed her mother had turned on her side and faced the wall. But she could still feel the comfort of the rise and fall of her body beside her and the gentle rhythm of the rain spitting on the courtyard outside.

How could she forget the glory of her mother's hair? It had once shone like the English penny her father gave her when he came back from the war. Only the other day, Audrey had told Attie that her beautiful hair had given her strength while Charlie was away. She had promised herself she would not cut it until he came home.

Then, a few years later during the wet season, she suddenly hacked it off with her pinking shears. Attie remembered her father's face, white with pain and shock. Suddenly, Audrey's skirts were shorter. She was soon bright and gay, sporting a neat little bob.

Only recently, Attie had seen Audrey delving in the Saratoga. Inside a rusting toffee tin with thatched cottages on the top, carefully wrapped in tissue paper, was her mother's long auburn plait. Kept intact for nearly twenty-five years.

Look, dear, she had held it out for Valerie. How remarkable it was to think the hair had not faded with time.

Attie always remembered her mother as young and vibrant. Audrey only ever wanted to remember the good things. Even now she would never allow herself to wallow in sadness.

Attie raised her father's military field binoculars and followed the aimless circles of the pelican. Up close, through the lens, she could see its long elastic bill-pouch quivering delicately above the water. It reminded her of that wobbly piece of flesh that hung from the upper part of her mother's arm.

*

The constant clicking rhythm of her knitting needles put Audrey into a kind of semi-hypnotic state of quiet and private beauty. But, for Valerie, the sound, with its monotonous regularity, was intensely irritating, worse even than a tap dripping. Headache shadows had begun to form around her eyes from the growing tension. If someone didn't speak soon and put a stop to it she was going to scream.

'It's no good moping around like that, Valerie. It won't do you any good. Why don't you do something uplifting, dear,' said Audrey. 'It might help to take your mind off things. I know what it's like to be homesick, believe me, after all those years in the tropics, but there's nothing we can do at the moment to change anything, is there?' Her voice had that soft, sing-song sound. 'Why don't you try some knitting? It's very easy, you know, and has a wonderful calming effect on the mind. I first took it up when Charlie went to war.'

Charlie this, *Charlie* that. Valerie counted to three to stop herself. She wanted to say *bravo Charlie, bravo bloody Charlie.* If only she had a pair of earphones she could block her out completely.

'I do find it's an interest,' Audrey went on. 'You could make a little cardigan for bubby. I bought some spare needles from Mr Singh. Would you like to have a go?'

'I couldn't, I'm sorry, Audrey, but it makes me feel quite ill looking down all the time. It'd only make my headache worse.'

'You should always try to look on the bright side of things,' said Audrey, 'that's what I always say.'

'So, what are you making this time, Mother?' called Attie, as she walked past.

'Just another pullover for Jasper.'

'I don't think he'll be needing pullovers up where he'll be going next,' scoffed Attie, 'or balaclavas, for that matter. You should know that, Mother. We lived in the tropics for long enough.'

'I realise that, you silly goose,' replied Audrey, unperturbed, 'but he's certainly going to need them when he eventually gets back to the farm, isn't he? Anyway, it gets rather tiresome knitting socks all the time.'

Valerie couldn't stay there another minute. All that bickering about Jasper. She put down the tea tray and stood at the kitchen window, looking out at the clear blue sky. Any minute she would cry. Pull yourself together, she said, pouring hot water out of the kettle onto the yellow soap. But, as she sloshed the cups, tears started rolling down her cheeks. If only she could be back in Lambeth at her parents' place. She closed her eyes and she could see the dairy on the corner and the way the road curved with its fancy façade of red-brick Victorian terrace-houses. *You've no idea what living in London's like at the moment, Valerie, everything's bedlam,* her mother had written. She thought of the cosy cups of tea in the front room, the family clustered around the fireside. She could smell coal dust and hear the trains rattling out from the sunken tracks. She had forgotten for a moment that half of the street had been bombed away. *It was three years now and the place was still a bloody shambles*, her father had written. But at least if she'd been home she could have caught the 202 down to Waterloo station. There'd be plenty of trains. It would be so busy nobody would notice her slip onto the lines and end it all.

Valerie's hands lay submerged beneath the suds. The water was cold. Only now did it occur to her that she still hadn't washed the cups. Outside gathering clouds had cast a shadow across the room. She looked at the clock. It was only 4.30, but she wished Audrey would come and light the lamps.

Chapter 12

Early in August, atomic bombs were dropped on Hiroshima and Nagasaki, each within two days of the other. They read of firsthand accounts from Allied aircraft carriers close to Japan, which described how the sky suddenly lit up in a magnificent sunset. More like an aurora, they reported, for there were no clouds to be seen. Now, everyone knew it was only a matter of weeks before the Japanese would surrender.

Audrey was energised, ready to celebrate.

'What about a tennis party?' she suggested, 'while the weather's fine.'

Attie felt in two minds. How could you celebrate a shocking atrocity even if it did mark the end of the war? But she finished up sweeping the court while the other two made cakes and scones for afternoon tea. On that unusually sunny Sunday afternoon, a small group of friends and neighbours gathered at the house.

Every now and then Audrey's head moved from side to side, tracking the ball as it was *pocked* backwards and forwards across the clay.

'It's good to see the young enjoying themselves,' she said, adjusting the shade of her pith helmet. Attie could hear her pattering on again about the tennis parties they'd had when Charlie was alive.

'Funny to think that that was how we originally met, back in the Old Country,' said Audrey. Charlie was the best partner in Kandy, with a stinging forehand and a serve to save your life. Goodness, what fun they'd had over the years. She wondered what he would have thought of young Valerie, were he still alive. Well, now that she knew her better, she'd grown quite fond of her really. It was hard to imagine the lass had been so sulky and nervy when she first arrived. Then again, hadn't she herself had a touch of the baby blues? It wasn't fair to judge. But never mind, Valerie had certainly brightened up over the last month or two. 'Just look at her out there squealing and leaping about in those new white shorts I made for her,' exclaimed Audrey.

Cam leant towards Attie. 'What do you reckon about those atomic bombs they've dropped?'

Attie didn't answer. The news had sickened her.

'Don't get me wrong, girl, as far as I'm concerned, the Japs have finally got their just desserts,' he said, 'but, Christ Almighty, fancy blowing a whole bloody island to smithereens.'

She shuddered. It was too horrific to imagine the civilian casualties. It made her feel sick but there was her mother beside her still blathering on and ...

'And oh, Betty, you can imagine, dear, how pleased Valerie looked, having scored young Noel Wheatley as her partner. He's the new accountant in the Bank of New South Wales.'

Attie could see the roll of her mother's brown eyes heading in her direction as Audrey leant forward and whispered in Betty's ear.

'A bit of young male company's just what my Adeline needs. Goodness knows what's going to become of her. Charlie wouldn't approve at all. Teaching in a bush school was bad enough for a young woman, but how's she ever going to meet anyone decent stuck on a farm forever? Oh well,' Audrey smiled and shrugged her shoulders, 'beggars can't be choosers. Nothing like a bit of good raw material, is there? So, Betty, what do you think of young Noel out there, eh? Perhaps he and Adeline could make a match of it. Of course, it would be rude to ask, but I can't help but wonder why he was rejected by the army.'

Attie clapped her hands over her ears as she saw Noel swish and clean miss an overhead. Perhaps he's flat-footed, she wanted to interject, or maybe, Mother, it was just that his work was considered an essential occupation.

'I don't think it's fair that some get off so lightly,' grumbled Betty.

'Come now, dear,' said Audrey. 'Someone's got to hold the fort.'

'Well, I'd keep my eyes on those two, if I were you,' Betty nodded to the tennis court.

'Dear oh dear!' scoffed Audrey. 'You're all doom and gloom, Betty. Let them have a bit of fun, dear, while they're young. You don't want them to end up old and bitter like us, do you now?'

Attie couldn't stand it any longer. She walked back to the house to get Virginia, who would be waking from her afternoon nap. When Attie entered the bedroom, the child was standing in her cot, her feet padding up and down.

'And how's my Ginnypin?' Attie's voice was light as she lifted the child out and laid her on Audrey's bed to change her nappy. Then she laughed, tickling her tummy and the child laughed back.

'Mum-mum-mumma.'

It was hard to believe her first birthday was coming up. Already, she was beginning to look like a little girl rather than a baby.

When I was one
I ate a bun
Going over the sea ...
going over going under, stand at attention like a soldier
with a one two three.

The tune came out spontaneously. Attie had taught it every year to her classrooms. It was an excellent way for children to grasp numeracy through a combination of voice, rhythm and movement. They loved it. Attie sang the song again. Virginia's bright eyes followed the various hand movements and she chuckled when Attie's three fingers sprang to her head in a final salute.

Out on the lawn, Attie sat the child on her knee and gave her a cup of milk.

'Ah, what have we here?' said Audrey, turning around with a smile.

'Goodness me, she's grown,' said Betty. 'Not sure who she's like. Can't say she takes after her mother.'

'She's not a baby any more. Can you believe she turns one in a week,' said Audrey. 'I'm making her a new smock for her birthday and you'll never guess, Betty, she'll soon be wearing her first pair of shoes. Of course, we had to send away, there's nothing much in town, you know ...'

Attie had watched the procedure in amusement a few days earlier. The piece of brown paper which Audrey had smoothed out on the table for the child to stand on, Valerie trying to hold Virginia steady, while Audrey attempted to trace around the shape of her little feet while they kept padding up and down, and the folded *foot-map* duly posted off with instructions to Charlie's old bootmaker in Perth.

'Game, set and match,' announced Noel rushing to the net. They all shook hands. 'Thank you partner, thank you umpire. Right, your turn Adeline. If you don't already know, we're playing a round robin.'

Taking her racquet, Attie walked out onto the court.

'Ladies first,' Noel bowed. 'Here, bat her up, Val, you can serve.' He smiled as he handed her the balls.

Attie flexed her knees and took a practice swing. Just a minute, what was that? Far away, she could hear the faint humming of an engine wafting in the breeze. Noel laughed loudly at something Valerie had said, so it was difficult to hear. She strained her ear while waiting patiently for Valerie's serve.

'Sorry, Val, just out,' Attie called. She could hear the same sound becoming louder. She thought of Jasper and prayed he was alright.

Cam's striped deck chair tipped over as he scrambled to his feet.

'Quick everyone, listen! There's a plane coming,' he shouted.

They all stopped and looked up, scanning the windswept sky. It was difficult to trace the sound.

'Over there,' Cam pointed his walking stick.

The plane was coming directly towards them. As it passed overhead they waved frantically.

'Careful! Are you sure it's one of ours,' warned Betty, drawing her cardigan across her shoulders. 'It gives me the heebie-jeebies every time I see one. Shouldn't we take cover?'

'Oh Betty, don't be silly,' said Audrey. 'Come now. The war's over.'

The plane continued on its way towards the state forest, then, as if changing heart, executed a large loop back towards them. With its engines revving louder, it descended rapidly, swooping towards the tennis court, so low they could see faces in the cockpit. A hand waved back at them.

'Christ Al-mighty! It's a bloody Lancaster,' roared Cam. 'What the hell's it doing over this part of the world?'

'I don't know,' said Noel, 'but crikey, that was less than two hundred feet! What do you reckon?'

'Probably heading back towards Busselton. You know, Valerie, there's a secret base there, but everybody within coo-ee knows about it. Any rate, I'm sure it was a Lancaster. Looked just like the one in the paper I saw a few weeks back.' Cam nodded. 'I cut my teeth on planes, you know, when I was a lad about your age. Got some shrapnel in me to prove it, too.'

'One thing's for certain. It's definitely one of ours.'

'What a dear!' cried Valerie, jumping up and down. 'The pilot actually waved at me! I saw his hand. Honestly I swear I did.'

'You know, I've done a bit of plane spotting since I've been in town,' said Noel, trying to regain Valerie's attention. 'They've got a lookout point down at the RSL and I'm part of a group that's rostered to do the twenty-four-hour watch,' he said puffing out his chest.

Attie lifted the baby and pointed.

'Look, Ginny,' she cried. 'Plane. See, over there. Plane.'

'Baba-baba,' gurgled the baby, waving her arms at the empty sky.

There was silence. No one felt much like tennis now. They sat around the wicker table watching the sun hiding behind the leaves. Shadows flickered across their arms. Audrey looked at the empty teacups and the butter melting over the drying scones.

'Oh dear, it's just sheer laziness,' she said. 'Either that or I'm getting old. I should get up at once and take these dishes inside.'

Suddenly, flashes of green and yellow flapped low over their heads.

'What the hell ...?' said Noel.

'Blasted pests!' Cam struggled to get to his feet. 'Where's Jasper keep his twenty-two?'

They all looked up. Parrots hung upside down in the date palm, their heads buried deep in the top of the fronds. They paused for a second, working their beaks, each with one eye on their audience in obvious amusement. Then, without any warning, they spattered the table with the debris of seed husks and took off in a screeching flurry.

*

Three days later, on August 15th, the news was announced. They were having dinner when Attie turned the wireless on.

The war is over, said the announcer. *Here I am in the thick of it, looking down on the streets of Perth. It is half past eight and you should see everyone. I am telling you that every person I see is going absolutely mad in celebration. The war is over. I say it again. The war is finally over. People are merry, kissing and dancing, and the air is filled with little pieces of paper floating down from office windows like flakes of snow.*

The national anthem was playing in the background. No one knew Valerie was musical. But her full soprano voice was quavering with emotion as she joined in to sing 'God Save the King'. Later, after their excitement had subsided, Attie went over to the gramophone. She looked through the old records in the cabinet and selected one.

'That sounds familiar,' said Audrey, as Attie wound the handle faster. 'Rather like a Beethoven symphony but I can't for the life of me think which one it is. Tell me, dear.'

'The, Fifth,' said Attie, smiling. 'You know, "The Victory Symphony."' Of course, they remembered it then.

Valerie sat staring at the fire. The recurrence of the opening motif throughout the first movement had not escaped her. That familiar pattern came back again and again in her mind. How strange, she smiled. Her radio training, which she hadn't been able to use for well over a year, had finally come into its own again. Those first few notes contained the same rhythm as the letter V in Morse code. How could she ever forget it? *V for Victor, Victory, Valerie ... Virginia. Over and out.*

Part 3

Chapter 13

From underneath the umbrella Gin could just make out the weatherboard cottages, black oily daubs half-hidden between the rocks and the peppermint trees. The three-roomed beach shacks were basic. Primitive by city standards but, as Valerie explained to her friends, 'that was what was so nice, no housework'. Ablutions were confined to a cold-water shower outside to douse off the morning swim and nearby communal lavatories camouflaged by purple bougainvillea and the lingering smell of phenol. The cottage furniture was sparse. A kero fridge and a table with an assortment of chairs, rusty iron beds covered in lumpy mattresses, which were mapped with wee-stains and had tufts of horsehair poking out of the ticking. This year there was no safe-cot. Dorothy insisted on sleeping out on the flywired veranda in a proper bed like her sister.

Each night, long after the hiss of lamps had been extinguished by Noel, Gin lay awake in the dark listening to the soothing sounds of the beach. Leaves from an overhanging branch of a peppermint tree swished softly against the tin roof above, and the constant sigh of the ocean and its waves slapping on the nearby shore soon lulled her off to sleep. But often she woke in the small hours of the morning to feel Dorothy's hand patting her face in the dark, and, within seconds, the cold sharp contact of tiny feet as the child slipped noiselessly in beside her.

It was funny how Dorothy always seemed to get her own way. It wasn't just Valerie and Noel. Everyone spoilt her. But how could Gin possibly be jealous of her? There she was playing on the shore where the water lapped the sand. Her cropped hair was white, matted with salt and sun and sticking up like soft peaks of mashed potato. Shirred seersucker bubbled around the contours of her body. She toddled backwards and forwards, backwards and forwards to scoop the water, her short podgy legs padding purposefully through the sand.

Gin shunted herself out from under the umbrella to expose her wet bathers to the sun. She frowned, rubbing the goose-pimples on her arms. It was late morning. The breeze was barely a whisper. Further out, though, was the beginning of a swell and, already, the sun's sting was drying her cheeks. She reached under the umbrella for Granny's old pith helmet, which lay half-covered by the towels. What had induced her to bring this ridiculous relic from the past, Valerie had wanted to know? Hadn't she a perfectly good tennis hat that she never wore? Noel had scoffed. It looked hideously old-fashioned, weighty, its colonial khaki masculine against the pink of her new bathers. She shook the sand and inspected the leather strapping and ventilation eyelets. The brim and domed crown were compact, but the hat felt surprisingly light on her head, and its shadow substantial, uncompromising, as her eyes scanned across the water.

The bay was protected. It faced north and was one of the few beaches, according to Noel, where you could look out to sea all day without being blinded by the sun. It wasn't just the light, Gin realised. Everything was more subtle, and here her thoughts tended to drift naturally into dreams. Far preferable to Cottesloe with too many waves, and the crowds milling around the shade houses and the spiny Norfolk pines. There was so much happening and it was always so overwhelmingly intrusive that Gin found it difficult to think, let alone imagine anything beyond the blur of Rottnest. Africa, for instance, seemed remote, something green and brown on the page of her school atlas. Even if she closed her eyes and tried to conjure up one of the vibrant images from Noel's *National Geographic* magazines, all she saw was a flood of colour on the inside of her eyelids. Down here in the bay, it was like being in another world. Quiet, a handful of families, the odd passing boat and only the gentlest of waves. Gin looked out at the narrow span of the horizon. A white wisp of a line delineated the reef. Today, it made her think of the equator. For some reason, she could readily summon up notions of Asia, of Ceylonese highlands where her father was born. Perhaps it was Granny's hat that made her imagine the tropical paradise. Perhaps she would go there one day.

The sun burnt into her arms. It didn't take long at this time of the day. Dorothy would be getting burnt too, thought Gin, flicking the sand from her beach coat. Beyond the break, the clinker boat rocked sleepily in a clear streak of turquoise. Noel and Frank Puddy were out fishing for herring and sand whiting. They would be coming in soon. Dorothy would be there to meet them, desperate to see the catch. Her sturdy thighs splayed, straining in the sand as she tried to help them heave the boat up onto the dry sand.

Gin felt detached from the brown-bodied children flipping and sliding through the water. There was no one her own age. Any day now the Leaving results would be published, and as soon as Valerie came out of the water and took care of Dorothy, Gin planned to walk up to the shop and see if the papers had arrived. Her heart quickened a little. She would soon be free, an adult, and there was nothing her mother could do about it.

Sliding her bather straps off her shoulders, she examined the light tan mark that cut across the white fullness of her breasts. She hitched at the bright pink cups without success. If only she was built like Denise Whitely, who could prance around in a skimpy bikini all day long with no self-consciousness at all.

Nearby, all the mothers were floating on their backs, toes nodding up and down in the water like heads in conversation. Gin strained to catch a glimpse of Valerie, her eyes following the ring of coloured bathing caps bobbing in unison through the ripples. Why was her mother taking so long? Had she forgotten?

'Look Ginny, fishy!' cried Dorothy, holding out her bucket.

'Let's see.'

Dorothy plumped herself down beside her and Gin caught the faint milky smell which the child's skin always breathed. Beneath the slopping water, a single shell lay settled at the bottom.

'Hmm. Pre-tty!' Gin smiled, inspecting the detail of her young face. Dottie's eyes were green and elusive like the sea. Already they had drifted and turned.

'I wanna swim.' The child tugged at her bonnet, exposing her face to the bright light. Tiny freckles shone like specks of seaweed against the white skin of her cheeks and runny nose. Apart from the fair complexion, there was nothing in her half-sister's features that Gin could remotely relate to. Even behind the broderie anglaise bonnet, the child still looked like Noel.

Dorothy reached up spontaneously to hug her. 'P-ease, Ginny. P-ease!' Her plump little body was dry with salt and grit and its grainy feel put her teeth on edge.

'No, don't!' Gin flung out her fingers. 'You're covered in sand, Dottie.' She stood up and brushed herself down. 'Oh, alright, then,' she relented. 'Let's go and find mummy,' she said, leading the child down to the water.

A small wave rolled steadily towards them. The circle disintegrated as the lip broke over the women's heads. Bright coloured caps and black costumes lurched forward towards the shore. Valerie emerged in the wash. Ankle-deep in the shallows, she stood, reaching out her pale arms towards Dorothy.

'Come, my darling,' she cried. 'Come and show mummy how you can swim.'

*

From the dusty lane, Gin could see the men squatting on the lawn. They were gutting and scaling fish over spread-out sheets of newspaper. Dorothy stood beside them in a gingham sun-frock pointing at the ground. The fresh bread was still warm in wrapping paper under Gin's arm as she stepped into the cottage, today's newspaper neatly folded in with the rest of the shopping she'd bought from the general store.

'Is that you, Virginia?' called Valerie from the bedroom. 'Could you rustle up some lunch, please? I'm just putting my hair in rollers.'

Gin set out the usual: thick slices of brown bread, ham, polony, cheese, shredded lettuce, and a tomato sandwich with a sprinkle of sugar for Dorothy. Only when they were all together at the table did she announce her results. Noel and Valerie both congratulated her. Then Noel went off to the bedroom and came back with a small red and gold box which he presented to her. Inside was a new Seiko watch he'd asked a fellow from work to bring back duty-free from Singapore for him.

Throughout the afternoon, Gin stretched the links over her wrist, examining the golden face again and again. It was small and sophisticated with modern notches instead of numerals. It placed a different emphasis on time, blending minutes into hours. The grey blanket prickled against her thigh as she lay on her bed pretending to read. It was nearly five o'clock. Any moment Noel would turn on the transistor radio to listen to the news. His voice drifted upwards through the louvered windows.

'Bloody Russians! Heck Frank, this Cuban fiasco could still escalate into a full-blown nuclear war.'

That night Frank and his wife Norma came over from their cottage next door. They ended up playing cards and drinking bottles of Frank's homemade beer.

'Do you think young Virginia deserves a drop?' Frank asked, leaning over towards Valerie, as if asking her permission. 'A kid doesn't matriculate every day of the year. Sounds like cause for celebration. Here you are lass ... congratulations!'

Moths flirted with the lamp light; everyone deep in concentration. Over its hiss came the periodic sound of Noel crunching salted peanuts. Gin lifted her eyes. From behind her open book, she could see Frank Puddy's hand on her mother's knee. Valerie looked up and slapped her leg.

'Mozzies are bad tonight, aren't they?' she laughed nervously.

'Must be your delicate English skin,' said Noel, biting into another pickled onion. 'I can't feel them at all.'

'No, they don't go for crusty old fishermen,' Frank smirked. 'They only like sweet-smelling flesh. Come on Norma, your turn.'

'Can we hold it there everyone?' Norma placed down her cards. 'I just want to pop over and check the little ones are asleep. I thought I heard something ...'

'Virginia.' Noel's shadow had fallen across her page. 'Do us a favour, would you lass? Go over next door and check on the little Puddies.'

Gin sighed. She put down her book and walked out to the veranda; Noel still chuckling at his wit as she fell into the dark. The moon was barely visible, a thin pearly piece of shell edging itself behind the peppermint tree. Within seconds she heard the crackle of twigs behind her.

'Want a hand to show you the way?'

'N-no, I'm alright, thanks, Mr Puddy,' her voice could only squeak.

'OK,' he called, 'suit yourself.'

*

Gin woke early. Noel, as usual, was out in the kitchen getting ready to go out fishing. She could hear him rustling around for biscuits and pumping the primus to make a thermos of tea to take out in the boat. Here, in the half-light beside her, Dorothy's body huddled small and still beneath the grey blankets on the bed. Good. While Dottie was still asleep, she'd take the opportunity for an early morning walk. Usually, at home, she didn't get to see the sun until after she'd done her practice. Gin shivered as the fresh salty air wafted under the canvas blind. Quickly she slipped out of her shortie pyjamas into shorts and a windcheater. From the cluster of peppermint trees outside, she watched the men pushing the clinker boat from the top of the beach down into the wide stretch of wet sand that marked the early morning tide. She heard a sputter and then the steady *putt-putt* of the motor.

By the time she arrived on the beach, the boat was already nosing its way through the lacy break. She stood on the beach smelling the last of the engine fumes. It was easy to guess who was who by their outlines: Noel at the helm, with Frank Puddy standing in the middle steadying himself with his arms. Yet it was impossible to tell where the silvery-grey ocean finished and where the sky began. In the pale light, the merging shape of the men and their boat looked like some ghostly beast making its way off into the land of the never-never.

Now to the east, over the silhouetted promontory of rocks, the sky was tinged coral-pink. An unusual cloud formation hung light and crimpy, like pieces of finely shredded lambswool. She was spellbound by the gradual transformation. Sunrays, finer than pins and needles, suddenly broke through rifts creating a silvery edge to the blushing clouds. *Arushi.* Strange how the word popped into her mind. Literally it meant 'red sky' in Hindu, according to Attie. What better name to call her red cloud kelpie-cross! Until now Gin had forgotten completely about her aunt's Christmas letter mentioning that the dog had died after picking up a bait. It was hard to believe it was nearly six years since she'd last stayed at the farm, two weeks of wet May school holidays during which Valerie and Noel had bunkered down in Cave's House for their honeymoon. Unloved, excluded, disposed of, that's how she'd felt. But the dog had been a source of comfort as soon as she'd arrived, had greeted her with such love and exuberance no human being had ever shown. From then on, every time the flywire door banged, Arushi would come trotting onto the veranda and roll over on her foot, golden eyes begging for a belly-rub. *Arushi!* She said it again out loud, as if calling her to come. It was a lovely name, soft, like the expression on her doggy face.

Gin walked on towards the promontory. In the new light, she could see the outline of her footprints, crisp and fresh in the salmon-coloured sand. As each step broke the crusted grains, she felt the ping of coming independence. What was that story Attie had told her? About Jasper and her climbing the highest mountain in Ceylon with Grandpa on their thirteenth birthdays to see the sunrise, their total exhilaration. Gin tried to imagine her father and Attie as teenage twins. At her age, they'd suddenly been uprooted from their island world. Everyone was affected by the Great Depression, Attie had explained. Almost overnight, Jasper had had to become a man; for six years, the hard relentless slog of twelve-hour days pursuing a farming dream in the Australian bush. And then, the heartbreak to come of him going off to fight another country's war and never coming home. The huddle of photos on Attie's mantelpiece came to mind. The double portrait of her father and Attie, and the last one taken of him in full air force uniform stood out. But even they were vague. No matter how hard she tried, she could gather nothing more substantial. Images of her father were always contained in one-dimensional shapes, missing fragments in a puzzle.

His plane was shot down but they never found his body.

But Mummy, maybe he's still alive?

It's been too long now, Virginia. He died a hero, always remember that.

It sounded important, her father being a hero, but it didn't mean a lot. Just words. Only recently, she'd become aware of the terrible sadness of it all, the sadness she'd once taken for granted as a child. What a tragedy, a young man in the prime of life suddenly vanishing in the sky—such a waste of thirty years of life. She wondered what sort of relationship she and her father might have had; how different her life would be now. Instead of that, she'd been brought up isolated in a world of women until things had suddenly changed and she'd had to contend with Noel. What a shock, confronting for the first time that strange intrusion of masculine presence at nearly thirteen years of age. She remembered only too clearly waking up the morning after Noel and Valerie had got back from their honeymoon and feeling too self-conscious to go the lavatory. She had held on until she was bursting—so many silly considerations. Were they awake or weren't they awake? And what if Noel heard her tinkling through the walls? As she'd tip-toed down the hallway there was that awful feeling lurking inside her, the trepidation that any second she would stumble in on something she shouldn't. A flicker of bottle-green robe had suddenly caught her eye through the open bathroom door. Noel was already there, bare feet planted on the tessellated tiles. One glimpse of those knotty purple-veined calves bulging beneath the hem of his gown had instantly revolted her. In those few split seconds she'd caught him frozen in the most repulsive pose: bum out, chin jutting forward and mouth drawn in a downward U. He seemed to pause, white-soaped face immobile and razor poised in hand—then, as she'd fled past the doorway, she detected the roll of his eyes following her and her own cowering expression in the mirror.

'Sorry,' she whispered.

'Damn! Damn, damn and damn!'

'What's wrong, my darling?' called Valerie from the kitchen.

'I bloody nicked myself, that's what!'

'Dear oh dear!'

'Bloody distractions!' Muttering, he flung out his foot to shut the door.

The bathroom was stifling when she'd eventually got there. Overcome by the smell of Old Spice and the warm steamy air, she'd heaved frantically at the bunged-up sash window. Overnight, the house had been invaded. Laid out neatly on the washstand were things she'd never encountered before: shaving brush, razor-knife and porcelain jug, and a tortoise-shell comb glistening with oil. Suddenly Valerie was standing at the door. She pounced.

'What on earth have you been doing in there all that time?' Snatching the leather strop from Gin's hand, she glared at her. 'Don't you dare touch things that don't belong to you,' she snapped, replacing it on the hook behind the door.

Noel's presence soon left a mark throughout the house. Even when he was at work or playing golf she could never quite escape him. Stale pipe-smoke always lingered in the air. The woolly reek of his hound's-tooth jacket still made her gag, as did the sight of sweat stains drying in his hat. Worst of all was the aniseed (Fisherman's Friends or whatever it was) she could smell when he came too close. But she never said anything. Just held her breath until he passed.

The knock-knock of his pipe on the back of his shoe was probably an attempt to break the silence. Furrows of concentration ploughed his forehead every time he performed this ritual. Gin had unconsciously made a study of it, finding a weird pleasure in anticipating exactly what he'd do next. She remembered him hunting around the garden for a stray cutting to scratch the inside of the pipe bowl, then emptying the ashes into the hydrangeas at the edge of the veranda. With mouth pursed, he'd taken a pinch of fresh tobacco from the leather pouch in his pocket and methodically packed it down in the bowl with his thumb. Then, with the pipe in his mouth and his left eyebrow raised in anticipation, he'd struck match after match, floating each one above the surface of the pipe while his cheeks popped in and out with each little suck. And when the pipe was finally alight, he'd leant back and narrowed his eyes.

'Well, then ...' he'd paused, pipe clenched in his teeth. 'About time you called me dad, hey?' he said through the corner of his mouth.

Her eyes smarted as a curl of smoke wafted up between them. The smell sickened her so she turned and walked away.

'What's wrong?' he called out. 'Hey? Cat got your tongue?'

*

Gin dallied in the warm shallows, watching eddies flush the rocks. Tongues of kelp licked the barnacles. Tiny fish nipped past and crabs scuttled away to hide. She looked down and wiggled her toes in the moving sand. Her bare legs were wet now and brown against her striped Bermuda shorts. Ah! No more school uniforms. Yippee! It'd be university in another month, she wanted to cry out and tell the world. Concert pianist, here I come! Quickening her pace, she headed back along the beach. The sea was still retreating, continuing to dump its debris on the shore. The wet sand glistened and mirrored in the early morning sun. Her recent footprints, embedded between the dank rows of weed, were rapidly fading as they became swallowed up into the shore.

*

The fish were not biting that day so the men were back by nine. From the shallows, Gin watched Noel draw a crease in front of the wicket with his foot. He looked gangly, like an over-aged schoolboy in his peaked cap and khaki shorts. Grinning at the bowler, he patted the wet sand with the bat.

'Hey! Virginia!' he called. 'Give us a hand, lass. We're a bit light on for fielders.'

Gin sank beneath a wave. It was so embarrassing, the thought of running in her bathers. Underwater she was deaf, out of sight, could luxuriate in her other senses. A blur of sand was churning around her feet but within seconds she could see clearly to the bottom. Schools of coloured fish darted through the shadows, which rippled across the sandy undulations, then disappeared into twirling strands of weed. She bounced off the bottom, reaching upwards to penetrate the crystal surface. Blinking away the sting of salt, she spotted Frank Puddy crouched in the nearby shallows ready to take a catch. Such a show-off. Flexed back and buttocks-outline bulging against his banlon bathers. What a creep. And that awful habit he had of winking at her when he thought no one was watching.

The *thwack* of bat on ball raised a full-blooded cheer from the shore. Frank lunged at the nearby plop. Instantly his shiny pate was steaming through the water; on either side, short overarm strokes slicing towards the tennis ball. Sodden and bald, it continued bobbing aimlessly up and down. Gin resisted an urge to retrieve the ball. Instead, she remained where she was, treading water, as the current dragged it away. Was she being passive or perverse, she wondered, not wanting to join in with the others? Part of her wouldn't let herself have a go. It was the same with swimming. She was naturally athletic but she'd never been able to trust her body entirely to the water. She wondered what it would be like to feel that sense of suspension, of being carried away by a greater force.

Not far away, she could see her mother, bobbles of black costume and white bathing cap floating in the water. Gin put her head back and closed her eyes against the glare. Whirling her hands harder through the water, she immediately felt her own resistance. No matter how hard she kicked, her legs managed to sink towards the bottom. Hair swirled over her face. She would have to wash it again. Such a fag putting it in rollers, such a stupid waste of time. Suddenly, from nowhere, something grabbed her legs. She kicked and thrashed, gasping slurps, snorting on the burning flush of salty water.

'Sh-shar-ark!' she spluttered at last. Hysteria relaxed into relief as a bald head burst out of a belch of bubbles. Up popped Frank Puddy beside her, sleek and dripping.

'Gotcha!' He flicked his excess spray on her. She flinched, but his hands had hold of her. Already they were sliding over her hips and squeezing into the small of her waist. Behind, the first lip of a set was approaching.

'Just a friendly old seahorse.' He smiled his slick smile. 'Quick, have a ride!' Before she could escape, he had hoisted her onto his leg, his body straining to keep afloat. He was making a jigging noise, like a horse trotting, his hands grappling at her, slime-ball eyes perving on her floating breasts .... Slap! The wave smacked her face, knocking her backwards. She pushed down, down, digging deeper, and when her feet found the sand she twisted hard and away from him into the oncoming wave.

Chapter 14

Suddenly the bay had lost its charm. Gin couldn't get back to Perth quick enough. But once she had, the Christmas holidays seemed to drag on. When she wasn't at the piano, she found herself encumbered with a list of chores which Valerie had conveniently delegated: window-cleaning, ironing Dorothy's clothes, polishing the floorboards, all to be completed in record temperatures. By the end of the first week, it was almost a relief to get out of the house, and, when Valerie asked her to babysit Dorothy on her bridge afternoon, Gin obliged without question.

Dottie didn't like being restricted in any way. Even before they left home she had taken off her straw hat and was sitting in the pusher playing with it instead.

'I'm going to eat these,' she said, picking at the decorative red cherries on the crown.

'You can't do that, you silly little nong,' Gin laughed. 'They're only plastic.'

'Dorothy, put your hat back on this instant,' scolded Valerie, coming into the room. She snatched it out of Dorothy's hands and pushed it down so forcibly on the child's head, Gin thought the straw was going to break.

'Lacky's hurting,' she pouted, tugging at it under her chin.

'You'll know all about hurting if you get burnt, young lady. You can't afford to go out without a hat, not in this heat, not with an English complexion. That poor little nose of yours has peeled once already this year.' Valerie frowned and waggled her finger. 'Now keep it on, do you hear me? Virginia, you're in charge. Make sure she does.'

Down at the river there was a children's playground with see-saws, swings and a set of monkey bars. It was a long walk there and back but Gin didn't mind. She cut through the tennis courts. She could see a number of middle-aged women waving their racquets as they lunged around the grass. A bit of hit and giggle is probably what they'd call it. The mandatory tennis lessons every Saturday morning had hardly been a laughing matter. Gin hated them. But Valerie was adamant. It was the social element that was important, Noel had stressed. What a drag it had been until last year when she'd finally been allowed to give them up.

The first thing Gin did when they arrived at the park was to let Dottie run around in bare feet. She could remember experiencing the same freedom when Valerie wasn't looking, the joy of feeling like any other Australian child. It was hard to fathom why her mother always insisted upon socks with sandals all through the heat of the summer. Another one of her silly English customs that looked ridiculous and didn't make any sense.

They stayed in the park all afternoon. Dottie played. Gin lay on the grass, feeling the cool breeze lifting up from the river and caressing the back of her neck. Ducks waddled in and out of the lantana. Dottie plodded after them in pursuit. Squawking seagulls stalked around her, beaks open trying to snatch the little pieces of fairy bread she threw to the water's edge. Gin half-read a book during that time, one eye on Dottie and the other reading the same page over and over again. She couldn't concentrate. She worried about the water, worried that Dorothy might drown or end up getting sunburnt. Then again, she was restless. Excited. Just biding her time until uni started. It was only two weeks to go and she couldn't wait. Right now she was itching to get back and do some practice. She stretched out her arms, peering at her new watch yet again. She'd mis-read the time. Heck, it was later than she thought. They'd better be heading home.

By late afternoon it was hotter inside than out, and humid. The house was old with high ceilings; cold and draughty through the winter, but in summertime the heat always drifted upwards and stayed there for days unable to escape. Only the sitting room would be cool. Valerie, of course, would have the fan going just far enough away from the cards so it didn't disturb her game of bridge.

Gin slipped inside through the back way as she always did, past the pink and blue hydrangeas wilting at the side of the house. The flywire door closed behind her with a sigh. She parked the pusher in the sleep-out where it was quiet, hoping the sea breeze would come and filter through the louvers. Dottie was still sitting in it fast asleep. Her face was damp and flushed, straw hat squashed against her cheek. Dribble trickled from her skewed mouth. She was frowning, probably because the hat elastic cut the plumpness around her chin.

Gin was about to take off the hat, when she heard the sudden *tick-tick-ticking* of Valerie's high heels down the hallway. Precise, like a metronome. Through the open kitchen doorway she watched her mother refill the soda siphon with cold water from the fridge, screw in a new bomb and release the gas with a *pffft*.

Valerie lit up a new cigarette. Hollows formed in her cheeks as she drew on the filter slowly and deliberately, and then tossed the silver lighter and packet of Benson and Hedges onto the kitchen table before leaving the room.

How long was this going on for, Gin asked herself? Bridge would have finished well over an hour ago. But from the sound of it they were still going, or, rather, had progressed, as her mother would say. Just having a quick one. One for the road. Glasses clinked. Voices suddenly lowered. Whispers. An explosion of laughter rippled down the hallway and then ...

'Dear, oh, dear, oh, dear ... you are a scream, Valerie,' giggled Norma Puddy.

By now Gin had had enough. She knew that any minute Dottie would wake up and need de-grumping.

'Hello Mrs Puddy, hello everyone,' she said, poking her head around the sitting-room door. 'Sorry to interrupt, mum. It's just that I ...'

'And how's my little baby?' enquired Valerie.

'Little baby?' Someone giggled. 'That's a bit rough, Valerie. She's taller than you now.'

'Well for once Dottie's actually been good,' Gin smiled politely. 'We've been down at the river for most of the afternoon.'

'What's the little pet up to now?'

'She's asleep. Drifted off in the pusher on the way back ... but she'll be hungry soon, mum, and you see I need to do my ...'

'Practice? Plenty of time, plenty of time. It's not as if you're going to be a ...' Her mother's voice trailed as she smiled around the room. 'Really Virginia, practice can wait. You know it's my night off.'

'Come in, dear,' piped up Betty Bentley. 'Let her play something for us, Valerie. I simply adore classical music.'

Gin wanted to leave there and then. But instead she went in and sat down at the piano as she'd been asked, trying to think of what to play. Her hands hovered for a moment over the keys. Suddenly she found herself launching into a Bach prelude, the Fifth, although she wasn't sure why.

'For God's sake, Virginia, can't you play something more suitable? Something lighter.' Valerie's voice was raised in irritation. 'You can only blame yourself, Betty,' she whispered.

Without pausing at the cadence, Gin broke straight into the fugue, cutting off a solitary clap from somewhere in the room. The piece was heavy and pompous, something she knew they wouldn't like. But for some reason she couldn't help herself. Its intensity suited her mood. She was sick of being treated like a nanny and a nobody. She didn't care, even if it was her way of trying to assert herself and make a point.

Low chatter and titters persisted, rising in competition. Gin wasn't concentrating. She slammed her foot on the damper to hear what they were saying. She found herself playing softly, more softly still, until she stopped halfway through the fugue. Paused. Looked around. Stood up and walked out unnoticed, unacknowledged, into the hall. She was seething but what else could she have done?

She sniffed. A nasty smell hung in the air. Something like ... what was it ... like burnt potato? As she started for the kitchen Dottie let out one piercing scream, then immediately fell silent.

'It's OK, Dottie. I'm coming! I'm coming!'

The child was ablaze when she found her, dancing up and

down on the spot. Flames licking higher and higher to the sizzle of shirring elastic and the crackle of straw, little arms waving wildly about, her mouth wide open grimacing in pain, wheezing, and the whites of her eyes rolling back, back, back into their sockets.

How long did it all take? It is difficult to say. But somewhere in those interminable seconds or minutes, Gin found the presence of mind to grab a tea-towel, and she kept blanketing every part of that little body until there were no more flames left to smother. Desperately, desperately, she tried crying out to her mother, but the smoke and the tightness in her throat strangulated her sounds and paralysed her tongue.

'Dottie?' she whispered eventually. 'Dottie? Say something, Dottie!' Gin felt at once the agony of burn against burn, body heat searing into her own red-raw hands and the awful limpness they embraced, but she was too frightened to take a look, too frightened to do anything except stay put, cradling the child's head with its white hair sticking up, charred and frizzled, and smelling of …

'What on earth's going on out there, Virginia?' Valerie's highly-strung voice rose from the sitting room. 'What are you doing to her now, for heaven's sake?'

It was then Gin spotted Valerie's lighter lying open at her feet. Suddenly a clump of hair fell away; black flakes floated to the floor. Gin looked down and thought she was going to vomit.

What broke the eerie silence was the sound of Valerie's shoes *tick-tick-ticking* down the hallway.

'My God!' she screamed. 'Oh my God! Norma! Norma! Quick! Don't just stand there. Call an ambulance! Quick!'

Chapter 15

Far away she could hear a boat. Was it a boat ... or was it something else? A sort of humming pulsation that came in waves, then the sound of water tinkling in a bowl. Perhaps it was a dream. Wake up, she told herself. But she knew she was awake by the smell, a nauseating jumble of boiled carrots, surgical spirits and carbolic soap and ... suddenly she retched.

'Quick, kidney bowl,' called an urgent voice.

Someone wiped her mouth, then held a glass of water to her lips. She tried to open her eyes but they felt thick and slabby, everything a blur of white. Gradually, she began to make out the sheets and pillows supporting her arms and the swaddle of her dressings. Her head swam in a sudden surge of pain, hands throbbing, bursting. Even the slightest movement was excruciating.

She followed a shadow moving by her side.

'Where am I?'

'You're in hospital, love,' said the nurse.

'Where's my mother? I want my mother!' she moaned.

'Just relax, sweetie. Close your eyes and relax. I'm just going to give you a quick jab to make you feel better. Your mum can't come right now.'

Later, through the whiteness, Gin saw something black moving on her hand. Calmly, her eyes tracked the object over the sheet and up the wall.

'What's that black thing crawling across the ceiling?'

'What thing?'

'That cockroach,' she nodded upwards.

'There's nothing there, love.'

'I can see it. Honestly. I know I can.'

'Don't worry. You're spooked out. It's just the pethidine.'

When Gin looked again the cockroach had vanished. She wiggled the pink tips of her fingers poking out from the bandages. Suddenly the cockroach returned. She wanted to point and say *look, there it is!* But it hurt too much to lift her hand. Gradually her focus began to fade and everything blanched back into the white surroundings. For a while she slept. Then the bedrail rattled beside her and she heard the swish of a starched uniform as the nurse reached up to adjust her intravenous drip.

*

Gin ran her eyes over the dressings. She had no idea why she was in hospital having to endure such pain. Every now and then, she would try to move her fingers on the supporting pillows but the pain was unbearable, her confusion overwhelming.

'It's the shock,' the doctor told her. 'Expect everything will be a bit fuzzy for a while. Don't worry. It'll come back to you. All in good time.'

When Gin asked the nurse what had happened to her she was evasive.

'Not privy to the details but you had an accident. There was a fire and you were burnt. Don't you remember, luvvie?'

*

Neither Valerie nor Noel came to see Gin in the first few days. Attie arrived instead and returned to see her several days in a row. She presented her with bunches of home-grown muscats and a box of expensive nougat, each rectangle individually wrapped in rice paper.

'Poor old Pom-pom. Promise not to touch you anywhere it hurts,' she said, kissing her on the forehead. 'I know you're in a lot of pain.' Gin welcomed the warmth of her aunt's brown eyes, the familiar pick-me-up of her voice. 'Not much consolation, I know, but I've brought you some special goodies. Here,' Attie bent down, 'these are the first of Dieter's table grapes, from new vines he's struck.' One by one she popped the grapes into Gin's mouth so she had no need to talk. Occasionally, she stroked her brow as she talked about the farm. 'I'm looking after a blind calf at the moment,' she whispered, her eyes softening again. 'Has to be hand-fed. Little devil has won me over. Doing well, all considered; well enough that I've left Dieter in charge. Good man, very capable. You know how suspicious I was when he first came. Don't know what I'd do without him now.' She paused and went on looking around the room. 'Things turn around, as they say. Apple-picking time again soon. Not much of a crop to speak of this year, thanks to the codling moth. Well then, I'll pop back as soon as I can. Meantime, Ginny, pecker up! You'll have to come down for a little holiday … when you're well enough, of course,' she added, 'and help me feed the calf.'

Gin was hardly listening now.

'Why haven't Mum and Noel been to see me?' Her eyes were closed when she interrupted. 'What's happened?'

'Goodness me, don't you know?'

'No. No one's told me. They just ... expect me to know.'

'Can you remember anything at all?'

'Absolutely nothing.'

Attie took a deep breath. 'Well, no one knows quite how it happened, but there was a dreadful accident. A fire in the kitchen. Dottie was burnt too, she's in the Children's Hospital only ...' Attie paused, looking down at the floor.

'Is she going to be alright? Attie, tell me quickly, is Dottie going to be alright?'

Attie paused again. Tears welled up in her eyes as she bent down and kissed Gin's forehead.

'Forgive me, Gin darling. I can't hide it from you. Poor little mite has third degree burns and now the wounds have become infected. I'm afraid she ... she's so critically ill, your mother and Noel are not able to leave her bedside.'

*

Gin woke to hear the plaintive tones of Toni Fisher singing 'West of the Wall'. She tried to pick out some imaginary notes of the song with just the tips of her fingers but every move was still excruciating.

'That's the shot, good girl.' Bent over the bed railings, with his face about a foot away from hers at eye level, was the registrar.

'You'll be out before you know it!' He was sitting looking at her notes. There was gloss on his voice, the spots on his bow-tie bobbing about brightly like a bunch of miniature balloons. 'I hear you play the piano, eh? Well, keep the fingers moving then.'

Gin braced herself for a couple of little wiggles.

'Bravo!' he said, issuing a round of hearty claps. 'We'll have you back home playing your favourite concerto in no time.'

*

Gin could tell it was Valerie by the sound of her heels along the corridor. But when her mother flicked into view she almost didn't recognise her. She looked skinny and drawn. What shocked Gin most was the colour of her hair. It was shot with white.

Valerie didn't even bend down and give her a kiss. Instead, she stood beside the metal locker, thin-lipped and staring at the wall.

'Well, aren't you even going to ask about Dorothy?'

In the flash that followed, Gin could see the whites of Dorothy's eyes rolling back against the red flames. Oh God!

Valerie had her hand on her hip, tapping her foot on the floor. This time she was even more reproachful.

'I thought I left you looking after her.'

'I'm sorry ... I'm terribly sorry Mum ... but she must have ... she must have ...' Gin was trying to remember, step by step. She'd finished playing the piano, gone out into the hallway, and the next thing ...

'Must have what?' Valerie raised her eyebrows.

Gin screwed up her eyes and buried her head sideways in the pillows. Trying to think made her dizzy. Any second, she felt, she was going to pass out.

But in the resulting blur, the pain seemed to ease a little. After a while, a light scratching sound started up. Through one half-opened eye, Gin could see Valerie's head tilting from side to side. Her mother was filing her nails with an emery board, systematically pushing back each cuticle in turn. The sound of her voice kept haunting her as she drifted in and out of sleep.

I used to only buff them but Noel says a bit of colour makes them stylish.

Gin awoke to hear a sniff. Valerie was trying to paint her nails but her hands had a mind of their own and wouldn't stop trembling. Gin's eyes flickered. A fusion of things slid before her: drops of red lacquer spilt into the glass full of raspberry cordial on her bedside locker, into the network of blood vessels flooding inside her eyelids, flooding inside her brain.

Memories shimmied from the past. Floribundas frilled against a window frame. She was a small child again watching Mummy out in the rose garden cutting off blooms. Mummy's sudden pulling away, having caught herself against a thorn. Red flecks on white skin, Mummy raising her bare arm to her lips. Her frown. In that flash of an image, her mother had looked quite plain and ordinary for once, in old golf shoes and corduroy slacks, sleeves pulled up, sucking her own blood.

Like most little girls, Gin had wondered what it felt like to be all dolled up like a grown-up lady. Once, having taken her mother's brown fur stole from the wardrobe, she had stood luxuriating in it in front of the mirror, and had caught the twinkle of rings spread out on the dressing table—for Valerie never gardened in her rings—together with her watch. Even now, through the pain, Gin could picture that watch. Granny had left it to Valerie to pass on to her when she was twenty-one. But her mother never seemed to wear it these days. Too old-fashioned, with its Roman numerals hand-painted and bedecked with tiny jewels.

'No point in going back to sleep, Virginia. Noel will be here any minute now and I expect there're things he'll want to ask you.'

'Bad news, I'm afraid, lass.'

Noel's face was stiff and hoary, little boat-like shadows moored beneath his watery-coloured eyes. He unfolded a handkerchief and wiped them, then blew his nose. When Noel told her that Dorothy had died, Gin wanted to curl up and disappear. She sobbed uncontrollably. How could her little sister have died? She was too tiny, too young. Only old people died. For three days, Gin cried non-stop. It wasn't just the continual gorging lump in her throat, her whole body ached so much that at one stage she thought that she herself was going to die.

That night she fell asleep exhausted only to be awoken by a dream leaving a strange image imprinted on her mind. Within seconds, the black-lined grey square had transformed into a misty window-pane positioned before her. She was looking outwards but there was nothing. Only a wash of grey; the constant drizzle of rain, drips melting the frosted pane outside.

'Wake up, we're going to wash your hair.' A nurse was running the shower.

Gin sat helplessly on a commode, her bandaged hands outstretched, bagged and bound in plastic, as sudsy water ran down her face and splashed against the white tiles. The image briefly returned again.

'Harder,' she said, hoping the nurse's working fingers would stimulate her brain into sustaining the image. But just as quickly it disintegrated and, feeling the misery of its loss, she instantly began to cry silent inward sobs. The sudden taste of salt came as comfort as her flush of tears merged into the clearing water.

As the days passed, her mind was less confused. Gin began to ask herself whether it really was her fault as Valerie had suggested. Gin had loved that child unquestionably, had always taken the utmost care of her. She remembered the fuss when Dottie was born and the notice which she'd carefully cut out of *The West Australian* to put in her scrap book. *Valerie and Noel are proud to announce the arrival of Dorothy Jane ... A little sister for Virginia.* She'd been so excited, couldn't believe she had a sister ... even a half-sister. All the girls at school were jealous. Dorothy Jane Wheatley, she had boasted, although she hardly ever got to hold her.

No Virginia, she's too tiny.

She's sleeping, Virginia, don't touch her.

Wash your hands, Virginia.

Be careful, Virginia, don't drop her.

Don't tease her, Virginia.

Are you happy now, Virginia, happy that you've just made your little sister cry?

Go to your room, Virginia, and don't come out until I tell you.

Don't you dare answer back, Virginia.

The quicker you get back to school, my girl, the better.

*

Noel did his best to hide his grief, as he tried to shoulder Valerie's. When Gin told him that she wanted to go to Dottie's funeral he said, 'I don't think you're up to it, lass, not in a fit state, and, anyway, it's hardly appropriate when your own mother isn't even going. You see, women don't usually go to funerals.'

How could Gin believe Dorothy was gone forever when here she was incarcerated in this horrible hospital bed with rails on the side? It simply wasn't real. When Granny died everyone was expecting it. She was old and sick, and you could actually see and smell the process happening. For some days after her death Gin could still hear her lingering cough, but that had faded as family rituals followed. She remembered how, on the morning of the funeral, the house smelt of boiled eggs. She could almost smell it now. Mrs Robinson, who'd helped look after Granny, over near the sink making a stack of mock-chicken sandwiches. Mummy polishing the last of the silver teaspoons, then covering the plates of sponges, sausage rolls and butterfly cakes with a white net, and finally setting out Granny's Spode tea-set over the starched embroidered cloth. She remembered the day as well as if it were yesterday, and she could picture quite vividly how she'd picked up one of the fine teacups when nobody was looking and caught the flickering outline of her fingers as she held it to the light.

Why couldn't I go to the funeral, Mummy?

Funerals are no place for women and certainly no place for little girls like you, are they Mrs Robinson?

Robbie had nodded dourly as she cut the remaining crusts off the stacked rounds of sandwiches.

But why has Attie gone then?

That's different.

Thinking about it now made her want to cry again, but she had no hands to blow her nose. Every time Gin sniffed, she recalled Granny's winter bulbs. When you picked them, snotty sap ran out of the stalks onto your fingers. Snowdrops, daffodils and jonquils that grew over where the angled half-bricks edged the curve of the drive, all bright and perky, straining to get the best of the short morning sun. They only lasted a few weeks before they shrivelled up and died. It was strange how quickly something else popped up in their place—what was the name of those flowers? So perfect they couldn't possibly be real. She'd broken off ten flowers. Counting them tenderly, so as not to bruise them, she'd then fitted the pink speckled bells one on each finger like the tips of a lady's glove. Then suddenly their spot-eyed tongues had vanished, could no longer tell what they had seen.

Virginia, you wicked child. Valerie's voice rang out. *What are you doing to my foxgloves? They're so difficult to grow in this country without your dear little fingers tweaking them off. I only have them a few precious weeks of the year.* Gin had looked up into the dim hall of sunshine on the veranda to where her mother was sitting, sewing basket and clothes hidden beside her wicker chair. *Come! There's something I have to tell you. It won't be for long*, she explained, without looking up from her sewing. Her white hand was shaking, needle and thread poised over the name-tag she was sewing on Gin's bloomers. *Just for a few months till I get things sorted out.*

From a distance she could already see the tower on the school roof, looking down across the park.

Look, Mummy, Micky Dripping's having a ride. The doll was tucked up inside the leather satchel strapped on her shoulders. There were other special things in there too. *The Water Babies* with 'Virginia Mary Partridge' written inside so that it didn't get lost, and a new wooden pencil case with a swivel top. She remembered her mother's hand, cold and dry, as she led her through the high iron gates of the school, and the oversized hat and brown lace-up shoes that she'd had to polish each day. She'd be the youngest but the older girls would look after her. Then her mother had held her by the shoulders while her mouth said *mmmmw* to her cheek.

There were six girls and six beds. It was dark and all she could hear was their breathing and their little night noises. And she was shivering. Someone had stolen Micky Dripping again and she couldn't get warm. With her head under the grey blankets and knees drawn up to her chin, she did what she did the previous night, and the night before, and the night before that. Breathed out hard to warm herself against the cold damp sheets until she eventually fell asleep.

*

It was humiliating, being spoon-fed like a baby. Gin felt helpless, degraded. Someone even had to wipe her bottom. The nurse lowered another spoonful of rice pudding in her mouth. Micky Dripping. That ridiculous doll. It was odd how he'd mysteriously disappeared. Truth be known, someone had thrown him in the rubbish bin. Probably Marjorie Wilson, the one who ended up a prefect. Girls had gathered around the dormitory in a semicircle. *What do you call that thing? Hey, you kids, she reckons that's a doll ... Micky?* they scoffed. *You can't have a boy doll, Virginia Partridge.* But Micky was a boy doll. He had to be a boy doll because there were no boys in the Partridge family. Not to her knowledge. And now Granny had gone, there was just her and Mummy and it felt so much better pretending there was a boy in the family. Sometimes Micky was a brother and sometimes he was her father. It didn't matter. He could be whoever she wanted him to be. At one stage Micky had even been her best friend. Or she could always prop him up beside her bride doll and then, *hey-presto*, she had a normal family like everybody else. It didn't matter then when other kids asked *how come you don't have a father?*

Chapter 16

The silence was the first thing she noticed when she came home from hospital. Particularly mealtimes when all three of them were pushed in tightly against the laminex table with no escape. The high chair had been removed, along with its place setting, leaving Noel at the head of the table and she and Valerie on either side. Gin had been wondering where the chair had gone. Then, yesterday, she'd seen it in the garage, stowed high up in the rafters alongside the folded wooden playpen.

The braised beef was stringy. She cut it into smaller pieces, trying to hide her tears. Head lowered, she watched Noel retrieve a pea that had bounced across the floor. Valerie *titched* but said nothing. Her mother hadn't eaten a thing as usual but continued pushing food around as if searching for corners in her plate.

'I wonder what the price of the English pound is today,' said Noel eventually.

Valerie put her knife and fork together. She looked up at him, drumming her fingers on the table.

'I wouldn't know Noel, but one thing's for certain,' she stood up, scraping back her chair. 'I wish to hell I'd never set foot in Australia.'

The Queen's long-awaited visit to Western Australia had

provided little consolation. Weeks before the accident, Valerie had been planning to take Dorothy to see Her Majesty and the dear little posy of Cecile Brunners she might present as they lined the gates of Government House, just as they'd done in 1954. But when the event finally arrived, Valerie was too overcome with grief to go. Gin had found her mother sobbing in Dorothy's bedroom. A beautiful little pink frock smocked by Noel's sister Madge especially for the royal occasion was laid out on the nylon bedspread, together with a pair of white cotton socks and a new pair of patent leather shoes.

Perhaps it was the size of them, and the velvet bow and tiny buckles, which sparked off Gin's own grief again. Ever since she'd come home, she'd found herself longing for the sound of Dorothy's feet padding down the hallway, her milky smell and infectious chuckles and high-pitched screeches of appeal. Gin needed desperately to talk about these things, but as soon as she mentioned Dorothy's name Valerie instantly clammed up with a stare that hit her like a stone.

Music might have eased the pain but, until now, Gin hadn't touched the piano. Better for her confidence, she thought, to start off playing something she knew well; nothing too long or complicated. She sat at the piano, now, flipping through pages of Schumann's *Scenes from Childhood*. Little pieces she knew like the back of her hand: 'Blind Man's Buff'; 'Pleading Child'; 'The Rocking-Horse'; 'Contented'; 'At the Fireside'; 'Frightening'; and 'Child Falling Asleep'. She sucked in her breath, told herself not to be put off by their titles. She would start with the first. Lifting her hands tentatively she positioned them on the keys. But her red scars were looking back at her angrily. And within the first few bars, she began to tremble, immediately feeling the pain, first in her fingertips, her hands, then up her arms and radiating into her shoulder-blades. Suddenly everything collapsed.

*

Most days Gin sat in her room, occasionally flicking through the yellow Kodak envelope of photos she'd taken with the Box Brownie Valerie and Noel had given her for her seventeenth birthday. There were shots taken of last Christmas as well. Dottie opening her presents under the Christmas tree and later playing in her new cubby house. There were more snaps of down south: Dorothy playing in the sand and outside the cottages 'helping' Noel and Frank Puddy scale the fish. She was such a dear little child.

Valerie no longer spent Wednesdays or Saturday afternoons at the tennis club with her friends. She seemed detached, embroiled in a world that no longer existed. One day Gin saw her mother stooped over, fussing inside the cubby at the end of the garden.

'It's still *tickety boo*, just how she left it,' she said with abnormal brightness as she came out of the pint-sized doorway. Valerie began hastily brushing away fallen leaves and peppercorns from the brick paving outside. 'I've been cleaning the windows,' she explained. 'Look,' she pointed. 'Now you can see all her toys lined up waiting inside. They'll be a comfort for her, poor little pet, after all she's been through.'

On another occasion Gin overheard her mother's imaginary conversations with Dorothy. Gin could tell by the tone and pitch of her voice and the simple sort of language people use when talking to the very young.

*

'For God's sake, Virginia, stop that incessant fidgeting,' said Valerie, 'it drives me mad.' She went over to the sink again and turned on the tap.

Gin squeezed her smarting eyes. The bleach fumes from her mother's liberal dousing were asphyxiating.

'You're not the only one, you know.' Valerie rinsed the sponge and continued wiping the laminex bench down even though she'd done it several times already. 'We've all been through hell. But, as far as I can see, Virginia, you've actually come out the lucky one.'

Later, Noel knocked gently on her bedroom door.

'Hey, I'm getting pretty browned off with things between you and your mother. Why don't you get back to the piano, lass? It'd be the best thing you could do. I know you don't mean to, but I think you're causing problems lounging around the house.'

'I can't play.' Gin's voice was higher than normal. 'It's impossible. My hands won't let me .... they ... the pain starts up and then I get the jitters.'

'Nonsense, of course you can,' said Noel. 'It's all in the mind. Let's have a look,' he said.

Gin snatched her hands away.

'Dear me. Self-conscious, eh? A few scars are nothing. Should be fit as a fiddle in no time with all those exercises you've been doing.'

'Well,' said Gin, hiding her hands behind her back. 'I don't know that I want to do music anyway.'

Noel paused, puffing on his pipe.

'What about office work, then?' he suggested. Fine bubbles of spit surrounded the stem of his pipe. He was stinking out her room. 'You'd be a good typist. And fast, after all the music you've done.'

'I don't feel I'd be able to ...' Gin could feel that sick feeling again, that lump rising in her throat.

'A business course with some book-keeping,' he added. 'You're a bright lass and with your head for figures you'd get through like a steam-roller.'

'I don't want to do a business course. For one thing, I can't concentrate on anything. And what's more, I'd hate it.'

'Well, I can't have you hanging around the house all day,' said Valerie, standing in the doorway.

She wants to punish me, thought Gin. She still believes it was my fault. But suddenly she felt her courage gaining.

'Then I'll go out all day, if that's how you feel,' she said, sliding past her mother.

Chapter 17

When spring came, Gin began going down to the university each day. She'd been isolated for so long, drifted apart from people her own age. People she thought were her friends now avoided her. They were too busy having a good time, to be involved with grief and tragedy. She tried not to think about it. All going well, she might enrol next year. Forget about music. Perhaps she might do Literature or History, something else instead.

Occasionally she'd come across people she knew walking through the campus: girls from school like Margaret Dunston and Denise Whiteley, with their new matching plum-coloured pixie haircuts, going into Geography. And, through the lunch-time queues in the ref, she'd seen the witch-like head of Barbara Wilson. On that occasion, Gin had inadvertently found herself behind her, looking up into that blond mish-mash of teased hair. The thought of harbouring insects had almost made her quake, but it was strange the secret pleasure she derived from checking out Barbara's heavy eye make-up and those thick powder-pale lips demolishing a vanilla slice as she scooped out the oozy yellow filling with her tongue. She might have been a prefect but how could any boy possibly want to kiss her?

Young people congregated around the courtyard. A couple

smooched against the embankment. Above, clacking honeyeaters plummeted in and out of the wattle bushes. Gin could smell their blossom wafting through the air. She stretched out her legs to try and catch the sun. For a second she glimpsed the blurred and languid movement of lips barely connecting, the tip of a tongue, slight wriggling of hips against the lawn. Quickly she turned her head and looked away.

All that bare skin, those rolled-back sleeves and trousers. It was warming up. Summer was almost here, she could feel it in the air. Ducks paddled idly through water lilies on the pond as strains of Beatles music drifted from the ref. It was that new song called 'I Wanna Hold Your Ha-a-a-nd'. Gin dug her nails into her empty palms. Who would want to hold her ugly scarred red hands?

After she had finished her sandwich she rose and strolled through the undercroft. There was something about the wandering gravel paths of the campus, the way they took her on a kind of journey around the world. She noted the plaques. Kaffir plums from South Africa, silky oaks, Moreton Bay figs and a tropical grove with date palms and kentia palms, and reputedly the biggest aspidistra in the world. She liked to step down into the Sunken Garden, sit enjoying its sense of enclosure and seclusion that encouraged contemplation. Late one afternoon, she'd stumbled on a rehearsal and, from the tree ferns above, had watched excerpts from *Ulysses*. From then on, the Sunken Garden always gave her the feeling she was in some ancient Greek amphitheatre as she looked up through the branches of the pines.

But, now, in the height of spring, the circular flowerbeds were ablaze with brightly coloured annuals and perennials. Snapdragons, delphiniums, foxgloves, gladiolas, she didn't know them all. Botanical tours, comprising middle-aged and elderly men and women, occasionally visited the gardens. Wouldn't her mother love it, thought Gin? If only she'd get out of the house, join one of these tours, it might help to lift her out of her misery.

Suddenly she noticed a boy carving something on a tree.

'Hey! Come here, son!' bellowed the gardener. 'I'm going to report you.'

Later, Gin scanned the wide girth of the oak in vain, searching amongst the most recently etched hearts, bows and arrows. Then she went back to the library. For days she had been immersing herself in novels. It didn't matter what it was. She'd read a chapter here and there, or sometimes a whole book in a day. If it was voluminous and took her fancy, she'd hide it somewhere on another shelf so no one could take it out. She started at the beginning of the alphabet on the shelves—Balzac and Baudelaire—and when she got to Chekhov, she quickly progressed onto the Russian classics which soon became a passion. It wasn't long before she wanted to know all about modern Russia and the revolution.

Noel was always going on about the *bloody commos*. Ever since the Cuban crisis, everyone had been on edge, particularly Valerie, worrying it could still spark off a nuclear war. But things seemed to have settled down since then. Kennedy had patched things up and was now talking to the Russians.

*

When the academic year eventually came to a close, Gin made her decision to enrol in Arts. The sun shone as she lay on the lawn, eyes closed, eavesdropping on the last of the exam postmortems. This would be *her* next year.

'Thank God that's it for the year. How'd you go, Greg?'

'Anywhere between fifty and seventy.'

'How's that for hedging your bets.'

'What about you Janice?'

'Lousy. Failed, for sure.'

'You always say that and come out trumps.'

They were discussing celebrations, offering each other commiserations, which of them were going to the Broadway stomp or slipping down to Steve's Hotel.

A tall gangly boy came running up, hands waving excitedly, panting. 'Hey, you guys, d'you hear the latest? President Kennedy's been assassinated.'

There was silence.

'No kidding?'

'Heck, eh? Geez. Go on.' The one with the longish hair turned around. 'Hey, did you hear that?'

Everyone was stunned.

'Apparently a sniper shot him dead as he was being driven through the streets of Dallas.'

Gin wanted to join in, hungry for details like the others, but the group walked on as if she didn't exist. She tried going back to her book but, for the rest of the afternoon, she couldn't stop thinking about the news.

Over on the foreshore, she stood taking in the drowning scent of the magnolia tree. What she'd overheard was scant but even that was too much information. It was almost unreal, like something out of a Hollywood picture. How, in that flash of gunshot, could anyone destroy the most famous face in America?

And, who, for that matter, could believe that Jackie K was now a widow? God! She was only thirty-four. Up until the accident, her mother had vainly tried to model herself on Jackie's style. *As for JFK, that man,* Valerie declared, *that man had to be the handsomest man on earth.* Even Noel admired him. The Kennedys had been an item, such a striking-looking couple. Incredibly photogenic. The perfect couple. The perfect family, for even little Caroline and Johnny Junior looked adorable as well.

Suddenly, the sun went behind a cloud. Gin buttoned her cardigan. Just then, a fleet of small yachts skittered around the point. The breeze was fresh although the sun was still warm. The group of children in the water remained frisky, rolling, sliding, and disappearing in and out of big black tractor tubes. Putting aside her sewing, their mother looked up at them anxiously and patted her perm. What a tragedy, thought Gin, those poor little Kennedy children now without a daddy. Would they be able to remember him when they were grown up?

Instead of catching the bus, Gin lingered outside the tea-rooms, delaying her journey home. She knew that if she left now she'd be home in time to see the five o'clock news. She wondered what Valerie would say? She could never quite predict her state of mind. The news might send her in a tizz. But it was getting late and Gin knew that soon she'd have to make a move. Noel would probably have stopped off down at the Flying Squadron for a few drinks before venturing home. Something he was doing more and more often, she'd noticed.

Gin took off her sunglasses. Out on the jetty was a young man walking a dog. So often she wished for the company of a dog. No words. No explanations. Just unconditional love. Noel had wanted to buy her one for her eighteenth birthday but Valerie wouldn't hear of it. The dog on the jetty caught Gin's eye: a short sturdy animal, well-defined with pretty patches of tan on black and white. A flurry of seagulls swooped, temporarily obscuring her view as they hovered, squealing and flapping their wings around the cluster of nearby garbage bins. The dog suddenly broke free and the birds began to scatter as it took off along the jetty. Ears flapped up and down, as it ran a steady lopsided gait. Look! It seemed to be coming straight towards her, smiling at her, tongue lolling out of one side of its mouth. She bent down to greet it. Pat it.

The dog kept grinning but ignored her as it nosed straight into the bin.

Within seconds a young man in desert boots and faded blue jeans came jogging through the sand. 'Rotten sod of a dog,' he muttered apologetically. 'Sorry about that.'

Gin looked up at the bespectacled face. How incongruous. Students and dogs didn't usually go together.

The fellow picked up the fallen leash. 'Come'ere, Barker,' he tugged. The dog rolled its eyes at Gin, but stood immobile, still clutching the remains of an old half-eaten bun in its mouth.

Gin laughed.

'Alright for you. Not as funny as you think.'

'Great dog.'

'Well, he's not exactly mine but you could say my responsibility.'

Gin looked at his face. His hair was dark and silky and flopped across his forehead.

'What did you call him?'

'A sod of a dog.'

'No, I mean his name.'

'Oh,' he smiled, 'Barker!'

'You're joking!' she laughed.

'Stupid name considering the mutt rarely barks. Too lazy, I'd say. Nose dominates his brain.' Grinning, he brushed aside his fallen hair. 'Well, I'm pooped after that.' He sat down beside her. 'Mind if I take a pew?'

The dog immediately sat down on Gin's shoe, drooling saliva as he wolfed down what was left of the bun.

Gin blurted, 'Did you know that President Kennedy has been assassinated?' There was no one else to tell and it was hideous, the strange sense of honour she felt in conveying the horrible news.

'No!'

'Yes,' she said, with growing confidence and authority, 'apparently a sniper shot him dead as he was being driven through the streets of Dallas.'

'Impossible!' He was all questions, drilling her for the gory details.

'Sorry, that's all I heard,' she said. 'It's absolutely shocking. Still can't believe it.'

'Guess the news will be full of it all,' he said.

Gin bent down and stroked the dog. The animal raised his head and looked back at her.

'I wish I had a dog,' she said. 'You're so lucky.'

'Looks as if butter wouldn't melt in his mouth, but don't be taken in. He's a wilful sod. Took a while to get to know him. I grew up with proper dogs, you know, dogs that do as they're told. But old Barker here is worse than a naughty child.' He laughed, looking back at the dog. 'If you had half a brain you'd be dangerous, wouldn't you, eh?'

His smooth tanned fingers were stroking the dog backwards and forwards between the ears. Gin noticed they were a funny spatula shape, much the same length but wider at the tips.

*

Suddenly, she realised how dense she'd been. She could picture the face clearly: its long angularity, high cheekbones, dark chocolaty eyes and olive skin, even his hands. She knew all of these things about him but she didn't even know his name. The fact that she knew his dog's name made it even worse. Yet stupidly she'd arranged to meet him here again at the tea-rooms.

'What happened?' he asked her within five minutes of sitting down.

He nodded at her hands.

Gin looked in disgust at the paper tissue she'd been unconsciously shredding in her lap.

'No, I mean your hands,' he probed, his eyes unflinching. 'Here,' he bent over her and scooped up the pieces of tissue, 'let me get rid of that pile of rubbish you're playing with. Then you can tell me all about it.'

He listened carefully, asking questions quietly and clinically, one after the other. When she'd finished, or when she'd told him as much as she wanted to, a silence fell between them. Then, taking hold of her wrist as if he were going to take her pulse, he turned it over and started caressing the inner white side, tracing its vulnerable map of blue veins with his index finger.

'Now there's more to that story than you're telling me,

isn't there?' he said, looking enquiringly at the tears that were swimming in her eyes. 'So? What happened?'

Gin sat there dogged, chewing on her lip.

'Fair enough,' he eventually conceded. 'I won't ask again.' He smiled, continuing to squeeze her hand.

'Excuse me. I don't even know your name.'

'Virginia. That's what my folks call me but I prefer Gin.'

'Gin sounds cool to me,' he shrugged. 'I'm Theo, by the way, except my folks pronounce it with a silent h like *Tao* ... as in ... *day-o, day-ay-ay-ayo ... day-de-light-come and I wanna go home.*

Nearby heads turned at his burst of song.

'Theo is short for Theodore,' he added, 'in case you didn't know.'

'I'll call you Theo,' she said. 'I like it, even with the h!'

Every now and then Gin could hear the slightest trace of a foreign accent. Perhaps it was the t's and the way he said his name. He spoke very quickly, in fact. Sometimes it was hard to keep up with him.

*

Theo told her he was studying engineering and lived in a granny flat near Hampden Road.

'What, all alone?'

'Yes,' he said. He told her his parents had abandoned him. 'Migrating immigrants you might call them. They'd fled to Australia from Java when the Japs came in 1942. After the war we were repatriated to Holland. I remember it being a horrible bloody place, cold and damp and crowded, and constantly having to dodge the bikes and dog turds. People were begging for the food which others fed their dogs.'

His top lip gathered into a curl.

'We hated the place,' he said 'and they hated us too. All that graffiti on the walls. *Indos ga veg!* Go back home, they said. Mum and Dad considered themselves relatively lucky. Some poor families had been living in Japanese POW camps, sick and starving for nearly four years. The home country had no idea of Japanese atrocities, considered them nothing to what they'd had to suffer under Nazi occupation. They resented refugees receiving any compensation. My parents were very proud and decided on migrating to Australia. We ended up living over at Graylands in tin sheds for a while, you know, Nissan huts, over behind the showgrounds. There were lots of new immigrant kids at school. Poles, Germans, Italians, Greeks, Slavs, you name it. I was alright. My nose was in front. I'd been born in Australia and brought up speaking English. A few times I felt a bit of an oddball. When I changed schools, kids ran around calling me a Dutchie and put me in the bin. Later at Hollywood High School, I caught a bit of flack. I'm an asthmatic and never liked swimming in the Baths. The phys. ed. teacher used to say, *You're soft Van Didden, about as soft as those nice Dutch ginger biscuits I bet your mum puts in your lunch-box every day.*

Theo said he supposed those sorts of insults only sharpened his wits, made him a survivor. He'd made light of it—given back some lip. It was the sort of thing he did when things didn't turn out the way they should. But it hadn't been easy for his parents. They'd left everything behind and had to start from scratch. Despite his father being an experienced pilot, he'd had to take a variety of menial jobs, which he supplemented by night-shift work as well.

'Funny, everything was going fine—we'd all been naturalised. Then suddenly my mother gets homesick. So, that's where they both are now—over in Indonesia trying to suss things out.' Theo said that, in the meantime, he was pretty much independent, putting himself through uni. He'd been lucky enough to earn himself a Commonwealth Scholarship. Things were good. He'd got through one year. Next week he'd be going up to Mukinbudin on a two-month contract working on the wheat bins. 'Not the best way to spend Christmas,' he laughed, 'but it's work, meaning money, see, so I'm not complaining.'

*

There'd been something pathetic about Valerie assembling the plastic tree with its gaudy baubles and obligatory fairy on the top. Gin felt flutters gathering in her stomach as, day by day, she watched her mother gradually filling a Christmas stocking with tiny treasures she'd retrieved from well-kept hidey holes. When Christmas Day eventually came, Noel took Valerie off to church. Gin excused herself, saying if they didn't mind she'd stay home and keep an eye on the turkey. She was bracing herself for the agony that she felt was sure to come.

After they'd gone, she sat in a cane chair in the sunroom with her knees drawn up under her chin. She looked at the mandatory Christmas tree. No laughter, no toys strewn around the floor. Only a year ago, Noel had given Dorothy the end of a long piece of string and they'd all watched as she followed it outside and the joy spreading across her little face when she discovered the other end was attached to a new cubby-house.

Now everything felt so strained. Any second something was

going to snap. If only Theo were here, she thought, it would have made things so much more bearable. The few short weeks she'd known him had been deliriously happy ones. It was so sweet. She hadn't expected a present when he'd left, and wished she'd been able to reciprocate. He'd kissed her, pressed it in her hand, whispering *I'll be back*. Unwrapping the paper, she'd found a record: 'Please Please Me'.

It was rather suggestive; she smiled to herself, as she listened closely to the lyrics. Gin knew she could only play it when nobody was home otherwise Valerie would have a fit. Noel would probably pick up the sleeve and grunt something like *Beatles, eh? Bloody awful. Noxious insects that should be exterminated. Where's the Mortein?*

Later that afternoon, after they'd got through lunch without too many dramas, Valerie and Noel wandered over to the Puddy's for 'open house'.

'Frank said to say you're invited too, lass,' reminded Noel.

'Thanks.' Frank Puddy was the last person she wanted to see on Christmas Day. Gin lay outside on the Li-Lo, looking up into Valerie's assortment of hanging baskets. Ribbon plants had multiplied; dozens of tiny offspring dangling down from the pergola near her head, fighting their way to the ground.

She wondered how much longer they would continue living here. The house was one of those Nedlands 'frown' houses, as Theo called them, a gloomy thirties bungalow with its downward angled portico and little natural light. Hibiscus partially shaded the leadlight windows in the front rooms. In the cooler months the severity of black-stained jarrah beams, panelling and architraves against the white walls gave the house a frosty feel whenever you came inside.

Not long after Dorothy had died, Noel had organised to have the kitchen renovated. New stove and fresh jade laminex bench tops for Valerie, the best they could afford. In one way the house was so convenient. Ten minutes from the city where Noel worked and close to the river and the university, but it was all so dark and depressing, thought Gin. Lately Noel had been talking about buying one of those new Corser duplexes he'd seen advertised in the *West*.

'Less to look after,' she'd heard him telling Frank Puddy. 'Val's not up to much these days. I've had my ups and downs myself, to tell you the truth, old fellow. Too many sad memories here. Think we both need a new start. Something bright and modern.'

It was clear her mother wasn't coping. Dark shadows clouded her eyes and she was always complaining of a headache. Recently the doctor had prescribed more pills, ones for her head and others to make her sleep. Noel was encouraging, told her she was looking more relaxed. From what Gin could see, the medication was having a marked effect. Her mother looked pale, remote. Most days she sat watching television and wouldn't leave the house. It still looked spic and span although she wasn't as obsessive. The edginess had eased. But it was as if she was trying to cocoon herself from the outside world.

Gin rolled her head from the Li-Lo. She sat up, feeling the crisscrossed pattern the nylon webbing had pressed against her cheek. The garden, she noticed, had been let go. It was the first year Valerie hadn't pruned her roses. Most of the pot plants were scruffy, dying, probably from lack of water. Leaves and fallen debris now littered the cement paving around Dorothy's cubby. Even Noel's interest had waned. The lawn had lost its crisp manicured lines, and piles of fallen lemons lay fermenting in the weeds. Feeling a pang of guilt, Gin took a bucket from the laundry. How many times had she walked past those lemons? Almost every day, yet it had never occurred to her to pick them up and put them in the bin. She'd had her own escape, been in another world hanging around at uni. Looking back, though, it was the best thing she could have done. Get away from the house and Valerie, away from all the sadness.

After emptying the rotting lemons in the bin, Gin washed her hands under the hose. She raised the head, spraying the row of pot-plants. From the steps of the patio she could see through next door's kitchen window. Someone waved. She waved back. Nice people, but she didn't know them very well. Valerie had always shunned them, closed them out, considering herself too good for them.

Between the steady streams of droplets, Gin could see the dividing hedge, long woody sprays of plumbago wilting in the hot sun. No matter how sad things were you had to have hope. *If you can't find it, you somehow have to try and visualise it,* Theo had said. Hundreds of people his family knew had a pretty rough time of it and it was amazing how many managed to survive. *Imagine being a bloody POW, would you mind? What kept them going? Not the half a blinkin' cup of rice a day, that's for certain. Hope, faith, call it what you will, but, crikey, Gin, you got to have hope in this world, otherwise you don't stand a hope in bloody hell.*

It was little more than a month since they'd met. Just thinking about him sent a rush of warmth rippling through her body, a new and faster rhythm to her pulse. Perhaps hope was staring her in the face: the plumbago, its blossoms, fragments of clear blue sky against the green. Perhaps hope was what she was feeling in her veins.

*

The Beatles' record Theo had given her must have been a kind of joke. The sort of music he really liked was jazz. He was always tapping out rhythms. Not that he could play an instrument or even read music, for that matter, but he was very knowledgeable, and had built up a good record collection which he quickly offered to show her in his flat upon her return. He explained that he liked the sophistication of jazz. The Stones were alright but he was sick of what he called *poncey melodies* and *gimmicky lyrics*; said he'd outgrown the sort of pop that plagued the radio all day long. Occasionally he'd flick on his transistor and they'd both laughingly sing along to something from the Top Forty. Everyone knew the Beatles. Some of it was good, she thought. But it didn't really have an impact on their lives.

Gin had always liked a syncopated rhythm. Back when she was about fourteen, she'd rather fancied herself as Winifred Atwell banging out her own version of 'Black and White Rag'. But that was as far as it went. The jazz Theo introduced her to at the start of the new academic year provided her with something totally fresh in her life, something that released her from the past.

Yet he was curious, jealous perhaps, of her classical training.

Crying shame, he'd said. *Waste of skills and knowledge. Only wish I'd had the opportunity. Why couldn't she play the piano any more,* he wanted to know? *Surely it was just a matter of trying to relax.*

One night they were at a party in Langham Street. It was the first time she'd tried Cinzano. After he'd plied her with one or two, he tried to wheedle her into playing.

'Come on,' he said, pulling out the piano stool for her. 'Have a go, Ginny. Don't be a party pooper.'

'I can't,' said Gin.

'Why not?'

'My fingers won't let me.'

'You can do it, Gin. It's a state of mind. Just relax. No one will notice. Look. Everyone's pissed anyway.'

Gin tried but she couldn't play a note. She remained seated, fingers stuck on the keys as if they were paralysed. Then, in a surge, a horrible burning sensation swept the length of her body and her heart began to explode.

'OK,' he said eventually, coming to the rescue. 'Fair enough.' He eased her shaking hands off the keys and took her away to a corner. For the rest of the night, his arm lingered protectively around her shoulders like a stole.

After that, Gin didn't bother to try again. Even the sound of classical piano music brought her pain. With jazz, she felt no pain. There was something lazy, unstructured and unpredictable about it that she could instantly relate to. She liked the freedom of it, the infinite possibilities of improvisation and the syncopated rhythms which suited the kind of off-beat existence Theo was living at the time. Theo was an elixir and Gin couldn't see enough of him. He had shown her how to smile.

Chapter 18

The first time she brought Theo home was during their mid-year break. Gin wasn't sure how her mother would react. For weeks, Valerie had been off-colour and Noel never seemed to be around. After Theo had nodded politely and shaken hands, the four of them stood in front of the fire; a homely kind of gathering. Valerie was unusually bright and rubbed her hands.

'Well, what a lovely surprise,' she said.

'It's hot in here,' said Theo looking around. 'Excuse me if I ...' He started stripping off his Alpine jumper. Perhaps he was nervous. His cheeks had a glow and his glasses were slightly fogged with perspiration. Gin could see her mother's eyes surveying him up and down, noting the missing buttons he'd been hiding on his unironed shirt. He'd just washed his hair, Gin noticed. It was still slightly wet, softer than usual, shining bluey-black. He looked almost respectable in a clean pair of corduroys and the brown brogues he had worn in place of his usual scruffy desert boots. There was an air of careless confidence about him, the tilt of his chin, fingers raking his hair like he was about to confront some sort of challenge.

He stood sipping quietly on the froth of the beer which Noel had poured for him.

'Theo?' Valerie sat back in the armchair. She crossed her knees and started twisting and turning her foot. 'Now that's a bit different.' She looked flushed, animated. She edged up to him. 'Would you like to stay and join us for dinner tonight, Theo?' she added as an afterthought.

'Won't be till after the footy's over,' said Noel.

Later sitting beside him at the table she said, 'I don't suppose you get anything like this batching by yourself, do you Theo?'

'Well, actually, I do alright for myself, thanks, Mrs Wheatley,' he said, nudging his glasses further up his nose. 'I quite like cooking. You could say I'm a dab hand at a joint.'

Gin kicked him under the table. His face didn't flinch and his dark brown eyes fixed on the bone-handled knife which Noel was sharpening. Theo watched him carefully core out the central layer of fat inside the leg of lamb, following each wafer-thin slice roll precisely off the knife. She knew he was starving. She knew he hadn't had lunch.

'Two or three slices?' asked Noel, directing his question to Theo without looking up.

'Three, thank you Mr Wheatley.'

Valerie clicked her tongue.

'But surely you can't manage a whole leg just by yourself, can you?'

'You'd be surprised,' replied Theo, watching her spoon out potatoes, cauliflower and peas onto his plate. 'To tell you the truth, if I cook a roast, I usually take some over to my landlord, old Mr Davis. He lives by himself. I keep an eye on him, you see, as part of the rent deal. What's left over, I clean up myself. Usually I don't eat anything else then until it's all gone. It keeps.'

'And where are your parents from Theo?' asked Noel.

Anyone else would have thought it was the beginning of an inquisition, thought Gin, but she was relieved when Theo retained his insouciance.

'That's a moot point. Gypsies, I suppose.'

Valerie choked.

'I kid you not,' he laughed. 'We've lived in so many different places, I can't remember them all.'

Theo reached over, helping himself to gravy and mint sauce. He looked around the table over the top of his glasses and then back at Gin.

'Something wrong, Theo?' asked Valerie, twiddling her beads.

'Actually … um … I wonder, Mrs Wheatley, if it would be too rude to ask if you might have a piece of bread … you know, to mop up my gravy.'

Noel turned his head to one side and blew his nose, as if stalling for time. He waited until he thought Valerie was out in the kitchen and then he said 'What does your father do for a crust, Theo?'

Theo took a deep breath.

'Well, a little bit of this and a little bit of that.' He was enjoying himself, thought Gin, leading them on.

Noel was not to be put off.

'Born in Australia?' he asked, green eyes shrivelled up like the peas on his plate.

'Yes, but my parents are Dutch–Indonesian, if that's what you're asking,' replied Theo, getting in first. 'We immigrated here when I was six but my parents have gone back to Java for a trial run. They're hoping it won't be long before Sukarno kicks the bucket. In the meantime, I'm here on my own and Dad's trying to get a job over there with KLM. He was a pilot during the war, see, and, after the Javanese evacuation, he joined forces with the RAAF.' His delivery was rapid, non-stop.

'How old are you, son?' asked Noel, after a pause.

'Just turned nineteen, Mr Wheatley,' he said, straightening his shoulders.

'Well, then, you might have a lot of responsibility on your plate next year. They're thinking of bringing in conscription.'

*

After Theo had left, Noel bent down and knocked his pipe against the grate. He stood up. 'I'm not joking. Communist terrorism is growing like a plague,' he said, waving the stem of his pipe in gesture.

Valerie remained by the fire rubbing her hands.

'We can't stand back and let ourselves be invaded, otherwise we'll end up like Eastern Europe.' He started hunting around for his tobacco. 'Bloody yellow peril,' he muttered.

'I'm fed up with all this talk.' Valerie's voice was high and tight. 'I've had enough of war, thank you very much, and enough bloody stress to last a lifetime. Goodnight.'

She rolled her eyes and, excusing herself on the pretext of tiredness, said it was time she went to bed.

Noel kissed her on the forehead and then continued as she left the room.

'Mark my words,' he warned, 'if we don't watch out, the domino theory will become a fact.'

Sometimes Gin tried to counter his theories but this time there was no stopping him; he was primed.

'Australia's a sitting duck,' he said. 'Japs proved that during the war. Menzies should up the numbers. If there aren't enough volunteers, then I say bring on conscription. Straighten out some of those long-haired layabouts into the bargain. Give 'em all a sense of purpose.'

Perhaps it was the alcohol and the heat from the fire. Noel's nose seemed larger than normal, thought Gin. It was red and glowing and all the pores had opened up. He was going on and on, loving the sound of his own voice. Times like this she despised him. She waited for him to draw breath.

'What part did you play in the war, Noel?' she asked, casually.

'I'd no choice in the matter. If I'd had my way, I'd have been in the front line. But I felt cheated. Had to stay home as I was in essential services.'

*

Gin soon became party to their constant bickering. All weekend it had been going on. She could hear Noel trying to remain calm and controlled.

'Look, Val. We can't go on like this,' he said. 'We've both got our grief, you know, only ...'

'Blaming me, are you? Haven't you thought for one minute it might be her ... Virginia, bringing home that ... that young ...' Valerie was crying. 'All this talk about war ... it's brought it all back again,' she sobbed.

'You mustn't let it offend you, sweetheart. There's nothing wrong with the lad,' said Noel. 'I'm sure he's a good kid, he's smart, and nothing that a good trip to the barber wouldn't solve. But at least he's not one of those real long-haired louts you see lounging about these days. All a kid needs is a dose of national service. Bit of work ethic and the discipline of short back and sides.'

'And you. You're just making things worse. You keep going on and on about war yourself all the time. You never stop.'

There was silence for a while. Then Gin heard Noel out in the kitchen. The *glug-glug* of whisky being poured out of a bottle, two short squirts of soda, the clink of ice-blocks. All of a sudden, she realised how bitterly cold it was in her room. She stood at the window, hoping Noel had lit the gas fire. Outside, everything looked motionless in the grey light. The pair of doves she had noticed earlier was still perched on next door's terracotta gargoyle, heads sunk in puffed-out chests and feathers fluffed against the weather. Mates probably, but where would they go now their roosts had gone? The mulberry tree was almost bare, the outline of the last scraps of leaves dark and bleak against the sky. The only sign of life out there was a baby mudlark scavenging in the pile of rotting leaves below.

Gin quickly slipped on a spencer under her skivvy and the pink angora jumper she'd recently bought. Its silkiness reminded her of the angora bolero she'd worn to the wedding. It was rather like stroking a little lost furry animal. When she looked up, the doves had barely moved. They were the same colour now as the sky. Birds were lucky; they didn't feel the cold. Their heart rate was faster, she'd learnt in biology, their body temperature higher than mammals. You could tell by their continual quick movements and their eating and foraging for food.

'Here, love. See if that perks you up,' Noel's voice filtered from the sitting room.

Thinking that might be the end of the matter, Gin sat down at her desk again opening a fresh page. Suddenly, they started up again. She could tell Noel had his pipe in his mouth by the way he was talking.

'I've been thinking, Val,' he said, through clenched teeth. 'What say we get right away from it all? Have a holiday. They're sending me up to Singapore again next month for a five-day convention. Why don't you come with me? I'll take some leave. We'll make a holiday out of it. Do us both the world of good, you know.'

Great, thought Gin.

'I couldn't possibly, Virginia's far too young to be left. What would the neighbours think with that young Van what's-his-name coming and going all hours of the night and day?'

Gin opened her bedroom door. She couldn't resist it.

'Don't worry about me,' she said lightly, walking into the conversation. 'I'm old enough to look after myself, I'm not a baby. I am twenty in case you didn't know. You should go, Mum. In fact, why don't you go back to England like you did before?'

*

But Valerie could not be tempted and Noel went up to Singapore by himself. One day, while he was still away, Valerie disappeared without saying where she was going. Gin caught a glimpse of her late that morning as she passed her bedroom door on her way to uni. Valerie looked rather like an aged film star, mouth pursed as she touched up her lipstick in front of the dressing table. Who did she remind her of? Vivienne Leigh, was it? Gin thought there was something a little odd and theatrical about the way her mother was dressed, that perhaps she was just reminiscing or playing some sort of game: old close-fitting tweedy suit from the early forties, and that ridiculous fox-fur that she'd played with as a child and hadn't seen for years. It looked macabre draped around her mother's shoulders. Clasped, pointy-nosed head looped across her bosom to bite its own tail, and beady eyes glinting as if in some sort of conspiracy. It never occurred to Gin to ask her mother why she was dressed like that or where she was going, in case she took offence. She was touchy enough as it was.

When the telephone rang the next morning, it woke Gin with a start. At first she thought it was Theo. They'd been up late the night before studying at his flat and he hadn't driven her home till after twelve. They'd arranged to meet between their lectures over at the tea-rooms. But, instead of Theo on the phone, it was Dulcie Bradford.

'Thought I'd ring and check how your mother is. Just that she's missed the last two weeks of bridge and I'm a wee bit worried about her. I'm not sure she's been at all well lately.'

'She's OK, but just a minute, I'll go and see if I can find her,' Gin said.

As she was running late, she simply put her hand over the mouthpiece and called up the stairs.

'Yoo-hoo ... Mum?'

She half-expected her to appear and say *How rude, Virginia. Too lazy to come and fetch me?* But there was no answer.

Gin didn't bother to check properly. She was looking at her watch.

'Afraid she's not here, Mrs Bradford. Shall I tell her you rang?'

When Gin came home that evening Valerie still hadn't returned, although the Mini was parked in the garage. On the kitchen table was the note she'd left her mother. There was no note of reply, none of the usual curt messages. Four loin chops were sitting in the fridge, waiting to be eaten. Nothing had been touched. Valerie's bedroom was as she always left it, immaculately tidy with the lingering smell of cigarettes, stale scent and make-up. Gin's eyes began searching for familiar objects. Rosy eiderdown pressed back in three even folds, white candlewick dressing-gown hanging behind the door, silver brush and mirror set angled together on the dressing table at the usual forty-five degrees, her prized collection of blue and white Wedgwood and the crystal perfume bottles all positioned as normal. The only thing that appeared to be missing was her mother's handbag and her pink sponge-bag from the bathroom.

'Theo, do you think I should ring the police?' asked Gin. 'I'm worried. It's totally out of character. The strange thing is her car's still here.'

'Hasn't your mum been acting a bit strange lately? What about those, you know, hallucinations and imaginary conversations you were telling me about.'

'Well, yes, but these days she doesn't like to leave the house.'

'P'raps wait a bit longer, Gin. You don't want to cause her or Noel any unnecessary embarrassment. Imagine the hoo-hah. You know what a snob she is. Why don't you wait till Noel gets back tomorrow?'

*

Noel had no hesitation in calling the police when he arrived home from Singapore.

'No disrespect but I've known the odd sheila to do this sort of thing to her old man,' he was told. 'Seems a bit odd but she'll be back, mate. Meantime, we'll keep a look out.'

For years Gin had listened to radio series like CIB and Missing Persons Bureau, always having to contain the vague expectation that her father might suddenly reappear from out of the blue. But how could her mother have disappeared off the planet with no clues as to why or where she'd gone?

Word quickly got out and over the next few days people came in dribs and drabs. Even after they'd gone, the house still harboured their whispers and sideways glances.

Perhaps she's wandered off and had a bout of amnesia ... the war affected her dreadfully ... fragile ... change of life ... she's been hospitalised in the past ... don't think she ever got over poor little Dorothy ... never been quite the same since ... no wonder poor Noel had to ...

These were the sort of comments bandied about. Gin was asked time and again if she remembered her mother behaving strangely, or if there was anything out of the ordinary happening at home. She didn't like to tell them that her mother had barely spoken to her ever since Dorothy had died.

*

Not long after, Frank Puddy came around and told Noel someone he knew thought they'd seen Valerie with a man outside the Palace Hotel. 'Face up to it, old man,' he whispered when he thought Gin was out of hearing. 'Keeps herself well. Only forty and still very good looking, Noel, and, as Norma said, you'd never know her hair was white.'

Policemen came and went. They searched the house taking

fingerprints and items of her clothing. They spent hours on horseback. Gin watched them tracking through the golf course and into the nearby bushland right up to the river cliffs where the grey of the grass blended into weathered limestone. And because someone thought they'd spotted her taking the footpath down towards the river, they searched there too, trudging backwards and forwards across the cliff-face, scouring beneath the banksias and sheoaks and underneath the dusty-coloured parrot bush. At the bottom they poked sticks in between the bamboos and the mud and the washed-up slush. Maybe she'd gone skinny-dipping in the hot spring and fallen in the water. But they found nothing and called off the search.

Then, about two weeks later, a fisherman noticed something wet and furry caught against the pylons of the boathouse jetty. When he scooped it up in his crab-net, he thought it was a dog that had drowned until he noticed the dainty face with eyes still gleaming. No doubt he would have dumped the fox-fur back off the jetty and not thought another thing about it had he not spotted Valerie's snakeskin handbag washed up in the nearby shallows. When he opened it, everything was intact. All her money, her driving licence and her small pink satin sponge-bag were still inside just where she'd put them. The fisherman immediately reported his findings to the police, and divers were sent down to search around the boathouse. If it hadn't been for low tide, Valerie might never have been found.

Gin insisted on going with Noel to the morgue to identify the body. They warned her. Valerie was unrecognisable, black and bloated, body straining against the turgid confines of her suit, her ankles swollen, bursting over the sides of her best court shoes.

'Then perhaps if you'd care to check the jewellery, Miss Partridge.'

Gin was almost sick and turned away. The kid gloves on her mother's hands had to be cut off, finger by finger; the rings were barely visible, embedded in her skin.

Chapter 19

Gin sat stiffly between Noel and Attie, shivering in her winter coat. To the dark solemn tones of organ music came the echo of footsteps sounding in unison as the pallbearers made their slow descent down the aisle. It was the first time she had seen a coffin. Perhaps it was the chrome trim and handles that made it look so awfully weird and chilling. Not for one second could she picture her mother lying inside, contained, silenced forever beneath that dark, dark lacquer. Over the white liliums adorning the top, a small spatter of raindrops glistened, tiny eyes staring back at her in question.

How could it possibly have happened? Attie squeezed her hand and gave her reassuring looks. Gin's lips involuntarily shaped soundless words of a hymn she knew so well but couldn't find the voice to sing. Her heart ached, literally ached; religious music often had that effect. Surely this was different. People were dabbing at faces. Beside her came the stifle of sobs, and out of the corner of her eye she saw Noel's handkerchief fluttering against his nose like a big white moth on a light bulb. The service came and went, fragmented like a dream.

Only once, during the eulogy, did anything seem real. Noel suddenly started jingling coins in his trouser pocket. From then on she couldn't concentrate on the words for the lump in her throat. Trying to swallow the hurt away, she blew her nose, drawing in the scent of rosemary from the sprig she'd been unconsciously fondling in the palm of her hand.

And she noticed, during that short, measured silence, the way the priest folded his hands and bowed his head in slow deliberation. Someone coughed. Then before she knew it, the organ was burping its final farewell, and within seconds she could feel the damp pressure of Noel on her arm as the coffin began to slide down and away out of sight.

How quickly everything became a blur; slivers of rain falling obliquely, a steady backward rhythm of darts against the black limousine. As it slowly nosed its way into their driveway, Gin noticed water overflowing from the gables on the roof, pouring in torrents over the outside of her mother's bedroom window. She wondered if the service was what her mother would have wanted, being herself someone who'd always avoided funerals. And would she like the wake which Norma Puddy and the bridge girls had so kindly organised inside for Noel?

Gin felt detached, everyone gravitating to the sitting room where the black beams and architraves seemed to frame the gathering into something resembling a period parlour scene out of a French painting: ladies leaning forward, refreshments elegantly perched on their knees, cabbage-rose faces blending into chintz. Then Frank Puddy suddenly came over and put his arm around her and gave her a squeeze. 'Where's that boyfriend of yours, eh?' The smell of his breath made her recoil. All afternoon there were hugs and kisses, pursed lips and powdery whispers, breathing the acrid warmth of tea and sherry into her face. Names were sounded. Some she knew, others strangers like Noel's bank colleagues and members of the Flying Squadron, who came with handshakes and light protective touches. At times, it was almost like being in remote control, forcing a smile, acknowledging this one, then that one, moving on and in between them all.

When Theo eventually turned up, the food had mostly gone. He picked at curling sandwiches and sausage rolls, flicking aside sprigs of wilting parsley. Together, they sat at the kitchen table looking at crumbs on plates and black dregs drained in the bottom of cups that still bore the half-smiles of ladies' lips.

Theo looked at her.

'How'd it all go, Gin?'

What could she say?

'There you are, Gin darling,' said Attie, catching her for the first time alone. 'Come and give your old aunt a great big hug.' As she wrapped her arms around her, Gin's tears began splashing down her cheeks. 'There, there,' said Attie between her gentle pats. 'There, there, there. It's alright. A damn good cry won't do you any harm, my girl. I've just had one myself.'

Theo stood up awkwardly.

'I'm Theo, by the way. Pleased to meet you. I guess you're Ginny's aunt.'

'How do you do, Theo, I'm Attie.'

Norma Puddy burst into the kitchen with a tray of dirty glasses.

'How about finding a taker for the rest of that butter cake, Theo, that's if you don't want it,' she said, handing him a plate. 'Needs eating quickly though. It'll be stale by the morning.'

Attie took Gin aside into the sunroom. 'It's a bit quieter here,' she said. 'Come and sit down, Gin. Here's a clean handkerchief,' she said, rummaging in her pocket.

Gin blew her nose and blinked away her tears.

'Nothing I can say will ease your pain. Guess your mother and I never quite saw eye to eye, but she had a difficult life, a lot of grief to contend with over the years. Take what you can from her life, Gin. It wasn't all bad. Your father, for instance. Don't forget he was part of her life just as he is of yours.' After a while she stood up and held Gin in her arms again. 'Now you sure you're going to be alright? I'll ring you in a day or so and we'll have a long chat. 'Fraid I have to go now, darling, I don't like travelling in the dark.' Attie kissed her and squeezed her arm. 'Remember, Gin, you've still got family. I'll be thinking of you. Your grief will take its course. When you feel strong enough, come down and pay me a visit, won't you? Bring young Theo and stay for a long weekend.'

When Gin went back to the sitting room, Noel was stretched out in the velvet rocker. He looked old, at least twenty years older than before. His eyes drooped, almost rheumy with confusion. Theo had just refilled Noel's tumbler with whisky, which he held precariously tilted on the arm of the chair. It looked like he was about to slop whisky all over the antimacassar. Any moment Gin expected to hear the *tick-tick-ticking* of her mother's footsteps down the hallway as she came to reprimand him. Suddenly he rallied, pushed himself up onto his feet, pumping hands as people made their parting.

After Theo had gone, the Puddys were the last to leave.

'Why?' Noel's shoulders slackened, his face suddenly frozen with the gravity of his loss. 'I still keep asking myself why, Frank? What have I done to deserve this? My little daughter gone and now my darling wife ... as if one loss isn't enough without another.' He wiped the drip that was hanging off his nose.

'You must think of the good times, Noel,' offered Norma Puddy, reaching up to kiss his cheek.

He sniffed.

'I adored her, you know ... from the moment I first set eyes on her on that tennis court.' He swelled out his chest like an old dove looking for its mate. 'So young and so beautiful,' he murmured. His eyes lightened, grasping at the past. Pouches unfolded on his face, and white sun-spotted lips cracked into a funny kind of smile.

'Well, I'll be off now, old boy, cheerio,' said Frank Puddy, clapping his hand on Noel's shoulder. 'Go and get yourself a good night's sleep. Might pop in and see how you are later on tomorrow. Don't forget lass, Norma said there's always a spare bed in the sleep-out any time you like.'

When everyone had left, and after Noel had finally padded off to the spare room, Gin had remained in the half-light listening to the silence. She felt drained, not even enough energy to turn on the lights. Everything was perfectly still apart from the ticking of the clock. Through the hush and the veil of shadows encroaching on the room, she could see a little red glow flickering. It looked like a cigarette, that ubiquitous cigarette that she kept seeing, and, suddenly, she felt the whole of her mother's presence emerge from that glow. Could see it and hear it so clearly, like a snippet replay from a film. The flick of a lighter, lips sucking on a draw and the little red glow burning through the darkness of the night.

*

A few weeks after the funeral, Noel asked Gin if she'd mind going through Valerie's things while he was out.

'Might break me up again. Anyway, women's things are best left with women, in my mind.' He offloaded some boxes from out of the garage before he left. 'Keep what you want and we'll box the rest for charity. By the way, lass, Norma Puddy's offered to come over later and take it off to the Red Cross.' He wasn't a rich man by any stretch of the imagination, but he'd always made damned sure that a wife of his would never go without. He could only hope now that the clothes would go to someone who'd appreciate a bit of style and knew quality when they saw it.

As soon as Noel had left, Gin rang Theo.

'Noel's gone out and left me to it. I can't face it. I know it has to be done, Theo, but I don't think I can ...' She broke down.

'Don't cry, Gin,' he said. 'I'll be over in a tick.'

As soon as she opened the door, Theo wrapped his arms around her. Gently he caressed her hands, the tips of his fingers lingering around her wrist. Cradling her in his arms, he took her to her bedroom and lifted her onto the bed. Backwards and forwards he rocked her, stroking her hair, soothing her, fingers tracing the delicate hollows in her shoulder blades. One by one he kissed away the tears. Covering her mouth with his, he swallowed her sobs and moans, again and again, until they finally subsided. Slowly he began pushing up her angora jumper, sliding its silkiness over her breasts, over her face. Side by side, they lay under the eiderdown. She could feel the entire length of his bare body, the comfort of its closeness, pressing against hers.

'It's OK,' he said. 'It's OK.' The warm hush of his breath, words whispered in her ear as he began moving little by little.

'Don't worry, Ginny, everything's going to be alright.' Exhaustion had overtaken her. Gradually her feverish body began to succumb to the tender rhythm inside her. She was barely reciprocating, barely participating, then ... suddenly she gasped and sank her head into his shoulder.

She had never intended it to be like this, something so quick and transitory. To happen at such a time seemed thoughtless, almost disrespectful to the memory of her mother. But as she lay in Theo's arms, the warmth flooding her body came as consolation; she was grateful for the huge sense of release that it brought.

For a time, they lay silently together. Then Theo looked at his watch.

'Shit,' he said. 'Been here over an hour. Gotta go.'

'Theo?' She held his arm.

'What?'

'Please stay,' she pleaded, stroking the curving outline of his chest. Theo slowly extracted himself from her arms and sat up.

'Sorry Ginny,' he said as he reached for his jeans. 'You'll think I'm a lousy so-and-so but I'm afraid I can't. Got an early exam tomorrow and I haven't even started yet.' He hugged her again, gently patting her on the back. 'You'll be OK. I know you will.'

Lousy so-and-so. She swallowed hard. Wiping away the fresh tears, she watched his lanky figure retreating down the footpath. Then she closed the door, dwelling in the silence over what had taken place. Funny to think that it had finally happened here rather than in the safe seclusion of Theo's flat; her bedroom had always been forbidden territory to Theo in the past. But what if Noel had come home and found them?

He'd told her he was going to see a real estate chappie about putting an offer in on the Como property. It was the up-and-coming place to be over there and a damned good deal, according to Frank Puddy. Brand new two-bed-roomed duplex, not far from the river when he wanted to fish, or he could simply hop over and do nine holes whenever it caught his fancy. Corsers were just putting the final touches to them. Good outfit they were. Far as Frank could see, he couldn't possibly go wrong.

Noel had said she'd have to make up her mind what she wanted to do when the time came to move, but he supposed there'd be enough room for the two of them until she'd finished her studies.

And what should she do? She would talk about it with Attie. Her aunt had been ringing her constantly since the funeral. *Call me if you need me, Gin darling. I'm here, don't forget.*

Time seemed to stop for a while as she considered her options. Then suddenly she noticed the silence disappearing. A variety of birds tweeted in the rustling leaves. Next door's dog barked once or twice. A few doors down she could hear squealing children, the occasional slap of a cricket ball. If she listened very carefully she could hear even smaller sounds, like the delicate cheep of a silver-eye, doves murmuring from the shadows of the mulberry tree down the back. The distant sound of a neighbour's piano, pounding out *Marche Militaire*.

Gin went into her mother's bedroom and turned on the light. It was strange how Noel hadn't slept in here since the funeral, preferring the spare room instead. She pulled up the venetians. Pink hibiscus greeted her. A fine dusting of pollen from a long crimson stamen brushed against the glass. Winter sun shone bleakly through the pane.

She gathered herself together. Nobody could help her do what she had to do. There was no other option than to do it by herself.

Beyond the faint trace of cigarette smoke, Gin could smell *Joy*, the lingering fragrance of duty free scent. Gin continued emptying out Valerie's underwear drawer. *Foundation garments*, her mother used to call them. *Always buy the best you can afford, Virginia. People can always tell. You never know when a girl ...*

Then Gin placed the folded garments one by one into cardboard boxes, which she stacked inside the sleep-out. Seeing the boxed clothes assembled together went some way to restoring her sense of order but it didn't erase the question of how her mother died. The recent findings of the coronial enquiry had declared Valerie's a 'death by misadventure'. There was no evidence, it said, to suggest she had been pushed or been the victim of foul play of any kind. Her handbag and the contents had all been found intact nearby, so it appeared she had either fallen accidentally or simply jumped into the water from the jetty.

*

It was only by a stroke of luck that Gin found the documents. Having cleared out all of the drawers from the cedar chest, she noticed a piece of yellow paper poking out below. Lifting out the drawer she could see a kind of secret panel hidden underneath. Inside was a wad of papers. Gin opened the bulldog clip. Letters, documents, postcards and sepia photographs in a water-stained manila envelope spilled onto the bed.

Seven grinning men in air force uniform were arranged in front of an aeroplane. Four behind and three squatting in front. A circle was drawn around one member who, she supposed, would be her father. Scrawled on the back was *Wickerton RAF Station,*

Christmas Day 1944. Gin looked at the other papers.

STATION COMMANDER'S CHRISTMAS MESSAGE

Group Captain H. M. Dudfield and the Officers of Wickerton Station wish all ranks a Happy Christmas and a Prosperous New Year. Our thanks go to those who have done so much to keep the Station running smoothly, efficiently and happily in 1944. If the same spirit prevails in 1945 and if all pull their weight and fulfil, with loyalty and devotion, and without regard to personal interests, the duty required of them, we need have no fear for the eventual outcome of the war and may be assured that the advent of a Christmas of real peace and good-will will not be long delayed.

Christmas Dinner Menu

OX TAIL SOUP

ROAST TURKEY

ROAST PORK

FORCEMEAT BALLS

APPLE SAUCE

ROAST & CREAMED POTATOES

BRUSSELS SPROUTS

CHRISTMAS PUDDING

RUM SAUCE

MINCE PIES, APPLES

BEER & MINERAL WATER

CIGARETTES

KRIEGSGEFANGENENLAGER
POSTKARTE

April 10th, 1945

Dear Bob,

One never knows where one will finish up, does one? I had hoped to be home by now but got called out for one last run. The other six came off second best. Lucky for me I came down with only a slight injury to my knee. The camp is not too bad. Bags of opportunity for sport etc. Jack Williams, whom you may remember, is here also. Drop a line home to my darling wife, would you please, and let her know what's what, otherwise I fear Kodak will leave her in the dark. Ask all the boys to write as well when you get a chance. Best of luck to yourself and crew. Keep smiling, Jasper.

KRIEGSGEFANGENENLAGER
POSTKARTE

April 25ᵗʰ, 1945

Dear Bob,

*Still plodding along and not doing too badly. Presume
you are the same although I haven't had your letter
in reply. It's not too bad here but as you can imagine
I won't be sorry to leave. I'm hoping to be in England
before too long. Well, look after yourself old chap. We'll
have a few beers when we get together again.*

Cheerio, Jasper.

The postcards had been addressed to Flight Sergeant Bob Anderson, RAAF Base, P.O. Kodak House, 63 Kingsway, London, then redirected to the RAF Station in Wickerton, Lincolnshire.

Gin sat down, suddenly aware of how hard and fast her heart was beating. There had never been any suggestion that her father had been a POW. Why hadn't her mother told her?

She opened a folded letter, carefully smoothing out the creases.

'The Grange'
Denham Village
Buckinghamshire,
England, U.K.
May 8th 1964

Dear Mrs Partridge,

I am a collector of Air Force memorabilia and am writing to you regarding the enclosed postcards which have come into my possession through the daughter of an ex-crew member of my old RAF squadron from the war. As you can see, the postcards were written by your husband Jasper as a POW in Germany and addressed to a friend of his, Bob Anderson, who was killed in action shortly before the cards arrived. They were subsequently passed on to Bob's family after his death, along with the rest of his possessions, and it was not until his daughter contacted me that I was aware of your husband's fate. As far as our squadron knew, Jasper was lost in action, presumed killed along with the rest of his crew when their Lancaster was shot down over occupied territory in April 1945. No doubt this was the same information you were given and today remains official Air Force record.

As far as I can see, these papers cast a totally different light on the matter and, bearing in mind the chaos that ensued in the last weeks of the war, it would appear that German authorities were remiss in not passing on details to the Allies of Jasper's survival and subsequent imprisonment. I knew the Jack Williams mentioned in Jasper's card and that he eventually arrived home safely after the war. With your permission I will try to contact him and the War Office and piece together more details about what happened to Jasper when the camp disbanded. I am aware that this news may disturb you and will not be eased by the passage of time. Should you wish me to proceed, my enquiries will be undertaken with the greatest respect.

I knew your husband well. Jasper was a fine man, a brave and brilliant pilot who was highly regarded by his crew and all those at the station. Shortly before he left on his last sortie he explained over a few drinks how he had been given his release. Being Jasper he was not content to wait and be repatriated by ship like the rest of his compatriots. Ever innovative and

an opportunist, he was, by some obscure and tenuous
arrangement and a stroke of good luck, trying to
obtain a lift home on the mail run through to Ceylon
and from there on to Perth by Catalina.

It has been a long and difficult time tracking you
down, Mrs Partridge, as you will appreciate, but I
hope my efforts may be of some value to you and
other members of the Partridge family. Please let me
know what you would like me to do. In the meantime,
I remain

Yours sincerely,
George Harrington (ex Fl. Officer) RAF

A POW? Gin couldn't believe it. Did that mean there was a faint chance her father was still alive? Pain began to grip inside her chest. After all these years, the prospect was almost too incredible to consider. She examined the wedding photographs, small black and white snaps taken spontaneously, probably by an amateur photographer friend. It was the first time she'd seen a picture of her mother and father together. It seemed strange, almost sacrilegious, looking at them standing arm-in-arm like that while not far away, on the new teak radiogram, were professional photos, taken thirteen years later, a colour bridal portrait of Valerie and Noel overlooking the river.

Gin felt guilty, a strange sense of betrayal, looking at the photos, secretly wondering if her mother had really loved her father. She turned the photo over ... *Valerie and Jasper married 12th January 1944*, she read, and started counting on her fingers.

It was a shocking thing to think, her mother barely into ashes. Hidden among the photos were two English aerogrammes from her father dated 1945. Carefully opening the fragile folds, she read and re-read words of love written to a war bride, not much older than herself.

> ... *My darling, it's a pity there's not more a chap*
> *can say on paper. Seems a wealth of material is lost*
> *with the limitations they place on the written word.*
> *Makes you think there's nothing left to write home*
> *about sometimes. But the one thing I can say, my*
> *darling girl, is that I love you more than you can*
> *imagine and can't wait to be back in your arms.*
>
> *Yours for ever,*
> *Jasper*

Reading the words again and again reassured her that her father had loved her mother. They made Theo's vague passing references to love and marriage look shallow. A poor nineteen-year-old student, what could he be thinking? Only the previous night there'd been various overtures, half-joking perhaps, half-serious, it was hard to tell.

'What am I going to do, Theo?' she'd wailed. 'Mountjoy Road is up for sale. I can't go on living with Noel.'

Theo had put his arms around her, hugged her, and lifted her off the ground. 'Then come and live with me, my sweet,' he'd said.

'You don't have to stay at the same address as that old toad. No way. I'll look after you.'

'Noel's not that bad, Theo. You know, some days, I almost feel sorry for him.'

'I mean it, Ginny,' he'd said, ignoring what she'd said. 'We could live together. Not here, necessarily,' he'd added hurriedly, 'that wasn't my intention, but we could find some other place.' He'd paused, grinning, as his finger traced the outline of her nose. 'We could even get married if you like? Only we'd have to put it off until after I get back from Mukinbudin.'

Gin smiled at the thought. She loved the things Theo did: his fingers sliding around the secret places on her body which previously she didn't know existed. There were other things she loved, his laugh, for instance, and the unexpected little presents that made her laugh in turn: a bunch of yellow-petalled sourgrass he'd spontaneously picked from the edge of the oval, a crumpled bag of liquorice, funny little rhymes he'd concocted on scraps of paper, his interest and concern. She loved the way he removed his glasses and said, *Can't see a bloody thing now but let me guess where I am kissing*, the sudden feel of his tongue hot and hurried, smothering every giggle and in her ears and all over her neck ... and *Gee I love you Gin.* That had been the extent of it. But now, things were different. Just thinking about their lovemaking sent ripples through her body. Was this what love meant?

Things were hotting up in South-East Asia; who knew what the future held?

'What about conscription?' she'd been quick to reply. Originally he'd told her it wouldn't apply to him because of his immigrant background. *Besides,* he'd added, *Australia's no longer my parents' normal place of residence.*

Until he'd read otherwise. Behind his glasses, his eyes had looked almost black with worry and uncertainty.

'Shit, Gin … shit shit shit! Think I'm stuffed. Just found out from the fine print that because I was sixteen and living in Australia at the time of my parent's naturalisation, I am in fact liable for call-up after all. Shit! What am I going to do?'

Sometimes, between lectures, the two of them had sat reading in the iron seat under the towering branches of what was known as the *Honeymoon Tree* in the Great Court. Amid passing footsteps and the rustle of leaves, she had heard nearby pampas grass whispering in the afternoon breeze. As a young child she had often played with the large clump which grew at the front of the old Swanbourne house. Once she had plucked a tall blond stalk and, pretending it was a hobby horse, hurtled around and around the lawn, calling out *look Mummy, look Mummy, I'm riding a pony.* Dismayed by the rapid disintegration of the feathery seeds, she had looked up to see a man standing with one arm around her mother, the other holding a pipe. *Making a mess so far as I can see, young lady.* It was probably her first recollection of Noel. She thought of the resulting wedding, remembering the horrible awkwardness of it all, and how embarrassed she'd felt as Noel and Valerie had slipped away on their honeymoon. Just over seven years ago. Her mother had been thirty-three years old, quite old for a bride.

Love and marriage were the privileges of youth, she had always thought. A couple of girls from school had already got married. You could tell Barbara Featherby's was a shotgun because she'd put on so much weight. The other, Coralie Simpson, the prettiest girl in their year, wanting in her usual competitive way to be the first, had got in early and recently married. Only the other day, Gin had bumped into her in the city and Coralie had been quick to explain that marriage was something she'd dreamed of since she was a little girl.

'Anyway, one thing's for certain,' she'd announced proudly, 'Ian won't have to do national service now we're married.' Her new husband didn't believe in married women working. 'Doesn't mean it has to be boring,' said Coralie, catching Gin's puzzled look, 'married life, that is.' She told her how she proposed wearing pink satin ballet pumps to do her housework in. She'd make a go of it, she said, floating around doing arabesques as she vaccied through their flat.

Others girls she knew had been steadily stowing away bits and pieces in their glory boxes in preparation. The thought of acquiring a glory box had never entered Gin's head, let alone marriage. Yet overnight she had inherited all of her mother's trappings. What should she do with them all?

Valerie kept gazing back at her from the silver-framed wedding photograph. It had been a proper affair; her mother not the slip of a war bride she'd been at her first wedding, that was for certain. Looking back again at the war wedding in the creased photo she was holding, Gin challenged herself to envisage for a few brief seconds the isolation, the separation and suffering of being married to a serviceman. How would she feel if Theo were called up and sent away to war? Menzies had promised that conscripted youths would only serve outside Australia voluntarily, but everyone knew that promises were made to be broken.

Quickly she slipped the photo into her wallet and then packed the rest of the papers away in the manila envelope. All this dusty information; it was history. In some ways she wanted to bundle it all up and throw it in the bin. How could it possibly change anything in her life? It wouldn't bring back Dottie. It wouldn't bring back her mother. It wouldn't take away all of those shocking memories.

She would discuss it with Attie in due course. Gin snapped the bulldog clip back on the wad of papers. For the time being, she would store the papers, along with whatever else of Valerie's she wanted to keep in the old tea-chest which Noel had brought inside. And talking of history, what had been its history, she wondered, suddenly noticing black stencilled letters on the plywood advertising the:

𝔉inest 𝔠eplon 𝔗ea since 1885
by appointment to 𝔥is 𝔐ajesty 𝔎ing 𝔊eorge 𝔙1.

Glory box indeed!

Chapter 20

The campus was too close, being almost part of the foreshore where Valerie had been found. Gin began avoiding the place, missing lectures and floundering around with unfinished assignments. Finally she withdrew from her end-of-year examinations.

The Christmas holidays, when they came, were like a kind of catalyst that began to release her from the past. Noel went over to the Puddys in the evenings. Theo was away working in the Wheatbelt. It was more a time of separation than celebratory gatherings. Then the Mountjoy Road house was sold and Noel moved into his Como duplex.

'Consider it yours, lass,' he said, referring glumly to Valerie's red Mini, 'but now you'd better try and find yourself a job.'

Attie, as usual, tried to be encouraging when Gin rang.

'Something will turn up.' She told Gin she had to come up to Perth for a medical appointment and arranged to meet her in town the day after New Year's Day.

They sat in the coffee shop face to face.

'Ever thought of being a primary school teacher,' Attie suggested, over the top of her cup of coffee. 'Don't know what it involves these days to get into teacher training.'

Gin looked away, feeling the sudden slump of her shoulders.

She had hoped to mention the letters about her father, but the weight of decisions was mounting and now her head was buzzing.

'I got in alright, you know,' Attie nodded brightly, 'and a jolly good teacher I was at that,' she said, taking another bite of her toasted sandwich.

Gin tried to summon a smile. Teaching was the last thing she pictured herself doing, having to stand out the front of a class, being the centre of attention, or inattention, as the case might be.

'I'm sure you were, Attie, but, no thanks, teaching's not for me. Anyway, too late,' she said, 'now we're into the new year.'

In the end, Gin reluctantly applied for a clerical position she'd seen advertised at the State Library. She was surprised when she was instantly accepted. By February she'd found board and lodging at a house in Subiaco. It was most convenient. From Hamersley Road she could easily take the Mini to work or catch a bus along Kings Park Road into St Georges Terrace. It was only a five-minute walk up Barrack Street past the Town Hall and over the railway line into Francis Street.

*

Gin's new accommodation, the front room of an old Federation house, featured a bay window that caught the morning sun. Often on weekends she curled up reading on the cushioned window-seat with the resident ginger cat, Christopher Robin, purring beside her. Everything was very comfy. The tea-chest she'd brought with her from Mountjoy Road sat in a corner shrouded in one of her mother's embroidered cloths. Mrs Maxwell, her landlady, provided adequate meals. The only drawback was her vegetarian Pekinese snuffling around her feet. But, it was easy enough, Gin found, to mind her own business, keep out of the way. She was earning money; she had a car and her independence.

When Theo lobbed up on the doorstep, having just arrived back in Perth from the Wheatbelt, she was somewhat distracted.

'I was just about to go back to the archives,' she explained. 'I want to do a bit of research.'

Theo was not to be put off. 'I've missed you, Gin,' he said, lifting her off the ground. 'How about going for a drive?' he said. 'It's a nice enough night. No food in the flat and I'm absolutely starving. Fancy a hamburger?'

After they'd eaten at Bernies, Theo took the short cut from Mounts Bay Road around the side of Bishops House along Mill Street, up and into the top end of St Georges Terrace. Facing them was the barracks with all its colonial grandeur, Norman turrets and Gothic arch.

'Can't believe they're going to bulldoze that just to make a freeway,' she said. 'No wonder everybody's up in arms. It's a crime. Such a beautiful old building, especially at night. You can build a freeway anywhere but you can't replace that sort of architecture. They want to take away our history, Theo, flatten it as if it never existed.'

'But what's the point of leaving the arch? How stupid's that going to look?' he said. 'What are the barracks used for, anyway?'

'There're over a hundred rooms which were originally used to house retired soldiers.' She knew this because, only yesterday, the Library had been inundated with the 'Save the Barracks' group and she was helping them with research.

But in a flash the barracks was behind them. Forgotten. They were climbing the hill and had turned into the wide avenue that led past the memorial.

'Bastard!'

'I think he's trying to tell you to dip your lights, Theo.'

'Well that's a bit hard isn't it, when there's only one bloody well working,' he said, leaning forward and peering through his glasses. 'I can't see a damn thing out there unless I've got them on high. I'll have to ask old man Davis if I can have a look at the wiring tomorrow.'

He pulled the Hillman over onto the gravel and drove into the parking area.

'Good a spot as any.' He switched off the lights and the engine, and stretched out his legs. 'There now, what more could you ask for?' he said, reaching over and putting his arm around her. They sat there in the silence taking in the view from Mount Eliza.

It was a balmy night. The water was black and smooth, opening out before them like an enormous puddle of ink. Navigation lights winked green and red around the bay. From the Narrows, the long line of freeway lights hung luminous as fireflies as far south as you could see. Matchbox cars whizzed and weaved along the lanes. Leaning forward Gin could see Canning Bridge, and the Raffles' flashing neon lights angled through the darkness. Everything was still. Just the hum of the traffic below and a boat putting around somewhere down near the Narrows. Above the skyline was a wedge of moon and plenty of stars.

'What do you reckon John Glenn must have thought from right up there in his spaceship?'

'Mind-boggled, I'd think.'

She remembered how the whole of Perth had been alight with porch lights and taxi drivers kept flicking their headlights on and off all night long. She had wanted to put a sheet on the lawn to reflect the light like her friends, but Valerie wouldn't let her. All those phobias her mother had about lights, especially UFOs.

Theo was quiet for a moment.

The 'City of Light' was what the astronauts had called Perth. Quite a label considering Paris was also known as the City of Light, being the centre of the Enlightenment. Yet Gin also knew of another place, a hillside town at the base of the highest mountain in Ceylon, sometimes known as 'Little England'. She couldn't remember its proper name but literally translated it meant City of Light.

Gin had always loved Attie's stories of Ceylon. The thought of other far-off exotic places excited her. She could quite easily see herself in Paris, walking along the Seine, black stockings and moccasins, a red beret perhaps, strolling around the Louvre and the Tuileries.

'Did you know that Perth is the most remote city in the world?' said Theo suddenly. 'We're really on our own, aren't we? So isolated. Sitting ducks, so to speak.'

The windscreen started fogging. Theo took off his glasses and wound down the window a little to break the condensate. On a still night up in the Park it was possible to smell the hops from the brewery below but tonight the smell of lemon-scented gums drifted sweetly through the window instead.

Theo leant over and took hold of her other hand. He was looking at her through the darkness. She couldn't see him properly but she could feel his warm breath on her face.

'Been doing a bit of thinking while I've been away. Fact is, Ginny, I really want to marry you,' he said in a rush. He was breathing fast, almost panting. This time, she could tell he wasn't joking. 'Well?'

'I just ... don't know what to say Theo ... it's sort of ...'

'Come on. Say something, Gin, for God's sake. I just want to know.'

'I'm sorry, Theo. I'll have to think about it.'

'And how long's that going to take?'

'Well, I'm not sure.'

'What aren't you sure about?'

'Just not sure, that's all.'

He started the motor. 'Fair enough,' he said.

*

One of the first things Theo wanted to do when he returned from Mukinbudin was take a walk along the river.

'I've missed that old blue snake,' he said on the phone. 'You get fed up with looking at miles and miles of flat treeless plains for weeks on end, nothing around but the colour of wheat. Sacrilege to live so close to the river and not make use of it.'

'No, Theo. Please,' she protested, 'Not today. I've things to do. Washing, ironing, changing my sheets, that sort of thing.'

'Nothing that can't wait,' he said. 'You're avoiding the place, Gin. What's more, you're avoiding me. You'll feel better when you've faced up to it all. Better that than pretend it never happened. Come on,' he said, trying to jolly her along, 'it'll do you good. We'll take the dog for a walk, won't we, Barker?' She heard a *woof* through the receiver. 'Hear that? Gee, you should see the look on his face, Gin. He understood exactly what I said.'

When they arrived, the sun was sparkling, water stretched

out blue against Matilda Bay. What was there to be afraid of? she kept asking herself. Just walking the dog by the river on a nice summer's day. She even tried to think of it from Barker's perspective, as Theo had suggested.

Everything was fine until the jetty began to wobble underneath them. Its warped, sun-bleached planks creaked against their weight. Behind them, Barker followed leisurely. Aloft in the breeze his wet nose dribbled with pleasure as river smells wafted around them thick and briny.

'Looks like no one's been in here for yonks,' said Theo. The jetty rocked as he yanked open the boathouse door. 'Careful,' he said, holding out his arm in front of her. 'Jesus, look at that. The decking's all rotten. I just can't imagine ...' his voice drifted away with the wind.

Gin knew exactly what Theo was thinking. What would have induced her mother to walk along the boathouse jetty dressed up to the nines? Through moving gaps, Gin watched the water swirl and slop against the barnacled pylons. Looking down made her dizzy, almost seasick. Suddenly, a jellyfish shunted forward through yellow streaks of weed. Barker followed it with eyes of suspicion.

Gin stood there mesmerised. Across the river she could hear the constant humming of boats, the sound of their wakes lapping against the shore. She didn't want to speculate—what purpose would it serve? It made no sense, but perhaps her mother had come here in the delusion of catching a boat back to England, or some sort of meeting up with Jasper. Gin thought of the letters she had found, half-trying to entertain again the possibility that her father might still be, somewhere, out there, alive. Conflicting thoughts tugged inside her; it was heartening to contemplate on the one hand but upsetting on the other, for whichever way she looked at it, mulling over her father's fate always resulted in bringing back memories of her mother's.

Barker pulled on his leash. Quickly they retreated along the jetty, the dog one step ahead, toenails clicking across splatters of seagull shit.

'Well, that's satisfied my curiosity in a hurry,' said Theo catching them up. 'If a dog senses it's unsafe, then who am I to argue?'

Out across the bay, remnants of a wake rippled towards them, fragmenting the water into a silver craze. As they reached the shore, the waves licked their feet, filling their footprints behind them.

'You OK?' Theo squeezed her hand.

'I'm OK.'

'Sure? Just checking. You're doing well.'

Neither of them had said anything for some time. Barker trotted on in hunting-dog style, nose to the ground, yet oblivious to the ducks waddling around in the shallows. They too looked unfazed. Bills continued to smile, shovelling through the slush in search of worms. Up ahead, near the yacht club, rows of boats were nodding up and down on their moorings. Jingling halyards clinked against their masts. A lone sailor stood astern, one hand on the tiller and the other taking up the slack on the mainsail, as his yacht slipped noiselessly out of its pen.

As they turned the point, Gin could feel the full force of the early sea breeze. Nearby, a dredge was restoring sand upon the shore, its engine droning from deep within its bowels. Every now and then it raised a bucket on a rope.

They continued following the path past the beer garden at Steve's and around the foreshore. As they came towards the Flying Squadron, Gin found herself thinking of Noel and how he was managing on his own. He had his clubs, she thought. He had his networks. This very instant, he was probably enjoying the lunchtime session perched on a stool in the bar.

Suddenly Barker broke free from the leash. He dashed straight towards the dank rows of seaweed on the shore. He nosed for a few moments in the wash, torso rigid, trawling in the putrid slime and debris, before disappearing off into the reeds. Only the tip of his tail was visible, like a little white flag waving above the salt-crusted reeds. Suddenly the dog emerged in a trot, teeth bared, with something either side of his grin.

'Barker! Barker! Come here!'

Theo let go of her hand and sprinted off.

'Quick, Theo,' she yelled. 'Catch him. I think he's got a dead blowie. They're poisonous.'

'Bark-er! BARKER! Drop!'

Now they were both running after the dog. Barker increased his speed, keeping just far enough in front of them to avoid their grasp. Breaking into a slow canter, he tossed the bloated fish into the air. A flash of white spun like quicksilver and plopped into the sand. Barker pounced in front of the fish, crouched, grinning saliva over it. Suddenly he snatched it back and dashed off. When he thought he was far enough away he dropped it again and with a sideways smirk rolled over and started rubbing his back into the stink.

Theo sprinted harder. Just as he reached Barker, the dog sprang to his feet making a grab at the fish. Theo lurched at him. Barker dodged. Theo tried again, missed, and then finally seized his collar.

'Drop! No!' he said sternly, trying to eyeball the dog, who was leering fixatedly at the foul spiky puffball lying at his feet. Barker panted. The wind whipped a lather of dribble as his tongue spilled pink out of his liquorice-coloured gums.

Heads or tails, silver scales. These words erupted inside Gin's head as she saw the fish in slow motion spinning through the air. *Heads or tails, silver scales.* There was a rhythm, a certain romance in their ring. When people talked about luck, they only talked about good luck, the luck of the Irish, so to speak. They never talked about bad luck and how much bad luck one person could have.

By now Barker was almost under control, minus his catch, but his eyes were bright and keen, his ears still erect. 'C'mon you mutt!' He pulled the leash, but the dog leaned backwards, stiff-legged in resistance.

They jostled in a battle of the wills. Once Theo had overpowered him, Barker acquiesced for a second or two, and then overtook, tugging forward on his leash to go home. Head to the ground, he knew the way. They followed him from the base of the limestone cliffs, winding their way up the sand track through wild figs, bamboos, banksias and paperbark trees.

At the top of the escarpment, Gin paused for a few seconds to catch her breath. Already there were a few little fishing boats out on the water. Here in the car park, the breeze was much fresher, dissipating the river smells.

Gin pointed. 'Look how fast it's going.' By now the yacht was scooting along at a good rate of knots. Angled hard against the rippling water, it carved a line neatly across the curve of the bay towards them. Suddenly it turned to go about. Its white triangle slackened as the sailor bobbed around the swinging boom in tack. The sail flapped and floundered for a few seconds, and then plumped out with a resounding slap.

She looked at her watch. It was nearly midday.

'Let's go back, Theo,' she said, feeling the dull sadness return. 'I've had enough.'

They took the shortest way back to Theo's down Broadway and across the Highway. As Theo opened the front gate, curtains parted in the window. Gin could see Mr Davis's nose pressed against the pane. Theo waved as they filed past. He threw Gin the leash and unspiralled the garden hose from under the frangipani. Thumb pressed hard over the end, he directed the spray at close range to Barker, gripped firmly between his calves. 'Get rid of that smile off your face,' he said frowning down at him. 'You're in disgrace.' Theo pulled open the door of the granny flat.

'I won't be two secs,' said Gin. 'I'm just going to duck under the shower and have a quick douse if you don't mind.' Water gushed down over her face from the rusty shower rose. *Heads or tails, silver scales*, the words came bubbling from nowhere. Gin spat out a mouthful of limey water onto the soap-slimed terrazzo. Where had the words come from? Probably some stupid nursery rhyme, she suspected. She bent down and picked up Theo's soggy towel off the floor to dry herself. But what did they mean? Was it something to do with 'luck'? She thought of Theo. He was always going on about luck. He said some people never stopped bitching about life, but, not him; he'd always considered himself lucky. Lucky that he was born intelligent, lucky that his parents had been fortunate enough to escape being thrown into a Japanese POW camp, lucky that they had made the right decision of whether to stay on the island for that extra hour or to get out while the going was good, and lucky, of course, in migrating from Holland to the lucky country, the land of milk and honey. Oh, and of course lucky that he had a scholarship and was doing engineering and ... then for a second he'd looked at her and, gently lifting her hair behind her ear, said just how much luckier could a fellow be, having a bird as beautiful as she.

She'd flinched at the backhanded compliment. 'Bird' grated on her ear.

But Theo had continued, oblivious.

I'm dead serious, Gin, he said. *To some extent you do have to make your own luck in life. You have to work at it and make informed decisions. Take a risk and make it happen.*

Gin wondered about the luck of the draw, how lucky he would consider himself if he ended up being called up in the ballot, whether he'd still try and argue that mathematical probabilities lay within any kind of personal control. Sooner or later, she thought, he'd know the outcome, one way or the other, and then what would he have to say?

She zipped up her canvas corded pants and stepped into the studio. Theo was sitting in a chair reading a book on planes. Gin tried to picture him in the sort of combat gear she'd seen servicemen wearing on newsreels and in magazines. He'd look handsome, and jungle greens would suit his olive skin, but she knew he wouldn't suit the army. He was too independent; he'd get out of line and be accused of insubordination.

Out of the sink she took two cups. She washed out the tea stains and dried the cups on the cleanest corner of Theo's only tea-towel, making a mental note to boil it up in a saucepan and hang it out on the line before she went home.

'*Heads or tails?*' she said without thinking.

'What?' said Theo in bewilderment.

'Tea or coffee?' She corrected herself.

'Coffee.'

Heads or tails? It came again. There was a compulsion to follow the rhyme with ... *silver scales*, she finished under her breath. *Heads or tails, silver scales.* She couldn't seem to erase the image. It kept returning, that flash of the fish spinning in slow motion, spinning around in her mind.

The flywire door banged. That would be Mr Davis, she guessed, snooping around outside on some pretext. Next thing he'd be perving in through the window at them. Theo leant over and dropped down the bamboo blind.

The only reason Theo puts up with him, thought Gin, is the rent's so damn good.

It was basic. A one-roomed studio. At one end was a kitchenette with a small table that looked out the window onto the Cape lilac tree. Included in the few pieces of furniture were an old chipped low-boy, a radiogram angled in one corner, and Theo's unmade bed—a blond-wood divan with an Indian cotton bedspread half-fallen across the floor. On the southern wall was a makeshift bookcase, its shelves a series of jarrah planks sitting on bricks, full of Theo's textbooks, his uni notes and files, and his beloved record collection. Above the shelves, rising damp had eroded the adjoining wall to the outside toilet and shower recess. The first thing Gin always noticed as she walked into the room was the smell of mildew.

Bacon spat in the frying pan. Theo broke the eggs one by one on the blackened edge of the pan. There were only two burners on the small stove but he liked to cook. He liked the order of it all, the precision of recipes, sharpened knives, and the practicality of kitchen utensils.

'Christ! You could ride to China on that.' He inspected the knife Gin had been using to slice off bacon rind and tested the blade with his thumb. 'Here, I'll sharpen it,' he said brandishing the steel.

As she took the cups over to the table, Gin stumbled on a corner of the rattan square that was sticking up, accidentally spilling coffee into the saucers.

'Leave it, don't worry,' he said. 'C'mon, let's eat, I'm starving.'

'Blast!' said Theo. 'The friggin' stacker has malfunctioned.' He went over to the radiogram and lifted up the arm manually and replaced it on its rest. He restacked the LPs on the spindle. Holding his breath, he pressed the start button.

The Dutch College Swing Band swung into action. They had breakfast in front of the open window. Yellow berries from the Cape lilac tree peppered the lawn where Barker lay stretched out on his side, wet fur fluffy and eyes slatted against the sun. Gin looked down at her plate and pushed it away.

'Don't you want that? You've hardly touched it.' Theo started forking her leftovers onto his plate. The music died. Now the needle was scratching between the tracks.

'I really dig this next one.' Theo picked up his sunglasses and started clicking his fingers and twitching his head with half-closed eyes. 'Just get a load of that lead guitarist,' he said, head craning through the half-opened French doors. He reached out, scraping the toast crusts and the bacon rind out on the lawn for Barker. 'By the way, old Pop's coming in for an inspection later on today. Better make an effort,' he said, turning on the tap and covering the dirty dishes with hot suds. 'And you'd better skedaddle soon, Gin. I know he turns a blind eye but he keeps reminding me that "no dames" is part of the contract.'

After they'd washed up, she made Theo's bed as if it were her own, wondering if that was what she would be prepared to do every day of her life. She could smell his body, his own peculiar testosterone. He was there but he was not there. Just his smell and his body hairs. She flicked them away and turned the sheet back properly, plumped the pillow, and brushed the end of the bedspread where Barker had spent the night. While she was doing that, Theo swept the small square of lino around the kitchenette. He looked to see if she was watching, then surreptitiously lifted up the rattan squares and flicked the sweepings underneath.

Chapter 21

It was Anzac Day and Theo had to take Mr Davis to the Dawn Service—the old man was adamant, said wild horses wouldn't keep him away. Why didn't they meet up afterwards? Theo asked. He told Gin he might have to wait with the old man until he'd marched or arranged a lift to the RSL. Gin didn't mind. She'd said she'd rather acknowledge Anzac Day in her own special way. Take an early morning walk instead. Pay her respects from Matilda Bay.

The boatshed was still in darkness as she parked the car. Already the sun had broken, the new sky raw against the silhouetted hills. Gin watched it rise, little by little, the cloudy darkness bruising around a wound. Gradually before her, out of the mist, emerged the river: calm, silent, mirror-like, and the shallows pink stained with yellow, like flavine.

Gin hugged her arms. It was cool but still, air barely breathing through the fog. Slowly her fear began to dissipate; now she was glad she'd come here on her own. But it was a strange kind of serenity. There was something surreal about it, as if she were part of an Impressionist painting, inconsequential, no more than a faded daub—the faint streak of a mast or the glimpse of a coloured hull.

Suddenly, two black swans toddled from the reeds. Gin held her breath, hoping they wouldn't see her. 'Swan River' was a misnomer. These days it was rare to see a swan. But there they were. Their haughty heads peered around, necks craning into question marks. Then their red bills *bipped* at her as they went past. Their sound was incongruous, almost comical. Ever since she'd arrived, she'd been waiting for the sound of the bugle, hoping that, even from this distance, she might hear its notes.

Then, without warning, it came, so faint, she wondered if she'd imagined it. Gin cocked her ear. Listen! There it was again. A haunting cry across the bay. Why did it sound so mournful? It was only a few broken chords hanging off a C. As the *Last Post* echoed through the mist, Gin saw the lonely intervals clearly in her head and her fingers replayed the notes against her thigh. Of the thousands of men who had given their lives to save their country, it was her father she always tried to picture whenever she heard its call. The thought that he might still be alive was worth considering. But, if he were, why hadn't he returned to his family? Amnesia? Surely it was time she wrote to ex-Flight Officer Harrington and sorted the matter out. But even if she were lucky enough to find her father, would he know who he was, who she was? What would he think of her? Would he be proud of her? After all, what had she achieved in her short life? An aborted musical career? An unfinished Arts degree?

Behind her lay the campus, silent, deserted. Across the highway cosseted in the pokey rooms of St Georges College were sleeping students, lucky rich kids as Theo called them, curled up in their beds. Distinctly British and castle-like, the college looked down on the rest of the campus from landscaped gardens, its red brick turrets towering above the turning plane trees and the tops of the Norfolk pines.

When she spotted Theo he was further up the foreshore, half-hidden by a Moreton Bay fig. He was taking a photo of the bay, squatting between the ancient phalangeal-like roots that spanned the dewy grass. He stood up as she arrived. After they'd hugged, he lifted a cardboard carton out of the boot of the Hillman and placed it on the bench.

'Abracadabra,' he said. 'And what have we here?' He lifted the cardboard flaps, then began unpacking the picnic breakfast he'd brought. Bread, Edam cheese, slices of mortadella, ginger biscuits and two scaly oranges, a thermos of milky coffee. Dutch style, he said, like his mother used to make.

Suddenly Gin felt hungry. The coffee was warming. They munched silently on bread and cheese. Any minute, she thought, he's going to bring up the subject of marriage again and make an ultimatum. But he didn't mention it, didn't appear in the least worried, by the look of his half-closed eyes. Before she knew it, the mist had lifted. Light cloud still hovered but the river shone like a sheet of metal.

'Did you know there was an American base here during the war?' Theo gazed at her dreamily. 'Just imagine it, Gin. Flying boats and Yanks everywhere, the constant roar of engines taking off and landing on the river, all that noise and smell of activity. Must have been exciting.'

Gin had never heard of the Crawley base, but she remembered Valerie and Norma Puddy prattling on about American servicemen on a number of occasions. It appeared their crew-cuts and accents and smart-looking uniforms were a bit of a novelty.

'Apparently Aussie women really fell for the Yanks,' she said. 'Thought all their dreams had come at once, according to my mother. Don't think they were very well appreciated by the wider community. I know Noel had no time for them.'

'Old Davis remembers the Yanks,' said Theo. 'He said it upset the Diggers that they took away their women by plying them with booze and expensive presents. There were always fights breaking out. But it must have been one hell of a big base, Gin. About two hundred American personnel alone. Apparently they annexed some of the university facilities, set up a sick bay there, he said, mess hall and galley, offices; rented surrounding houses; took over Nedlands so to speak.' Theo paused and gave a chuckle. 'Sometimes all hell'd break loose according to Mr Davis. They'd meet their women off the trolley buses and start canoodling on the grounds. University authorities had to put a stop to it in case students got the wrong idea!'

What Theo was really interested in were the flying boats on the river. After hours and hours as a kid playing around glue, balsa-wood and benzene, creating models, he was an authority on planes. Even still had his battered tin collection his dad had bought him. Strange how planes were one of the few things they'd had in common.

'Guess there's always been a bit of tension,' he said, 'far back as I can remember. Poor sod was away for the first two years of my life, back thrashing it out with the nationalists in Indonesia. How'd you be, having already fought one war, to have to start all over again? Apparently I wouldn't have a bar of the old man when he got back. Suspect the feeling was mutual. Trouble was, neither of us liked competing for Mum's attentions.' Theo grimaced as he stuck his thumb in an orange and began peeling it. 'The one time we weren't fighting was when we were by ourselves out in the back shed talking about the war. Funny that!' he laughed. 'Ever been up in a plane, Gin?'

'No,' she said. 'Scary thought.'

'It's absolutely exhilarating, I can tell you. Guess I've been hooked on planes ever since Dad took me up in a German Klemm when I was a kid. Perth's very first flying boat. Believe it belonged to a fellow called Harry Baker. Back in the twenties he used to give joy-rides from here to Mandurah and Rottnest and roundabout.'

Theo bent over, slurping on his orange.

'But the Catalina they had here during the war was special,' he said, wiping his mouth. 'Ugly duckling in appearance, sort of cumbersome, but, gee, what an amazing piece of machinery.' He said his father had flown them in the Marine *Luchtvaartdienst*. Most of the Dutch planes got blitzed by the Japs but some survived. They fled to wherever they could—Australia, Ceylon—regrouping into Allied squadrons.

*

As soon as she got back to her room, Gin whipped aside Valerie's lace cloth and began delving in the tea-chest for the documents and letters she'd bundled together. She unclipped the bulldog clip, searching amongst the war documents for anything relating to her father. Besides the letter from George Harrington and her father's postcards as a POW, she found the letters he'd written to her mother in 1945. Ah! Here was the part she'd been looking for

*... with a bit of string-pulling I'll try to get home
the quickest way I can. Kangaroo-hopping if you get
the gist of it. Then it might be a case of waiting for
a black cat. Tell Mother there's a chance I might be
holed up in Ceylon for a while. Old Dumbo can only
take a couple of extras ...*

Her father's words mystified her. It seemed he wrote in riddles. She had yet to discuss the matter with Attie. Then, again, she worried it might only upset them both.

Gin had put off writing to George Harrington at the prospect of some wild goose chase that might raise her hopes only to burden her with yet another loss. But, surely, she thought, as she re-read his letter, it was only polite to reply. First, she needed more information. There was so much she didn't understand.

Delving in the dark and dusty archives, she found bundles of newspapers with photographs of flying boats floating like giant birds on the Swan River. Others featured American servicemen in leather bomber-jackets, casually leaning on a plane or sprawled in groups on the shadowed Crawley foreshore smoking cigarettes. *Old Dumbo? Black cats?* Her father's own words. War-time jargon perhaps, but what did it mean?

Her own ignorance at times surprised her. Gin had been brought up in a house where one dare not mention the war. As a war baby, her recollections were limited to the vague aftermath of protracted rations. From her earliest childhood she'd been led to believe that war was a nasty game, played by men far away from home in old crumbling European cities. Such were the settings of war films like *The Dam Busters,* which featured moustachioed English officers and blond, blue-eyed, jack-booted Germans but made no mention of Australians. Even the American musical *South Pacific* was staged on some remote tropical island bearing no direct relevance to Australia. And the hard green textbook of Australian history she'd had at school was merely a compilation of words and dates shedding no sense of reality on the war. Until now, Gin had no idea that her own city had been under any sort of direct threat of invasion. Yet from the little research she'd done lately, she could see that war had been virtually on her own doorstep.

'Who are you telling?' replied Theo, when she told him the following week of her discovery. 'The Japs dropped bombs on Broome. Crikey, I should know, Gin. Don't forget my mother was there at the time. She could tell you all about the bombings, how many of her friends were killed. Only it was all hushed up in Perth.'

Once Gin had started researching it was hard to stop. All these off-shoots and ramifications were never-ending and confusing. But at least she now knew something about the Japanese invasion of South-East Asia and the islands. Darwin had been bombed. Katherine had been bombed. Broome had been bombed. Australian and foreign civilians had been killed. She looked at a map, suddenly conscious for the first time of just how exposed Australians must have felt.

Then she became sidetracked looking at articles on Catalinas, or black cats, as she found they were called at the time. After Singapore had fallen, Ceylon replaced it as the main air stopover between England and Australia. To serve the connection and a mail run, another Catalina base was established, adjacent to the existing American Crawley base. She wanted to picture it in her mind, this connection with her father that had been the source of his faith in getting home to his family again.

When Gin hurried to tell Theo about the Catalinas, he wasn't surprised at all.

'Yes,' he said, 'probably only about three hundred metres away, between Pelican Point and the Nedlands baths.' He knew all about the Qantas Double Sunrise Base. His father had told him. But, during wartime, Perth had been kept in the dark as to the nature of this top-secret operation. 'Those pilots flew non-stop, Perth to Koggala in Ceylon, three-and-a-half thousand miles in their black cats. Incredibly brave they must have been. Imagine the stamina … twenty-seven hours it took—two sunrises. How'd you be, Gin, flying off in the dark with nothing but the Indian Ocean below, no radio control, just navigating by the stars? It was all hush-hush back then.'

*

Theo looked so young and vulnerable that Saturday morning queuing up with other students, and apprentices and bank clerks, to sign on the dotted line—smaller than usual. That gung-ho attitude of his had gone and his face was a paler shade of putty. He held her hand, kept squeezing it, and wouldn't let it go.

The wind whistled down the street. Shivering, Gin broke away from Theo and stood against the wall, retreating into her duffle coat. Suddenly, for the first time, she felt older than him. Up until now their twelve-month age difference had been irrelevant. He'd always seemed more mature and independent than other boys she knew; smart and wise, so damned knowledgeable it was almost as if he'd been reincarnated. But now, observing his slump in the jagged line, she began to see him for what he was, an innocent boy on the brink of his twentieth birthday. For the first time, she realised the seriousness of his current situation. Legally old enough to be sent to war but not old enough to vote. Next month she'd be twenty-one, an adult twelve months ahead of him. Funny to think she'd be registering herself on the electoral roll.

*

Theo was upset. Why hadn't she told him before, he wanted to know? Why all these secrets? It wasn't her fault, she said. She thought he knew or, at least, she didn't know that he didn't know she was a full year older than he was. Her mother had kept her back a year from starting school; she thought everybody knew.

The fact was that Gin hadn't wanted him to know, initially. She knew she'd been remiss but, the longer she'd left it, the harder it became to tell him.

'Anyway,' she said, trying to dismiss the matter. 'What difference does it make? It's my twenty-first. Noel's invited us both to the Adelphi Steak House to celebrate.' A party, she said, was out of the question.

*

'Well, well, well!' Noel stood up and greeted them. 'Haven't seen you for a while, young man. Almost didn't recognise you with your hair like that.'

Theo was in his element as Noel ordered a bottle of Cawarra

Claret. Later, when the two of them went back for seconds, Gin sat looking at her steak. She would have much preferred a Chinese or an Italian meal, something different, but Noel wanted none of that *splag* as he called it, every forkful tasting the same as the one before. He wanted proper food he could cut and chew.

Strangely, she found it easier to talk to him than in the past. Since he'd moved into his duplex, he'd rung her several times, and she'd felt none of the old hostility. She suspected it was a relief for him; the encouragement of her independence had disguised his abrogation. It was obvious, though, he still liked to keep in touch. She noticed that he'd aged considerably, looked more like a grandfather than her step-father, sitting on the other side of the table in his navy jacket and cravat. He asked the usual questions. How was she liking work? Was she OK for cash? As soon as he could, he'd see about setting up a trust fund for her. She was worried that any minute he'd bring up national service and the latest in Cambodia. But, in the end, it was easy enough. He and Theo talked about cars and the introduction of decimal currency, then Noel raised a toast.

'Here's to Virginia,' he said. He laughed as he lifted his glass, pausing with a nervous little cough. 'I can't exactly hand you a key to the house, can I? You've already got your own.'

In her mother's absence, Gin had begun to see Noel in a different light. Whenever he turned his head to speak to Theo she could see the brown mole that used to irritate her so intensely, popping up and down above his collar. It was still roughly the same size, but she noticed that stiff brown hairs were growing out of it. Perhaps it was the wine, but, for some reason, now it didn't seem to bother her at all.

Gin's real birthday was a week later. Attie arranged to come up to Perth for what turned out to be another celebratory dinner. With her childhood behind her, Gin felt the sudden weight of responsibility. She really must speak to Attie about those letters, adult to adult.

'Oh, by the way, Attie, I've got something very important to tell you when you come up.' Gin thought it best to forewarn her when her aunt first rang.

'Ooh, hope it's good news!' her aunt had replied. 'Don't tell me we're in for more celebrations,' she laughed. 'Keep a lid on it, dear. I've got to dash into town to catch the post.'

*

When Gin turned up at Theo's in a short mod skirt and new black skinny-ribbed top, he seemed annoyed. Why couldn't she wear that high-necked silky blouse she'd worn the other night, the romantic one with the granny print and the leg o' mutton sleeves? She turned on the iron she'd brought with her and unfolded the large piece of brown paper.

'Going to iron my shirt for me,' he grinned cheekily.

'Sure,' she said, tossing back her head, 'after you've done me a favour first.' Her hair was still moist. Already it had begun to frizz. 'Here,' she said, handing him the iron and the paper. 'Could you straighten my hair, please? Now you know what I mean about having a mind of its own.'

'What do you want to straighten it for, Gin, it's beautiful.' He was standing behind her, threading his fingers through her long tresses. Then he held the curling ends up to his lips and kissed them.

'Well, it's driving me crazy,' she said. 'Actually, I'm thinking of getting it cut.'

'You're not,' he said.

'Yes.' Gin knelt down on the floor and spread her hair out on a towel. 'Just you wait and see,' she said. 'I'm going to shed my shackles.'

'Oh Gin,' he pleaded, 'don't do that. Please.'

'Why?'

'You know I prefer birds with long hair.'

'Sorry?'

Theo didn't reply but just asked, 'How short?'

'Short,' she said. 'Mary Quant short, geometric style.'

*

Attie didn't like driving in the city at night, so Gin told her they would pick her up. After he'd greeted Attie, Theo pushed forward the bucket seat and climbed into the back. As she drove the Mini along Thomas Street, Gin glanced in the rear-vision mirror. Theo was scowling, hunched up, head almost touching the roof, with his knees drawn up under his chin. When they arrived at the Golden Dragon, Attie asked him how uni was, what were his future plans. He told her how he'd registered for national service but it depended upon which way the marbles fell.

'And what if you are called up, Theo, what then? Do you actually want to go?'

'No way,' he shook his head violently. 'Not on your Nelly.'

'Well, we'll keep our fingers crossed. In my mind, it's an outrage. They've no right to be conscripting young men. Australia should keep its nose out of other countries' business. But let's not talk about war on a birthday.' She patted his hand. 'War is certainly nothing to celebrate.'

Gin knew she should bring up the matter about the letters and her father being a POW. But how could she with Theo around? It was neither the time nor the place, she realised. Opportunity missed now her aunt was going back first thing in the morning.

Attie bent down and reached into her handbag. 'Here, Gin, I'd like you to have this,' she said. 'Happy birthday!'

Unwrapping the present, Gin found a small moth-eaten velvet box. Inside was a charm bracelet.

'Your granny and grandfather gave this to me for my twenty-first birthday.' Attie smiled. 'Made in Ceylon. No good these days on my thick old work-worn wrist. Needs to be worn by someone young.'

Gin held out her hand, and taking the silver bracelet examined the charms one by one. Amongst them were an elephant with its trunk pointing upwards, a horseshoe, a fish, a key, a monkey and a coin. She tugged at the cuff of her sleeve, then draped the bracelet over her wrist, opening and closing the heart-shaped clasp with its ornamental keyhole and tiny safety chain.

'Thank you Attie.' She reached over and hugged her aunt. 'It's really beautiful! Thank you so much.' For the moment she'd forgotten about her scars. Apart from a few keloids on her right hand, they weren't that noticeable in the dimmed light. She beamed at Theo and back at her aunt.

'I reckon you could do with a bit of good luck, Gin.' Reaching down, Attie began rummaging in her bag again. 'In any event, I thought this might come in handy.' She flapped an envelope at Gin. 'Don't open it now, Gin. Save it until you get home.'

Chapter 22

Theo was devastated. Not long after he'd received his Certificate of Registration, a letter arrived from the Department of Labour and National Service confirming his number in the call-up.

'Don't worry, Theo,' said Gin, hugging him. 'You'll easily get a deferment on the basis of your studies. Hundreds of kids are applying. Think of the positives. You've still got another year to go till you get your degree. By then the war could be over.'

Through the studio window Gin could see Mr Davis limping down the path with his stick. He rapped three times on the weatherboard wall, then poked his head inside. Fortunately, he couldn't see her; she was right behind the door.

'Hey, young fellow.'

'Yes, Mr Davis?' replied Theo.

'Listen, could you go and get me a couple of packets of Craven A when you've got a moment?' He coughed and spat on the lawn. 'Oh, a bottle of Bex and some Irish Moss if they've got any,' he said. 'Here's ten bob and bring back the rest. Make sure you don't short-change me like you did yesterday, either. You diddled me, you rascal.' He turned to leave, his crippled-up frame hunched over, as he shuffled back to the house on bandy legs.

'He's been forgetting things lately, Gin,' said Theo. 'But he's a Light-Horse veteran and he's not going lightly.' Suddenly, in a change of heart, Mr Davis turned around. 'You can borrow the Hillman again if you like, son, if you need to go anywhere special,' he called. 'Keys are hanging in the usual place. Oh, and another thing ... that young sheila of yours. Hey? Saw you holding hands yesterday. Makes me jealous. I can remember like it was yesterday when I was sitting next to this young lady in a railway carriage and ...'

'Sure thing, Mr Davis, I'll be back in a tick,' said Theo.

*

There was something about train stations, thought Gin, as she leant over the balustrades of the Horseshoe Bridge. The station-master's whistle, pistons hissing, the tootle of a horn, and the mingling smells of coal-dust and diesel, the smell of action, of people coming and going with different destinations. Myriad emotions conflicted when you travelled on a train. She knew this primarily from books; nineteenth-century European novels, in particular, Russian ones like *Anna Karenina* and *War and Peace,* in which long journeys were part and parcel of the transformation of character within a narrative. She could imagine perfectly the suspended excitement of anticipation, the unknown, the unexpected; sadness in separation; or the ominous sense of awaiting disaster at the other end, or even along the way.

Within her own limited experience, Gin had felt the frustration of grappling with fragments of human life flashing past a swaying window. The daily boredom of travelling to school at thirteen had been temporarily shattered by the close-up glimpse of a drunken woman on the platform punching another woman in the face. As the train pulled away from the platform, she'd wanted to cry out. But, in one blink, that splinter of life had vanished as if nothing had ever happened, the train *clickety-clacking* onwards to the next station without a care in the world. What other option had she but to sit shivering helplessly in shock until she'd eventually stumbled out of the carriage at her stop. And, although she'd instantly tried to erase that grotesque image from her mind, it still flipped into recall in photographic detail whenever she travelled by train.

The containment of a moving carriage encouraged sly observations, stolen snippets of other people's lives. No sooner had the empty Claremont showgrounds flashed past than the train would start pulling up at Loch Street. Then, as foreign-looking migrant families clambered into her carriage, she would find herself trying to guess which country they were from. Wasn't that the problem? For too long, she'd been a spectator, watching other people, waiting for things to happen.

The balustrade felt cold and hard against her hand. Below, a steam train was shunting its carriages on grimy tracks. Gin looked down at the station clock. The big hand was nearly on the twelve. It was time she went back to work. She knew she'd been stalling. Attie's cheque, which she had just deposited in her account at the St Georges Terrace branch of the Bank of New South Wales, offered innumerable possibilities. *Go and take a holiday, Gin,* Attie had written on her birthday card.

Hastening her steps Gin continued walking back up William into Francis Street. By the time she'd climbed the steps back into the great limestone fortress of the State Library, she'd made her decision.

Even Noel, when she told him, thought that going away would be an excellent idea. Broaden her horizons, he said, and whenever she gave the word he'd make damn certain she got a special deal through the manager, mate of his, in the travel department. Only yesterday, wading through recent English newspapers in the archives, she'd spotted excellent jobs advertised in London: one with the *Folio Society* and another with *The Daily Telegraph*. Just the shot. And she would finally be able to meet her English cousins. What was she waiting for? It was just that Theo …

*

Gin had no choice. She would have to tell Theo before uni broke up. So why not tell him now?

The flywire door of Mr Davis's house slapped shut. Barker, sensing the onset of the sea breeze, flopped down on the grass. Wafting through the open French doors of the studio was the sound of Theo's transistor. Gin could tell the news was on because Theo had his finger to his lips. Suddenly he jumped up to greet her.

'Ooh-hoo! Thank God for that, Ming's out!' he whooped.

'What on earth are you talking about?' Gin asked.

'Menzies, he's retiring. About time, silly old coot.'

'Who's taking over?'

'Harold Holt, I suppose.'

'Do you think he's likely to put a stop to conscription?'

'Not bloody likely. Need a general election to do that.' Despite his elation, he seemed distracted. 'Sorry, Gin,' he said, grappling for his keys. 'I'm just on my way out. Got to take Mr Davis down to the Repatriation Hospital.'

Gin waited next to the letter-box as Theo backed the Hillman out of the driveway. She smiled and waved. The old man looked glum as he returned her wave. It wasn't just his hip. He was also having problems with his chest. For some time the bluey-whiteness of his face, his chronic cough and shortness of breath had been reminding her of Granny. Then, there'd been the globs of blood-stained mucus on the lawn and the tests that Theo had talked him into having.

'Shouldn't your relatives be informed, now you have to be admitted?' Theo asked, helping Mr Davis into the car.

'None of their bloody business,' he snapped. 'What they don't know can't hurt them. The only thing they care about's what they can lay their hands on—my house and my bloody money.'

Bracing herself, Gin walked back along the street to the Mini. The wind was unusually blustery, batting fallen box-tree leaves around her feet. Council pruning had stunted the trees along the verge. Thick foliage concealed their deformity throughout the year so that they always looked the same. But there was something poignant about deciduous trees, the way nature stripped them clean. She remembered the flame trees in winter, how their bare distorted branches looked grotesque against the silvery sky with streaks of scarlet blossom.

'The prognosis didn't look good,' Theo told her the next day on the phone. He'd been so worried about the old man that he'd stayed with him until after his admission.

'Crikey, Gin. Must be bad. Maybe I should put off going away for Christmas. Old fellow wants to make me power of attorney but how can I when I'm not twenty-one?'

There was never a good time to break the news, she found. There were always unforeseen obstacles. On top of that, Theo was constantly preoccupied with all his responsibilities: Mr Davis's health problems, end-of-year exams looming up, and then all this paraphernalia about national service and applying for exemption. Theo had talked about it often enough. There were ways and means, he said. Conscientious objection was the buzzword, although a difficult thing to prove, and despite student rumblings of demonstrations he didn't want to defeat the objective and end up in the clink. All right for some, fellows like Tony Lloyd and Tom Burns, threatening to set alight to their draft cards, but then they probably didn't have to support themselves through engineering like he did. It was a tough haul, engineering.

'What about the Kings Park rally?' she asked. 'Why don't you go to that? The more protestors the better, I'd say.'

'Probably will when the time comes,' he said, 'that's if I *have* time'.

'Is there another way out?'

'Well, yes,' he replied, 'there is.' He'd been talking to some med students about how to fail the medical.

'Like what? Eating toothpaste?' she said. 'That's an old trick from school, Theo. All that does is raise your temperature for five minutes.'

'No fear. What we're talking about are serious health issues; displaying symptoms a bit more serious than the lousy common cold.'

'So, tell me.'

'OK, then. Here's the plan. Just before you go for your medical you get an egg, see, and you crack it and dip your fingers in the white. Then, when they send you off to the toilets to pee in a specimen jar you 'accidentally' come back with egg white in your pee.'

'So, what's that do?' she asked, bemused.

'Well,' he pointed at his head, 'you know what egg white's composed of, don't you? Albumen, get it? Otherwise known as protein, and protein is one of the things they test for. Any bloke who has protein in his urine is bad news, sick, really sick. No way they want to recruit health issues that serious. But there are always other serious health issues you can get exemptions for, and by that I don't just mean physical,' he said. 'If you don't want to crack eggs, you could always get a shrink on side, or plead you are a poofter.'

Gin shook her head; the smile had quickly vanished from her face.

'You can't be serious, Theo,' she said. 'Lying like that. You'll get found out.'

'Why not? Who's going to prove it?'

'Because it's wrong,' she said, 'that's why.'

'Alright for you to take the moral line,' he huffed. 'You're a bird. Fancy-free. How do you think you'd feel, though, being a bloke, bonded by the law? Don't you know what's happening up in Vietnam? Fellas having their brains and guts and limbs blown apart—for what? It's not even our fucking war.'

What could she say?

'Don't you read the papers, Gin? You got blinkers? Too caught up in the past, I suspect, reading up about the last fucking war.' His eyes flashed as they searched her stricken face. 'And if you want to talk about morals, what sort of morality is conscription?

I ask you, what sort of morality is that, hey? A morality that discriminates between men and women.' His top lip curled as he walked towards the door. 'Anyway,' he called over his shoulder, 'it's obvious you don't love me, otherwise you wouldn't want me to go away whatever the cost. At least I know now where I stand.'

*

When Gin opened her eyes, her room was bathed in morning sunlight. Christopher Robin was lying on the pillow six inches from her face staring from the downward slits in his pale yellow eyes. It was a smug look, as if he knew the precise moment when she would wake. His unblinking, penetrating stare was a challenge for her to do the same, but her eyes soon began to water and she blinked and looked away.

Poor Theo. It was a week since they'd last spoken; the incident was still spiralling in her mind. Not to mention the guilt. Delaying the inevitable made it even worse. But lying back with her hands behind her head looking up at the ceiling rose, she couldn't help feeling that perhaps she should give him just a little more time to cool off before letting him in on her plans.

The morning sun was getting hotter. Perspiration was dripping down her neck. She leant up and adjusted the blind. Catching the back of her hair in her hand Gin sank back on the pillow. She ducked her face as the ginger cat suddenly pounced at the charm bracelet swaying on her wrist. Ouch! A tiny drop of blood rose against the whiteness of her skin. Probably after that little fish, she half-smiled. Shaking the bracelet aside she lifted the wound to her mouth and quickly sucked it clean.

Chapter 23

Ever since she'd made the decision to go, there was momentum in her life, a checklist a mile long of things she had to do and only a month left to do them in. Packing up her belongings, bills to pay, goodbyes, and she still had the Mini to sell. Then the phone call came from Attie.

'I'm so excited for you. But do you think you could squeeze in time to come down and see your old aunt before you leave?' she said. 'Once you're over there, you never know how long you'll stay, and I mightn't live to see you again.'

'Oh, Attie,' she said. 'Don't be silly. Of course I can.'

'Lucky doer,' she said. She sounded almost jealous for the moment. 'Wish you could put me in your suitcase. Missed my chance, you know, when I was young. Granny was determined to take us back to the Old Country when your father and I turned eighteen, but then the Depression came and put a stop to that.' There was a pause and then she continued brightly. 'But how exciting! Now you'll be able to go and do the things we only dreamed about.' The phone went dead for a moment. 'Now, Gin dear, there's something else. I don't want to put a damper on your plans,' she continued. 'I should really tell you this in person but, now that you've already booked to go, it's better you know sooner than later. It's about your father.'

'What about him, Attie?'

'I'll get straight to the point. Some time back before your mother passed away, I received a letter from an English fellow who'd been in the same squadron as Jasper.'

Gin could hear her heart beating in the silence.

'Don't quite know how to say this, Gin—doesn't come easily even after all this time. Well, this fellow says your father didn't die when his plane was shot down, as we were all led to believe. He bailed out and was captured and taken prisoner.' There was a long pause. 'Are you still there, Gin?'

Gin knew what was coming next. 'Yes, yes, Attie,' she said, 'go on.'

'Well, the fellow asked for your mother's address,' said Attie slowly, 'so I wrote and told him. Didn't breathe a word of it to Valerie, of course. Knew she wouldn't take kindly to hearing it from me. Thought it best coming straight from the horse's mouth.' Attie paused. 'Dare say it was her right to know, same as yours, now you're twenty-one.' Attie paused as if trying to gauge Gin's reaction.

'It's OK, Attie, think I already know what you're about to say,' said Gin. 'I found his letter to Mum some time back when I was going through her things.' There was another pause. Why hadn't she answered it? She didn't want to raise her expectations unnecessarily. To have them dashed would have been more than she could bear. Instead she'd been getting bogged down in related detail, learning all there was to know about Catalinas, all the time skirting neatly around the whole issue of whether her father was even still alive. How could she explain that, even to Attie? And now, after everything that had happened, did she really want proof that her father was dead, she wondered, feeling the old ache of grief return?

'Oh, I see,' Attie's voice sounded distant and Gin thought she heard a sniff. 'You already knew about it then.'

'Yes. Sort of.'

'Oh well, in that case ... funny thing is, I've just had a letter this week ... anyway, it can wait until I see you.'

*

Gin didn't mind making the four-hour journey down to the farm. She promised Attie she'd stay the weekend. There were questions she wanted to ask her. Answers she needed to know. She was amazed driving along how everything had changed. All of the old signs and reference points seemed to have gone. Older homes had been demolished and replaced by brash dwellings of salmon brick. Even the road was not how she remembered it, widened now and re-routed with progress.

At one stage, she worried that she might have missed a turning, but suddenly the landscape became more familiar and she brightened up a little. In the distance she could see an old weatherboard house which she thought she remembered. It was derelict and surrounded by a tangle of rusted car parts and farm machinery. A scarifier lay upside down, discarded, its giant orange prongs pointing upwards as if questioning the sky. Half-hidden behind wild oats was an old bus chassis relegated to blocks. Nearby were stockyards and a broken-down assortment of corrugated iron sheds. Barbed wire shimmered in the sun. The house flicked past; a stiff row of washing on a fence. Shafts of sunlight filtered through gathering clouds of dust and in the moving haze, a small herd of cattle lumbered along the fence ready to be milked. A man slouched against the open gate, hand on hip. His strange weathered face turned to look at her as she passed. In a flash he was gone. There must have been some connection because she started to think about the man, what sort of life he lived, the circumstances of his poverty and isolation. How old he was. Probably the same age her father would have been, around fifty at a guess. Was he married with a family? And did he go to war like her father? Had they known each other back before the war? And could her father really still be alive?

Gin thought of these things as paddocks flitted past. Charcoal-striped shadows continued to deepen over the golden stubble. In between, sheep stooped motionless like primeval rocks, rounded backs immersed in a whitewash of late afternoon sun. The car was stifling. She wound down the window a little and twisted the visor to shade her eyes from the glare. She realised how tense she was. A little hammer was ticking away in her temple. Her hands felt taut and sweaty in her mother's leather driving gloves, which she wore for protection from the sun. The buff gloves looked old-fashioned and pretentious with a fan of keyholes. But she was glad she'd remembered to retrieve them from the tea-chest. The sun was still penetrating and they covered up her scars.

It was dangerous driving when she felt like this. Gin knew she should have stopped and rested for a while at the general store ten miles back, had a Coke or a ginger beer. Her mouth was parched. Beads of perspiration gathered under her eyes, which felt unusually heavy. But she pressed on, conscious of Attie's afterthought: *Keep an eye out, the kangaroos can be deadly at dusk*. She remembered how they could leap out at you without warning, stove in the front end and the radiator, or even write off a car completely. A Mini wasn't much bigger than a kangaroo and she didn't fancy the thought.

The sight of the state forest looming up didn't help matters. Karri trees towered above, their inward lean forming a kind of tunnel over the road. Darkness suddenly descended, closing in as it hollowed out her path. She knew it was silly but she couldn't stop her heart racing and the wave of nausea which swept over her. Light continually flickered through the canopy of branches, making her even more dizzy and light-headed. Goosebumps rose on her arms. Shadows played tricks as they merged into the bracken either side of the gravelly cut. The crisscrossing of long dark stripes across the road seemed to rise into the gloom. As she switched on the headlights, she started shuddering, involuntary shudders so strong that she could barely keep her hands upon the wheel.

'Don't be a fool,' she kept telling herself, 'just follow the lines. You'll soon be there.' She tried hard to focus but the lines seemed to move and smudge into the whiteness of lilies dotting their way through the ferns at the side of the road. Arum lilies were noxious weeds. Pretty but poisonous, Attie had told her. Yet wasn't that what her father had called her mother? *Lily. My dearest darling Lil, you've no idea ...* Gin could feel herself fading. Could she hold out? Her thirst was rapidly gaining as she looked for the creek that fed the dam. Suddenly, she could see light and a bridge on the bend. Good. She remembered the bridge, and as she got closer the curve of its railings emerged like a smile.

Out of her half-closed eyes, Gin could see a maze of blues and greens. Attie was bending over her. Her cool hand lightly touched her brow.

'You've slept for nearly twenty hours straight,' she said, holding out a thermometer. 'Here's a drink for you, but, first, I want to pop this in your mouth.'

Attie's face was shiny and exposed. Her hair was shorter than when Gin had seen her last, freshly washed with wet waves neatly fingered behind her ears. A practical style, like the cotton shift she was wearing.

'Does this old bed bring back memories?' As Attie plumped the pillow, the smell of camphor wafted from her muted batik print. Fine threads of gold caught Gin's eye in a streak of afternoon light. 'It should do, you know,' said Attie. Her eyebrows lifted like fine golden wings. 'You slept in it while your mother went to England.'

Gin felt her face tightening as she tried to smile back.

Attie took the thermometer from her lips.

'Goodness me, you're burning,' she said. 'Now you just forget about having to get back to Perth. There's no hurry. No point in going back when you're feeling like death warmed up. Why don't you lie back and concentrate on getting some more shut-eye?' Her thongs *slip-slap, slip-slapped* across the floorboards. 'There, that might be easier on your poor old head,' she said, having pulled down the blind.

But within minutes Gin was shivering again. She drew up Granny's patchwork quilt and its coloured patterns began swirling around and around in her head. In the pearliness of fever, she saw an apparition of her mother. Somewhere far away in the distance she could hear a ship's horn. Valerie seemed to be calling, gesturing to her through the fog. But Gin could feel herself being taken somewhere else, limbs aching and flailing as she tried to swim towards her. Next thing she was floating on her back, feeling the waves carrying her away, away in the opposite direction from her mother.

When Gin eventually came to, she found her eyes were wet and Attie was standing beside the bed.

'You've been hallucinating. Calling out for your mother, you were. Wouldn't mind betting it's an overreaction to your smallpox injection,' she said. 'Over the worst, I suspect.' Attie sat Gin up, plumping pillows behind her. 'Here,' she said, placing the tray upon her lap. A grey blob of sago wobbled in a bowl.

'Tell me about her. Mum, I mean,' Gin said, gingerly picking up the spoon. 'What it was like during the war?'

'The war changed everything, Gin. People, places and relationships. Your mother was proud, but, as I said, an anxious person, full of insecurities. She'd had a terrible time in London during the Blitz, night after night of it, as a teenager. Even witnessed half her street blown away. Imagine continually waking up every night to the sound of sirens, bombs exploding, searchlights, watching bodies being pulled out from under fallen rubble. Your mother told me how little fires continually broke out from the shattering explosions, joining together into huge uncontrollable rings which kept sweeping through the city causing havoc. Beacons, they were, for the next wave of bombings. Imagine, Gin, having to run frantically to escape falling bombs, only to find yourself losing your way amongst the fires. Imagine the terror. Joining the forces was probably a kind of escape for your mother, although I suspect she was also attracted by the glamour. Even so, she would have known the other side of the coin, the things we didn't know. The losses in the air were horrific. She would have known only too well what your poor father was going through. When she arrived here, Gin, she had you, dear little darling though you were, and somehow I don't think she was quite ready for a child. She was still looking for an escape, I guess, wanting to get away from the war and all its privations. Trouble was, she came with all sorts of preconceptions. Australia really wasn't at all what she'd expected. The farm wasn't what she'd expected. Everything topsy-turvy. Grasswood didn't come easy for the Partridge family. It was gruelling work day in, day out, but we all made a go of it. Your father worked his body and soul for everything that's here, Gin, and I wanted to keep it to pass on to you.'

Attie stared at the patchwork quilt, trying to gather her thoughts.

'Life was stressful back then for all of us on the farm. The only person your mother really got on with in the first year, until she met Noel, was your granny, who of course got on with everyone. And then the dreadful mix-up. We didn't know anything was wrong, of course—the telegram got sent to the wrong address. Months of waiting. Official notification that Jasper was missing didn't arrive here until almost the Christmas, and even then there was nothing certain. One way or another, Valerie had had enough by the end of the war. She was a city girl and wasn't waiting around anymore. Granny had had enough too; she needed treatment for her chest. Housing was pretty hard to come by after the war, but Granny pitched in, and, together with Valerie's war-service loan, they managed to buy a place, and that was the end of that,' she said, clapping her hands together. 'There was no way I was leaving here. But the stress took its toll on our health. Your granny, your mother, even me. It was only when I was recuperating from cancer that I had the time to think, so I started writing things down to get the war years off my chest. There was a lot to tell. Enough to write a book, so I thought at the time. But you know, Gin, I got sidetracked. Dieter came along and somehow he changed my storyline. But there are hours and hours of it there, page upon page inside the old Davenport, should you want a read. When I'm dead and gone you can get rid of it—burn it all.'

'I'd like to read it Attie.'

'Now that I've mentioned Dieter, I suppose I'll have to let you into a little secret. Don't laugh, Gin, but Dieter and I are getting married.'

Gin nearly sent the sago flying. She sat up, flabbergasted.

'Married? Attie! Really?'

'Yes. Married. Ever seen a fifty-year-old bride before?' Attie gave a hoot. Then she whispered, 'Bit hard living in sin all these years in a country town, tongues wagging like they do. But it'll be a quiet affair, no fuss, before you leave. Only a handful of people. We'd like you to be present, Gin.'

Attie went on about how Dieter was keen to buy back the original twenty acres she'd had to sell fifteen years ago. 'You probably don't remember old Fitzy, Gin. Poor old geezer's on borrowed time.' She looked thoughtful for a moment, then gave a chuckle. 'I remember he had a bit of an obsession with your mother when she first arrived. Used to turn up at ungodly times in the night, headlights shining into the house, war-time and all, mind you. Used to frighten the dickens out of her. I felt it best not to cause a fuss, otherwise he might do it all the more.'

Suddenly Gin remembered the man. She pictured the figure she'd seen years ago swimming naked in the dam, that strange man who'd invited them over to pick cherries, the demented stare as she clambered over the branches, handing the ripe fruit down to Attie below. At one stage, she'd been so petrified she'd almost lost her balance and fallen to the ground. Couldn't get back into the car quick enough. Just a bit of an oddball, Attie had tried to reassure her. Just a strange lonely man. It was he, Gin realised, whom she'd seen on the trip down, standing next to the gate waiting sadly for his herd of milking cows.

Attie paused and smiled. 'But I'm talking too much,' she said, folding back the counterpane. 'Gone on and on so much I've made myself dry. I'll be back directly. Just going to make a cup of tea. Oh, by the way, Gin, that boyfriend of yours, Theo, has been ringing up. Worrying himself sick you'd had an accident. He'd rung Hamersley Road and found you'd been away for the weekend and hadn't come back. I told him not to worry, you were sick, bailed up with a fever, but otherwise OK. Might be a few days before you're on your feet.'

Gin rolled her eyes and squeezed her forehead. The headache had come back again. It was all very well saying not to worry. Any day her passport would be arriving. After all that angst about her name not matching that on her birth certificate, what if there was further delay? For the last eight years she'd called herself *Virginia Wheatley*, in accordance with Valerie's instructions.

Easier for all concerned. How could she forget that awful day, and the anger she'd felt, as she'd scratched out *Virginia Partridge* in her school books and written *Virginia Wheatley* below? *Easier for all concerned?* Even now it was causing all sorts of unnecessary complications. But how was she to know her name had never been changed by deed-poll?

A few hours later Attie came back with a glass of homemade lemonade. 'Been years since Dieter saw you last, Gin. Dare say he'll barely recognise you. He'll probably remember an awkward, shy twelve-year-old with a bit of a stutter. Don't hear it much these days. Your mother was always anxious, closeted you in some ways. Kept you back from starting school because you'd had chronic tonsillitis. You didn't say much as a wee child, but when you did talk nobody could understand a word you were saying. Dare say you inherited that stutter from your father. But a stutter didn't stop him doing what he had to do. He was quite a man, Gin, your father. But I shouldn't talk for too long or I'll exhaust you. Now, don't forget,' she said, refilling the glass, 'drink lots of water. It'll help to bring your temperature down.'

It was hard taking everything in, piecing everything together. Attie had been talking for almost an hour. Gin closed her eyes beneath the cool lavender-soaked flannel her aunt had laid across her forehead. The smell brought back so many memories.

*

'Now,' Gin opened her eyes to the sound of Attie's words. 'About that letter from England I was telling you about on the phone. The one from George Harrington, you know, about your father.'

Gin frowned for a moment, uncertain of what she was talking

about. She pushed back the bedcovers and sat upright. Then she remembered.

'Are you sure you're ready for this, dear?'

'Yes, yes,' said Gin. She swung herself around so that she was sitting on the edge of the bed, face to face. 'Of course,' she said.

Attie started out brave and rather business-like. 'Well, I'm not sure how much of this you already know. But for whatever reason, details of your father's capture were never relayed to the Allies. Perhaps the mayhem of the final few months before the surrender caused a breakdown in communication. Chap said German administration would have floundered: their documentation had gone to pot and Geneva conventions were abandoned. And all that time your father was alive and well, at least well enough to do a bunk. It appears he survived on the run making his way across Germany into Holland. There's a story floating around about an Aussie airman, walked into a small village late one night during the final weeks of the war, sick and disorientated. They didn't know who he was, as he'd abandoned his uniform and was disguised in stolen civvies. Eventually they twigged he was a POW on the run.'

'What happened then?' asked Gin, her voice slow and flat, as she looked up at Attie.

'Well,' Attie took in a deep breath, but immediately her chin dimpled and her bottom lip began to quiver. 'Well, by that time, poor darling had contracted pneumonia from sleeping out.' Gin looked away as her aunt struggled to find her words. 'Some villagers gave him shelter in their cellar but ... but he died before he could tell them his name and squadron.' Attie covered her face with her hands, releasing a long deep groan. 'Oh Gin,' she sobbed,

'I don't want you to see me cry.'

'It's alright, Attie,' Gin had jumped up and was giving her aunt a long hard hug. 'It's OK. Take your time. It's alright.' This time it was she who was doing the comforting.

But already Attie was composing herself. 'Word is, Gin,' she said, blinking away her tears, 'that there's an unmarked grave in the village churchyard they say is Jasper's. Apart from the stolen clothes, the only possession he left behind was an unusual watch. They've asked me to go over so they can put a name to the grave. The family who looked after him need me to identify the watch. Now, that watch, I suspect, Gin, was the one that belonged to Grandfather Charlie. It was a gold fob watch, distinctive in its Arabic numerals and engraving. Father gave it to Jasper on his arrival home from war.'

The floorboards creaked as they wandered out into the sitting room. Gin, still in her pyjamas, stood at the mantelpiece studying the photos of her father. Attie came up beside her and put her arm around her shoulders.

'I'd dearly love to go, Gin,' she said quietly, 'but you can't just walk out on a farm and leave it to its own devices. So, it's over to you, dear.'

Chapter 24

Gin inspected her Bank of New South Wales travel itinerary. Perth–Singapore–Colombo–London–Amsterdam. It was quite some business changing flights at the last minute. Noel's mate had even managed to find her a stopover in Ceylon on BOAC from Singapore.

Gin fastened her seat belt.

'Boeing 707,' Theo had informed her, although she was none the wiser.

'Doesn't stop me being scared,' she'd replied.

Theo told her not to worry; she'd be right once the plane was at altitude. 'In actual fact, more accidents happen during take-off than any other flight procedure,' he'd pointed out, unnecessary detail that made her worry even more.

When she'd told him the news about her father, he'd appeared shocked. 'Never knew all that history. Didn't even know he was a pilot. Why didn't you tell me, Gin?' He'd given her a look of the wounded. 'Talk about a dark horse.'

How could she explain that the subject had been overshadowed by existing troubles, become too much to bear in the pain and aftershock of other events?

'You never asked,' she said.

'Bit hard with Noel being in the picture,' he'd shrugged, as if reading her thoughts. 'Just presumed your parents' marriage had gone the way of a lot of other war marriages—divorce.'

She peered through the cabin window, wondering if he would stay to watch her leave.

An hour ago they had stood together outside the front of the airport, fingers loosely linked together, watching black swans making lazy circles in their pond. Theo was ecstatic. He'd told her he'd just received his deferral. For a year at least, or until he'd finished his degree.

'What happens then?' she'd asked.

'Well,' he'd smirked, 'once I've finished my degree, I'm obliged to have a medical!'

'Fingers crossed, Theo, let me know.'

'Write to me, Gin, won't you?'

'Of course I'll write. On the condition you write too.'

''Fraid I'm not much of a writer, Gin,' he said, as he bit on his bottom lip, 'least that's what my folks say.'

'Tell me. How did you find out I was going, Theo?'

'I've got my spies,' he replied, his penetrating dark brown eyes seeking out her own. 'You can't keep secrets from me forever, Gin.'

As the plane was being taxied to the runway, she looked again for Theo. But he was nowhere to be seen. Deep down she knew Theo would be alright—he lived by his spirit and his wits. She was grateful for having known him. But would she ever be able to quell her suspicions that he'd only wanted to marry her as a means of avoiding national service? Others had. Coralie

Simpson's husband, for instance. The condition in the fine-print cited such marriages had to have taken place before registration. Funny how, once Theo had registered, he'd never mentioned marriage again. But what did it matter? It was history now, she thought, with a sigh of relief. There was no going back, although she nearly hadn't made it. Her passport hadn't arrived in her hand until the death-knock.

Gin opened it again, examining the photo of herself. *Bloody mug-shot*, Theo had commented, quickly tossing the passport back to her. What's more he didn't like the cut. Wasn't that bad, she thought. In fact, her new hairstyle rather suited her, blunt fringe and cropped an inch below her ears. *Virginia Partridge*, she read. Sounded funny after having been *Virginia Wheatley* all these years. *Virginia Partridge.* Fancy that!

Surprisingly, she felt no fear at all as the plane gathered speed along the runway. Her heart was beating rapidly, but lightly, like a bird's. Accompanying it was a sense of freedom and elation. She wasn't Theo's 'bird' anymore, nor was she anybody else's for that matter. She was flying on her own and independent.

In no time, the plane was in the air. Higher and higher it rose, circling back towards the city. Beneath she could see the Swan River snaking from the dried-out hills through the suburbs and the city to the sea. The Narrows Bridge flicked past, the wide stretch of Melville Waters opening out into Matilda Bay below. Craning her head back she quickly tried to locate the boathouse and the university, but already they were gone, out of sight, and, for the moment, out of mind. Within seconds she was up over the Indian Ocean looking down where the blue of the sky meets the sea, toy-like ships disappearing into clouds.

As the plane continued climbing higher, she re-read the safety instructions again and again. Just imagine having to bail out like her father had to do. She thought of the hours and hours he must have spent in a plane, always conscious that the flight might be his last. His nerve and untold bravery were real stories. *He was a hero, Virginia.* She had never forgotten her mother's words but now they held some meaning. The bulk of research lay in front of her, almost another story in itself. After all these years, would she finally meet her hero at his grave?

Then would she still ponder how different life would have been had her father come back to Perth by Catalina? For the time being, she was on her first aeroplane flight, making the first leg of a journey in reverse.

Gin closed her eyes. Her fingers began following the Chopin nocturne that was playing in her head. The piece always reminded her of dear Mr Penworthy, who had taken her love of music to another level. She'd forgotten to ask Attie about him. She'd hoped he might have played the piano at the wedding. As the hours ticked by, she half-dozed, observing changing colours in the clouds. Occasionally she would glance backwards at the jet engines on the wing. Closing her eyes again, she would pretend she was inside a Catalina flying boat on a flight so slow and arduous she, too, would have the privilege of seeing a double sunrise.

Author's Notes

Finding Jasper is a work of fiction within a framework of real places and events. Grasswood is the name of the farming property pioneered by my great-grandfather near Brazier in the South West of Western Australia. The setting I describe as Grasswood in the novel, however, is a composite of a number of settings in the South West with which I have strong links. The RAF base, 'Wickerton', is a place of fiction representative of a typical English air force base during World War II. The 'double sunrise' refers to the two sunrises seen by the courageous pilots of the Catalina Flying Boats which were used in the secret Perth-to-England mail run during World War II. The Catalinas flew 5,630 kilometres non-stop between Crawley Bay in Perth and Koggala in Ceylon (now Sri Lanka) for up to twenty-eight hours in complete radio silence and with virtually no navigational aids.

Beethoven's Fifth became known as the 'Victory Symphony' when it was cleverly utilised during the BBC's 'V for Victory campaign' as a means of raising public morale and galvanising the Allied effort against the Germans. The dramatic rhythm of the first four notes, 'dit-dit-dit-daaaah', spelt out 'V for victory' in Morse Code and was incorporated as the call sign of all the BBC's European services, mocking the German nationalism intended by the symphony's composer.

The characters in *Finding Jasper* are imaginary and the narrative is intended to represent life as it could have been in the historical and cultural context of Western Australia during the 1940s to 1960s. While drawing from some of my own memories and understandings, I have gained valuable insight from a variety of non-fiction sources, as well as memorabilia, letters, recordings and real-life conversations with people whose experiences spanned the relevant years.

Sources

The bulk of historical research for *Finding Jasper* was carried out between 2004 and 2006. I relied heavily on online resources, some of which are no longer available. News reports of specific dates and events were consulted. Mentions of the London Blitz were based on some of the many eye-witness accounts of the time. ABC and BBC archival websites provided word-for-word reporting of the Allied bombing of Dresden, Churchill's Victory Speech, and the atomic bombing of Nagasaki. The account of people's reactions in the streets of Perth when the Japanese finally surrendered was taken from a transcript of the AM Radio National broadcast of 'Australia Remembers Victory in the Pacific' presented by Tony Eastley. Numerous non-fiction books provided information on the social implications of war. Of special mention were Margaret Geddes' *Blood, Sweat and Tears: Australia's WWII Remembered by the Men and Women who lived it* and Carol Fallows' *Love and War: Stories of War Brides from the Great War to Vietnam*. For a wider understanding of those who served in Bomber Command during World War II, I referred to H. Nelson's *A Different War: Australians in Bomber Command*.

The RAAF Aviation Museum at Bullcreek provided a fantastic display of real aircraft, letters and recordings, which helped me to portray the war years. For information on flying boats, I consulted A. M. Koenig's 'Catalinas on the Swan River – Perth', A. McMillan's *Catalina Dreaming*, and D. Pedley's *Catalina comes home to Matilda*, as well as an electronic publication 'Perth to Ceylon Flights' put out by the Catalina Organisation of Australia. Collections at the Australian War Memorial enabled me to research online the part played in the war by the Dutch. This was mostly sourced from Albert Pallazzo's account 'The Netherlands East Indies and the Pacific War' in *Allies in Adversity: Australia and the Dutch in the Pacific War*. For details on national service for young Australian men during the Vietnam War, I consulted Sue Langford's 'The National Service Scheme, 1964–72', Appendix from *A Nation at War* by Peter Edwards.

Two texts which helped jog my memory and provided a social and historical context for Perth in the 1950s–1960s were Jenny Gregory's *City of Light* and Tom Stannage's *The People of Perth.* Gillian Lilleyman and George Seddon's *A Landscape for Learning: A History of the Grounds of The University of Western Australia* was also of great assistance.

A number of creative works are mentioned in *Finding Jasper.* Quotations from Mary Grant Bruce's *Captain Jim* were taken from an early 1919 edition. Numerous lines were also taken from Banjo Paterson's poem *The Man from Snowy River.* Both 'Going Over the Sea' and 'The Banana Boat' song are traditional folk songs. Lyrics were also taken from online versions of the popular sing-a-long songs of the time: Harry Woods' 1926 song 'When the Red Red Robin Comes Bob-Bob-Bobbin' Along'; George and Felix Powell's 'Pack up your Troubles', composed in 1919; and the slightly earlier 1915 song, 'I've been Sailing Down the Old Green River' by Bert Kalmar and Joe Cooper. The legend of Ganesh was sourced from 'Stories from Hindu Mythology: Ganesh', one of many online versions.

MATILDA BAY BOOKS

What do you think of Finding Jasper?

Join the discussion online at

www.lynneleonhardt.com/finding-jasper

or at

www.facebook.com/LynneLeonhardtAuthor

First published in 2012 by Margaret River Press

This edition published 2018 by Matilda Bay Books,
Western Australia

Cataloguing-in-Publication data is available from the
National Library of Australia
ISBN 978-0-6483788-0-8 (paperback)
ISBN 978-0-6483788-2-2 (ebook)

Edited by Richard Rossiter
Designed by Tracey Gibbs
Typset in Linux Libertine
Printed by Lightning Source / Ingram, Australia
Photograph by Massonstock

www.ingramcontent.com/pod-product-compliance
Lightning Source LLC
Chambersburg PA
CBHW020702110726
47901CB00001B/274

* 9 7 8 0 6 4 8 3 7 8 8 0 8 *